BARRY'S WALK

Here's round
2!

Ted
Nutry

'17

BARRY'S WALK

Book2 of the GONE FERAL Series

Ted Nulty

Braveship
BOOKS

Aura Libertatis Spirat

BARRY'S WALK

Braveship Books

www.braveshipbooks.com

Edited by Sara Jones

Cover Design by Milan Jovanovic

Selected graphic elements licensed from 123RF.com

ISBN-13: 978-1-939398-77-2

Printed in the United States of America

AUTHOR'S NOTE

This is not a sequel. I know many of you are expecting the story to pick up from the end of *Gone Feral*. It doesn't.

This story runs in parallel, overlapping the time period of the first book. It tells Barry's story from the start of the attacks, then briefly expands on his time with the National Guard. Finally, it follows him as he searches for a way home.

If you enjoyed *Gone Feral*, then I hope you enjoy this book as well. Barry, Mark, Jake, Mel, Terry and the others thank you. So do I.

For all the people who have taken the time to participate in my world. I had fun building it, I hope you have fun visiting it, and I hope none of us have to live in it...

(Even though I think it would be kind of cool!)

PROLOGUE

Camp Pendleton, CA

The sun was getting low in the western sky as the young man crested the hill and stared down into the valley in front of him. He could see the backs of the four classmates ahead of him as they followed the trail back down to the school house. A glance behind him showed a line of fellow classmates struggling up the hill toward his location.

Dragging a dusty sleeve across his brow to wipe away the sweat that was running down his face and dripping off his nose, the young man hitched his pack a little higher and fingered the small figurine hanging from a piece of paracord around his neck. With a look of grim determination, he made sure his M4 carbine was secure on its sling but readily available, and began to trot down the hill. A .45 in an old canvas holster bumped against his hip as he jogged down the steep incline.

As he picked up speed, he began to gain on the classmate in front of him. He had almost caught up, when the man he was gaining on turned with a startled look on his face.

Seeing the determined look on the younger man's face, he began jogging as well. Soon there was a small knot composed of the 2nd through 5th place students bearing down on the leader. Try as they might though they couldn't catch him. As soon as the leader hit the road with a half mile remaining to the finish line, he took off like he wasn't carrying a forty pound pack and rifle.

His scarred face was set in grim determination as his ground eating lope easily kept a safe distance between him and his fellow classmates.

Rounding the last bend in the road, Jim Norris trotted across the finish line and checked in with the class' lead instructor. After that he moved back to the curve in the road to cheer on his classmates. He watched as the next two people to come into view bore down on the finish line in a dead heat.

He was surprised to see the smallest member of his class pumping his legs madly to try and get second place. It just didn't happen, as Barry Metzler came in third, having passed two classmates since his pause at the top of the ridge. Both men crossed the line breathing like locomotives. Barry turned and staggered over next to Jim to lend motivational support while Ernie Wright collapsed on his back, not even bothering to remove his pack.

It took over two hours for the rest of CCTC-1 to cross the finish line. The final stragglers crossed the line followed by the medical HMMV with two students aboard.

The group had just passed the final hump before graduation, which was two days away. The first class of the Marine Corps' Civilian Combat Training Course would graduate 82 students, the oldest being a fifty-six year-old former carpenter, and the youngest was a fourteen-year-old orphan from Bemidji, Minnesota.

CHAPTER 1

14 Months Earlier

"You can't doooo that!" Andrew Petty complained as his older brother Will turned the hose on him, easily overpowering the Super-soaker that Andrew was aiming back at him. The rules stated that the hose was neutral territory. The squirt gun fight had elevated to a water balloon fight which then devolved into a mud wrestling match. "We get to fill our guns too!"

"This *is* my gun butthead, and if you want some water, come and get it!" Will yelled as he sprayed Barry before he turned the hose back on his younger brother.

Barry used the distraction to dodge in and grab the igloo ice cooler that had been the ammunition depository for the water balloons. It was now half full of water and the remnants of several popped balloons. He picked it up and heaved the contents at Will, drenching him thoroughly and ending the water fight with a resounding victory for the underdogs.

Will, who was a poor sport in victory, became an absolute bully when shown up by his younger brother and Barry. He lunged at Barry with a balled fist and a curse on his lips, which changed to a yelp of surprise as he tripped on the cooler that Barry threw at his feet as he nimbly skipped away. Will went down hard on the muddy lawn, giving Barry and Andrew the opportunity to run away.

The two friends took off for Barry's house, knowing that it wouldn't be safe at Andrew's house for quite some time. They cut through the woods, making sure to stop and look down into Ms. Allensworth's back yard. The

6th and 7th grade social studies teacher was immensely popular with the students, especially the boys. The 5'9" blonde had worked her way through college as a model and was stunningly beautiful. This was not lost on the male population, and a lot more fathers began showing up at PTA meetings.

Peering through the trees, the boys saw a towel on the chaise lounge in her back yard. The boys exchanged a knowing grin and immediately went into stealth mode. They dropped down onto their hands and knees, and began to crawl down the slope towards her fence. If they could get there unobserved, they would be able to get a near perfect side on view as she was getting a tan.

Movement at the kitchen window caused both boys to freeze as Justine Allensworth finished making a tall glass of sweet tea and headed to the back door. The boys watched as she made herself comfortable and picked up her tablet to read. The two twelve-year-olds got comfortable and just stared at what had to be God's most perfect creation for a while.

Andrew was really feeling the sun on his neck and was starting to fidget when Barry gave him an elbow to make him be still. Their clothes had quickly dried in the summer sun and they were now beginning to sweat profusely. Their discomfort paid off though as she stood up and laid the lounge down flat. Both Barry and Andrew were coiled tight as springs as she undid the strings to her bikini top and laid down on her stomach. The brief glimpse of her magnificent chest would be the subject of both boys' fantasies for some time.

The boys watched for another half hour before Justine got up and went inside for some reason. This provided the boys with one last look at her chest and then allowed them to slip away to the fort where they would talk for hours about how they would propose to her as they worked at putting the finishing touches on their hideaway.

Their fort was located almost exactly halfway between Ms. Allensworth's house and the back fence line of Barry's farm. The entrance was a cleft between two rocks on the side of the hill overlooking the farm. This was camouflaged by dragging some vines across the opening and attaching them with a piece of rope to a wooden frame. Both boys were avid science fiction and war movie fans, so they had developed a super-secret protocol for getting to the entrance unobserved. This protocol involved looping back to check their back trail to see if anyone was following them. While watching out for any spies trying to follow them, the boys talked about various horror films and discussed defending the fort in case of a Zombie apocalypse. Once sure that they weren't being followed they slipped past the vines and entered their sanctuary.

Once past the boulders. The cleft in the rocks opened out into a space twelve feet wide by fifteen feet deep. This immense cavern had a set of shelves along one side which held various items important to fort defense including an old battery powered radio and a pair of old binoculars. A small red cooler provided food storage, while two lawn chairs completed the furnishings. The boys had scavenged a small A-frame ladder that allowed them to climb up onto a small rock shelf that looked out over Barry's farm in the distance. This platform would eventually mount a hyper speed turbo-laser to be used in defense of the zombie hordes.

Neither of the boys knew it, but that was exactly what they would be facing by the end of the week.

CHAPTER 2

Dale Metzler walked out of the Wal-Mart in Bemidji with a bag in each hand. A stock investment in his retirement plan had paid off a handsome dividend and he had slipped into town to get some presents for the wife and kids. Two thousand dollars later, he had a set of diamond earrings (not from Wal-Mart), a Tablet for Cammie his oldest daughter, a new Archery set for Barry, a Teddy bear for Kristine his youngest daughter, and last but not least a huge smoked beef bone for Bert the dog.

Feeling that he had earned a little self-indulgence, Dale had also ordered a new shotgun to use on a hunting trip he had planned with his oldest son. Henry was from Dale's first marriage. He was much older than Camille, Barry, and Krissy, and lived in Minneapolis.

He paused to take a long drink from a public water fountain and shift the bags in his hands. He didn't notice the slight odor of chlorine in the water, and had no idea that he had just ingested enough toxin to poison a horse. The summer sun had him sweating by the time he made the short trip across the parking lot to his big green pick-up. After setting the bags in the back seat of the crew cab, he decided to get a large soda from the local stop-and-rob before driving home.

He was inside the convenience store when a man in camouflage clothing came in holding his wrist, blood was seeping from between his fingers and he had a shocked look on his face. Dale grabbed a handful of napkins from a dispenser next to the soda machine and used them to apply direct pressure, while one of the clerks went in back to get a first aid kit.

"What happened? That looks like an animal bite." Dale asked as he held the appendage over the man's head while maintaining the pressure on the wound.

"I got attacked by a couple of squirrels!" The man said still not believing it himself. "I swear to God they were rabid or something…Oh shit! I bet I've got rabies now or something!"

"Well let's wrap this up, you should definitely get to a doctor if it was an animal attack." Dale used the first aid kit to apply a proper bandage and tape it in place. "The good thing is rabies shots aren't nearly as painful as they used to be."

"Oh thanks!" The man grinned at him. "It was the craziest thing, they just jumped out of the tree right on me."

"Maybe they had a baby on the ground that you didn't see and they were protecting their young." The clerk offered. "I've seen normally gentle animals get pretty nasty when their young are involved."

"Could be." Dale nodded in agreement.

"Maybe, my name's Steve Dickson, and I thank you both for your kindness. It doesn't look too bad, so I'll make an appointment to have it looked at." He put out his hand and Dale shook it and introductions were made all around. Steve left while Dale helped Chris the clerk clean up the mess.

Dale left the store with a forty-four ounce Coke, compliments of Chris, and climbed into his truck. As he was pulling out of the driveway he noticed a squirrel lying on the side of the road with its legs straight out and breathing heavy. He almost stopped and collected it. Thinking that animal control should be notified if there was a wave of rabies going through the rodent population. He settled for calling the animal control number, but the line was busy so he just went home. He wanted to get the gifts wrapped before his wife got home from work.

Barry left Andrew at the fort and trotted home. He crawled under the pasture fence and snuck around the barn, peeking inside to see if any of the field hands were still there. Not finding anyone, he was headed to the house when Bert came flying around the side of the house and began doing the doggie greeting dance. Barry spent several minutes bonding with Bert by rolling on the ground and wrestling with the hound.

Bert was some sort of lab/hound dog mix and had been adopted from the animal shelter. He had the biggest set of floppy ears that hung way down the side of his head. The ears gave him the most comical of looks, endearing him to Cammie who refused to leave the shelter without him. Although Barry was the one who took Bert on the most walks, it was 'KK' who he absolutely adored. The eight-year-old and the dog doted on each other twenty-four hours a day. They slept together and unless school or chores required it, were practically bound at the hip.

Barry looked up to see his younger sister coming around the side of the house from the same direction the dog had come from. She rushed up to Barry and was dancing from foot to foot as he brushed the leaves off his clothes.

"Hey KK, what's going on?" Barry frowned at what he thought was the Pee-pee dance. "Do you have to go to the bathroom?"

"No! I do not have to go to the bathroom! That's gross!" It seemed that anything and everything having to do with boys or bodily functions was 'gross' right now. "Dad got us some presents and we just have to wait till after dinner!"

"Wow! Well when is dinner? Is Cammie home?"

"Mom says she's on her way from Allison's right now." KK continued to dance her way towards the house. The mood was infectious and Bert bounced right along with her. They were almost to the back door when their mother appeared with her hands on her hips.

"You will not come into my house with all those branches and leaves stuck to you, young man." She turned her gaze on KK. "And you could stand a little cleaning yourself missy! I swear you kids must love rolling around with each other."

"That's gross, Mom! I don't roll around with anyone but Bert!" KK said casting a wary glance at Barry in case he got any funny ideas.

The kids dusted themselves off and went to the bathroom to wash up. Both of them noticed that the door to their father's office was closed. KK covered her mouth as Barry walked up and knocked on the door. It was a given that you did not disturb Dad when the office door was closed.

"I'll be out in a few minutes for dinner!" Dale's voice floated out from under the door.

"Okay, Dad!" Barry looked at KK and whispered, "it was worth a try."

They both went down the hall giggling. As soon as they got to the kitchen they helped lay out the place settings and get drinks on the table. While they were doing this, Cammie came through the front door and made a beeline for her room, seemingly oblivious to everyone in the house. She closed her door a little too loudly though, alerting her mother to her presence.

"Was that Cam?" she asked poking her head into the dining room, where Barry and KK were busy guessing what treats their father had gotten them.

"Yes ma'am." Barry replied while KK just shrugged.

"Well tell her to wash up and come on, dinners ready."

She got another "Yes ma'am." From Barry as he trooped down the hall towards his sister's room. He was brought up short when his father stepped out into the hall. Barry was just starting to smile as he looked up at his father, but he was taken aback, when he saw the bright red patches of skin on his father's neck.

"Are you all right, Dad?" He asked in an alarmed tone.

"What?" Dale looked down at his son, and seeing the alarmed look on his face crouched down in front of him. "I'm Okay buddy, I'm feeling a little warm though, why?"

"You need to look in a mirror, Dad! You have a rash!"

"Really? Well let's go take a look then." Dale turned and they both walked into the bathroom where Barry pointed out the obviously flushed skin.

"Wow! You're right bud. And I am feeling a little warm. I wonder if I picked up a bug somewhere?"

Dale was running a hand over the warm patch of skin on his neck and remembering the incident at the convenience store. "You know what this means."

"Cluck, cluck!" Barry started making chicken sounds and grinning. Cassy Louise Metzler lived to fuss over sick people. She was a walking pill dispenser and advice giver on any and every ailment known to man. She was such a mother hen when anyone was sick, that they had taken to 'Clucking' at each other when one of them was about to be on the receiving end of such ministrations.

Dale grinned at his son as they both went back into the hall. Barry banged on his sisters door and told her dinner was ready, to which he received no reply. Dale stepped over to the door and after rapping loudly on it twice said 'Now young Lady!'

Cammie's door flew open and she was stepping into the hall when the sight of her father's neck brought her up short.

"Oooohhh, Momma Hen's gonna be so happy to see you, Dad!"

The three of them made their way down the hall with various chicken sounds coming out of the two kid's mouths. They were all grinning as they entered the dining room and began to take their seats. KK caught on to the clucking noises as soon as she saw her father's neck and joined right in.

"I can hear you all, you know that right?" Cassy said as she brought in the baked ham and a bowl of mashed potatoes. She looked around the table before her eyes settled on her husband.

"Here it comes..." He managed to get out before she set the food down and went storming over to her husband.

"Dale Metzler! What in the world did you get into?" Not waiting for a reply, she immediately started pulling back the collar of his shirt.

"I am feeling a little warm but I didn't really notice until Barry pointed it out to me in the hall." He said covering her hand and ending any more exploring and diagnosis for the time being. "Let's eat dinner, then I have a surprise for you guys."

Meals didn't usually take that long at the Metzler household, they were all hard working country folk and had healthy appetites, and with the added incentive of whatever treat was coming at the end, the food seemingly vanished. Although KK frowned at Barry when he put seconds on his plate, he managed to wolf it down by the time Cammie was finished. Once everyone was finished, Dale leaned back with a satisfied smile on his face and returned the expectant looks of everyone at the table.

"What?" He grinned. "Oh you're waiting for me... Cam please help your mother with the dishes."

"Why don't..."

"Because young lady, they set the table while you were nowhere to be found and another word will result in you not only NOT receiving your present, but a weekend of chores as well." Cassy cut off her argument before it even got started. Weekend chores would mean no dance on Friday night at the Community center, a fate far worse than death to the teenager.

"Yes ma'am." Cammie knew she was right and immediately got up to help clear the table.

"Barry, you come help me carry this stuff in." Dale said tilting his head back down the hall.

"Okay, Dad."

As the men went down the hall to the office, KK got up and helped with the dishes anyway. In the office, Dale handed Barry two boxes and carried three out himself. The packages didn't have cards but the recipient's name was written in black magic marker on each gift. Barry set the large box at his mother's seat and a smaller one in front of Cam. He noticed his father putting a long skinny box next to Barry's chair, a weird shaped lumpy thing in front of KK's place, and what was obviously a wrapped dog bone in front of himself.

"Okay guys, a few years ago, a friend told me about a company that was developing solar panels that worked really well. We had a little bit of money at the time so I invested fifty thousand dollars in it. Last week the company sold for almost 1.8 billion dollars. My buyout on the stock was almost Seven hundred thousand dollars after income taxes." He waited as the information sank in. "For the past week, I've been paying off our debt and getting some things set in place for you guys. As of yesterday the farm is paid for and the car and truck notes are settled."

"What do the car and truck have notes for, Dad?" KK asked.

"Well honey, I borrowed money from the bank to pay for them when I bought them. That loan is called a note sometimes."

"So we're rich?" Barry had to ask.

"No son, not even close. But we're a lot more comfortable now. I thought a little celebration was in order though, so I booked us a seven day cruise to Mexico and..."

He picked up the package in front of him and opened it to reveal a smoked cow thigh. "Come here Bert!"

The dog went bouncing over and after a quick sniff, attempted to take the eight-pound bone in his mouth. The weight caused his head to plummet towards the floor. They all laughed as Bert had to drag the bone by backing up into the living room.

"So who's next?" Dale asked.

All the kids looked at their mom who blushed and said, "Oh no, I can wait."

"Come on, Mom!"

"Yeah , Mom. You're next!"

"You might as well show them babe, it's just a toaster..."

"Aww Dad!"

"Nuh-uh!"

"Okay, okay!" Cassy said and began to unwrap the box in front of her. Inside was some stuffing and another box. "Look I got a present for a present!"

The kids started sending Dale the evil eye when the second box was opened to reveal a third even smaller box.

"These are like those Russian Homely dolls..." Cammie said.

"Russian Nesting dolls." Dale said.

"Whatever, Dad!"

Two minutes and three boxes later, Cassy was holding up a pair of sapphire and diamond earrings. The reactions around the table ranged from a smug look on Dales face, to one of envy on Cammie's, to one of almost boredom on Barry's.

"KK your turn." Dale said.

The stuffed bear was a big hit with the youngest member of the clan and immediately became the inhabitant of the chair next to her.

"Son" Dale nodded to Barry.

The outer box was opened to reveal a quiver with twenty-five target arrows in it. The inner box had a complete Archery set including a bow with five more arrows, an arm guard, and a trigger type release for the bow string. Barry had all of it laid out on the table and was immediately nose deep in the instructions.

"There are going to be rules on that just like the guns son. That is a serious tool and not a toy. I'll help you build a practice range with a target tomorrow."

"Thanks, Dad!" Barry said glancing up from the instruction booklet. "This is so cool!"

Cammie, who thus far had displayed more patience than usual to this point, didn't even wait for words to come out of her father's mouth when he looked her way. She tore the wrapper off the box and had the Electronic Tablet out in ten seconds flat.

"Oh My God! A 64 gig tablet!" She glanced at her father. "Does it have internet?"

"Yes honey, you can do everything on it." Dale grinned at his daughter as she began unwrapping the USB charging cord and other accessories out of the box.

With the two older kid's eyebrows deep in their instruction booklets, and Cassy clunking around in the kitchen, Dale turned to KK, who was holding her bear up and staring at it intently. She slowly turned the stuffed toy around looking at it from every angle.

"What are you doing KK?"

"Do you think this is a boy bear or a girl bear? I can't tell the difference." She said with a serious look at her father.

"Well honey, I think that's up to you to decide." Dale struggled to keep from laughing at the girl's inspection of the androgynous animal.

"Uhmm... Okay." She continued to stare at the bear for a few more minutes before nodding her head and setting the toy back down on the chair next to her. "Because I have to give it the right name, I hope you know."

"Yes you do honey." Dale smiled at her. "A name is very important."

"I think her name should be Jo Jo Humperdink!" She said finally with a smug look on her face.

"Jo Jo Humperdink!" Barry repeated. "That's a great name Kristen!"

KK smiled up at her older brother as he gathered his new belongings and headed to his room. She picked up the wrapping paper and began clearing the other debris from the table, she even got a smile from her older sister who was busily downloading applications and reading the instructions to her tablet. With the help of her father the dining room was put back into order and she headed down the hall to her room.

Cassy came out from the kitchen drinking a glass of water. She set it on the table and wrapped her arms around her husband who had sat back down. She recoiled at the hot feel of the feverish skin on his neck.

"Oh honey! You are going to the clinic tomorrow to have that rash looked at! Lord you are warm."

"It's funny how I don't feel feverish, but I feel hot, like I just ran five miles." Dale said wiping away a bead of sweat from his forehead. "I will definitely go in tomorrow, right after I get Chuck to work on the back fence line."

"I think you need a day off, what's the point of being a big Wall Street investor if you can't take some leisure time?" She said poking fun at him. "Especially if you're not feeling well."

"The clinic won't be open till 9, so I might as well get him going on it. He should have done it last week. Besides, I feel fine…fine enough to get a little lovin'" he said as he swooped her up in his arms and carried her down the hall to their bedroom.

"Dale Metzler! What about the children?"

"I think they can tuck themselves in, besides, it's summer. They can bathe when they get dirty." The two of them continued down the hall, laughing and giggling. Dale carried his wife to their bed and set her down gently, while kicking the door shut with his booted foot.

The two of them began to strip off their clothes like they were teenagers. Dale feeling an animal rush to be with his mate. Their love making was passionate and vigorous, and a little loud. Cammie walked down the hall after downloading her Apps and heard the activity inside her parents' room.

"Ewww!" She muttered and quickly went to her room and shut the door.

CHAPTER 3

The toxin floated freely through their blood stream. Seeping through the walls of their blood vessels and concentrating in the cells of their brains. Their bodies immediately began trying to rid themselves of the chemical by concentrating it in their saliva and sweat, but it was too late for the brain. Psychosis began to set in.

Dale woke up covered in sweat and moaning. He stood up and began to get dressed out of habit, glancing down at his wife who was tossing and turning. He noticed the bright red rash running from her neck down across her left breast. The sight nudged something in his brain and somewhere in his muddled thoughts, he knew it should concern him but his mind couldn't focus on it. There was something else he had to do.

He staggered down the hallway and began to mutter "Fence, fence…"

After stopping at the kitchen sink to take a long drink from the faucet and rinse out his mouth, he staggered outside and began walking towards the barn. He stepped inside the cool space and stood there trying to remember what he was supposed to do. His eyes came to rest on a shovel and he pulled it off the wall hooks. Holding it in his hands he became very angry at something but he couldn't tell what. He began breathing heavy when he heard a truck pull up outside. He stepped over to the window and looked out as Chuck, the farm foreman stepped out and stumbled to the back of the truck.

Drunk! Dale's mind fixated on the thought. *He's shown up drunk! To work on my farm!*

A small growl escaped his lips as he walked out to the truck. He got there and Chuck was nowhere to be seen, having walked around the other side of the barn and headed off across the drive to a utility shed. Dale stood there not comprehending what was going on. He felt an incredible rage at Chuck for showing up at work drunk, but in the back of his head, he knew it wasn't a reasonable thought, but then again he had run away.

After standing there for a minute trying to process the information, he was finally brought out of his funk by the sound of his tractor. He looked just as it came around the side of the barn with the bucket raised. The auger bit had been installed on the back the previous week so that it could be used to drill out the post holes. Chuck stopped it and turned the motor off with the bucket next to the back of his truck. He hopped down and walked over to the tailgate.

"Fence, fence, fence..." Dale muttered as he looked at the poles in the bed of the truck.

"Yeah, they weren't in last week, remember?" Chuck asked in a somewhat belligerent tone. He had a headache, and a rash and didn't feel well.

Dale picked up on the tone and turned to face his longtime friend. He was gripping the shovel in both hands across the front of his body. Seemingly of their own accord, his arms drove the shovel blade up into Chuck's neck, under his jaw. The curved blade tore through his jugular vein, carotid artery, and crushed his esophagus. Chuck's eyes widened for a moment before his body collapsed, falling between the tailgate of the truck and the tractor bucket.

Dale looked down at the body and then held the blade of the shovel up to inspect it. Inside, a part of him recoiled at the act and the blood. But the bigger part of his mind reveled in the sight and the smell of the blood. A rush of confusing emotions swept through him before he recoiled in horror at what he had done. With a low whine he turned and ran into the woods.

Barry was up before anyone else in the house. During the school year, his mother normally had to resort to a crowbar to get him out of bed in the morning. During the summer it was a whole different ball game, he didn't want to waste any free time. He put on some jeans with a belt (His mom bought him clothes a size or two big now because he grew out of them so fast) and a tee shirt before heading out towards Andrew's house.

Stopping in the kitchen to grab a bite, he poured a glass of milk and grabbed a chunk of Mrs. Smith's pineapple upside down cake. He stood at the sink and devoured the sweet, letting the crumbs fall into the sink and occasionally dropping a chunk to Bert, who sat there patiently, willing to dispose of any dropped morsel. Barry washed down his last mouthful of cake with the last of his milk and rinsed his glass.

Noticing that the dog's water dish was almost empty, he filled it from the tap and set it back down on the placemat that held his food and water bowls. He gave Bert a pet as the dog began to lap up the water. He noticed that Bert's fur felt warm. Barry figured the dog had already been outside in the sun.

Barry was out the door with the instructions to his new bow stuck in his back pocket to show Andy. He stopped by the barn to grab a couple of bottles of drinking water and then took off through the woods to the fort. He only used minimal 'Counter surveillance' techniques when he came from his house, because the main concern was not someone following them from Barry's house, it was more to keep Andy's older brother Will from finding it and taking it over.

After making his way inside, he put one of his bottles in the cooler, even though there was no ice, it was in the shade and would stay cool, and took the other with him up top. He brought the radio to listen to as he sipped the clear water. He had almost finished the bottle when the music he was listening to stopped and the warning tone from the emergency broadcast system began to sound through the speaker.

Barry looked at the device in annoyance, leaned over and started to change channels. Every station that he tried had the same annoying tone coming out of it. He was sure it was one of those tests and was just about to turn it off when a voice began to tell him that it *was not* a test, and to standby for important information. The message repeated itself several times, then the warning tone started again.

Barry had had just about enough and was standing up when a different voice came out of the radio.

"This is the emergency broadcast system, the United States has been subject to a chemical attack. Parties unknown have managed to taint most of the open source water supplies in the US. Do not drink water from any public source or city supplied tap water. The chemical causes fever and in some cases violent behavior. The National Guard has been activated and all members are ordered to report to their units immediately. Civilians are urged to remain in their homes and only drink from known safe water sources."

The emergency tone started again, and Barry just stood there with his mouth open for a minute before turning it off. He then climbed down into the fort and took stock of his supplies. The boys had two boxes of Pop-

Tarts, a big bag of sunflower seeds, and a bag of Teriyaki beef jerky stashed away. The cooler held a couple bottles of water plus a couple of boxed fruit drinks.

The Jog back to his house was far scarier than the trip out. The young boy's imagination was running full force and he kept expecting to have some boogeyman jump out at him. He was still a quarter mile from his fence when he heard something crashing through the brush off to his right. He ducked down into a depression and tried to see what it was, but all he could make out was a man sized silhouette running through the trees.

He was slipping through the fence when he noticed Chuck's truck and the tractor parked next to the barn. He angled over that way but didn't see anyone so he continued on towards the house. He walked through the mudroom off of the kitchen, stopping to brush off some leaves and dirt before stepping into the kitchen.

"Mom! Dad!" He shouted into the house. "There's an emergency!"

Then the smell hit him and he stepped towards the living room.

Cassy drifted up from unconsciousness with a pounding headache. She was sweating and her mouth was coated with some form of thick slime. She staggered up from her bed and went into the master bath where her muddled brain told her to turn on the faucet. She rinsed out her mouth and then took a long drink, bending over and almost sucking on the tap. The water running across her cheek felt so good that she began splashing it across her face and neck, grunting in pleasure. By the time she was finished, she was soaked to the waist, but the pounding in her head had lessened somewhat.

She walked out of the bathroom and looked around her bedroom like it was her first time. Her mind was trying to sort out the various signals her body was sending it. Her head still ached, and she was feverish, but she also had a sore feeling between her legs that wasn't entirely unpleasant. She looked down her naked body at her crotch and gently touched herself there before grunting in pleasure, knowing that something was good about the feeling, but not exactly sure what.

Eventually the hunger took over again and she opened the door to her closet. After poking through it and realizing that it wasn't the way out, she went to the window. She heard the sound of a motor and instinctively knew that it meant someone was around. She considered busting out through the window but a flash of memory had her walking out to the hallway and down towards the living room.

She walked in and saw Bert gnawing on a bone and growling. Her stomach grumbled at the smell of the bone. Dropping to all fours she approached the dog and began to growl herself. Bert stopped his chewing and bared his fangs, not liking the chemical sweat smell coming off of the woman.

Cassy lunged forward and attempted to grab the bone and received a bite to the hand for her efforts. She only pulled back her hand for a second before launching her entire body at the dog who was now barking ferociously at her. She sprawled across Bert who gave out a startled yelp before biting her again on the upper arm. She managed to pick the squirming dog up and bring its neck to her mouth before one of the dog's claws caught the corner of her eye, tearing the eyelid away, and leaving a small cut on her cheek.

Cassy let out a howl of rage and bit down on Bert's neck causing the dog to yelp again. The struggle was short lived as she tore into the dog using her hands and mouth. She continued to rip the dog to shreds until a scream brought her up short.

KK and Cammie had both been woken by the commotion in the living room. KK was the first to make it down the hall and screamed in horror at the sight of her mother, covered in blood, literally pulling a leg off of her dog. The scream resonated through Cassy's skull, causing a wave of pain. She hurled the partially dismembered dog at her daughter and clamped her hands over her ears before snarling at her in a rage.

The throw was high, and Bert's body flew over KK's head and impacted the wall in the hallway, leaving a smear of blood and entrails, before landing on the floor and sliding along the hall, coming to rest against Cammie's door as she was opening it.

The shocked teenager stared down at the mangled body before looking up in time to see her little sister yanked into the living room by her arm. She ran down the hall as the screams from the living room reached a crescendo. Cammie rounded the corner just in time to see her naked mother, covered in gore, rake her finger nails across her younger sister's face and neck. KK was trying to protect herself by holding Jo Jo Humperdink between herself and her mother. She was only partially successful and the fingernails left a set of long furrows down the side of the young girls face.

Cammie, who had the beginnings of a rash starting along the inside of her thighs and armpits, became enraged at her mother and stepped forward, swinging her new tablet at her mothers' head. The slender device snapped almost in half as it crashed across the side of Cassy's face and shattered, sending fragments of the glass screen into her already damaged eye. Cassy let out a howl and turned on her older daughter while hurling KK across the room. The little girl, who had not been exposed to the toxin, slammed into the edge of the coffee table, shattering her collar bone and mercifully knocking her unconscious.

Cassy leapt on Cammie with a snarl as the teenager slammed what was left of the broken device down on her mother's neck. The jagged edge penetrated the opening between the collar bone and the scapula, tearing through vital blood vessels and collapsing part of her throat. Although the wound was fatal it did not stop Cassy from clamping her teeth on her daughters' neck and ripping out a chunk of flesh. The two fell to the floor clawing and flailing at each other as their strength ebbed. The struggle only took another twenty seconds before Cammie lay dead on the floor.

Cassy staggered to her feet and made her way unsteadily to KK. The smell of blood and the hunger in her stomach won out over whatever was left of her psyche. She bent over and bit down on her daughters' neck. She leaned over to take a second bite when the internal hemorrhaging caused her to slip into unconsciousness and die.

The blood from the bodies was still running down the walls and seeping into the floor when Barry stepped into the room. As he crossed the threshold into the living room, he glanced down the hallway and immediately recognized the lump of mangled fur lying in the doorway to his sister's room. He froze in his tracks and slowly turned his head to take in the carnage in the living room. His mother's naked body was draped across KK's torn and battered corpse. The blood matted Jo Jo Humperdink still interposed between them. Cammie was lying with one leg folded under her as a pool of blood expanded under her blonde hair.

The enormity of the situation stunned Barry to his very core. His mind began to shut down as the images were burned into his memory. He stood there as shock began to take hold of him and he became light headed. He had no idea what he should do to help his family. He stumbled to the wall and leaned against it.

The sound of his mother's bowels letting loose startled him. The stench of the outgassing finally causing him to move. He stepped back into the kitchen and called out for his father. When he didn't receive any response, he woodenly walked into the kitchen and picked up the phone. He was raising his hand to dial 911 when he realized that the headset was making the busy tone. He tapped the disconnect bar of the ancient machine, but got the same result. He was afraid to search the house further so he walked outside.

He began walking towards the barn, and remembering the truck, walked around to the side. As soon as he rounded the corner he saw the body lying beneath the tailgate. He was too terrified to approach the scene and stood rooted at the corner of the barn. As he was staring at the jeans with work boots sticking out from them, under the back of the truck, he heard a scream from across the field. It was the straw that broke the camel's back. He turned and fled.

Barry began running towards the woods, looking over his shoulder to see what had screamed so loud. Just as he was entering the tree line he saw a man loping up his driveway. He paused and stared at the familiar figure of one of his neighbors as he trotted up the drive. It took a second for Barry to figure out that the dark bib the man was wearing was actually blood stained gore dripping from the man's mouth. Barry watched until the man went out of view around the front of his house, then turned and ran deeper into the woods.

Barry ignored the fort and cut an angle towards Andy's house through the woods. He came out just between Ms. Allensworth's' house and Andy's. He ran full tilt around to the front of their house. The sight that met him there causing him to skid to a stop.

The Petty's front door was open and there was a trail of blood leading out to the street. Barry's gaze followed the trail out to a misshapen lump lying on the other side of the road. Barry immediately recognized some of the clothing as Will's, and a sliver of hope sprang into his head. He turned and rushed through the front door. Stepping across the threshold, he took in the entry foyer and living room. Aside from the blood smear which came through the archway from the kitchen and went out the front door everything seemed in order.

Barry considered calling out, but decided that discretion was in order. Instead he walked up the stairs and down the hall to Andy's room. The door was open and Barry stepped into the doorway. He took in the wreckage and displaced items strewn about the room. The bed cover was dragged halfway onto the floor among the clothes and toys strewn about. It was the first normal scene Barry had come across since leaving the fort.

Not finding his friend in his room, Barry wandered about the house but didn't find anyone. He picked up the cordless phone in the living room but got the same busy tone that he had heard earlier. He walked back out the front door and looked up and down the street. Way off in the distance he saw a person leaning over another. It took him a moment to realize that the one kneeling was chewing on the arm of the one laying there. He immediately decided to get off the street and start using cover. The decision saved his life.

After cutting back around the Petty's' house to the woods, Barry made a beeline for Ms. Allensworth's house. He made it to her back fence and looked over into her back yard. Not seeing anyone he called out softly.

"Ms. Allensworth!" He peered around before calling out again. "Hello?"

He waited a few minutes and when no reply was forthcoming he went to the side door and knocked. He waited for a few more minutes again before he began moving down towards the Smith's. He was in the tree line and was about to break cover and head to the Smith's back door when he heard a grunt behind him. Crouching down in some bushes he watched as a blood spattered figure came around from the front of the house.

The man stopped and looked around for a few seconds before hearing a noise behind him. He turned and charged back towards the front of the houses and out of Barry's sight. Barry wasted no time and rushed to the Smith's cellar door. Finding it unlocked he slipped inside and was just closing the door when the sounds of a horrible fight came from the front of the house. He crawled behind some shelves and hid.

Justine Allensworth had always been very fit. She maintained her stunning figure with a disciplined workout routine which made her that much more dangerous when the chemicals coursing through her brain turned her into a cannibal. She had ingested plenty of the toxin the previous day in her sweat tea, and had woken up that morning fully disoriented. She had staggered around the house with a horrible headache, until a commotion from next door sent her over there in a rage.

Mr. Smith had beaten his wife to death with a kitchen chair and was stumbling through his house howling like the madman he was, when Justine came through the door. The athletic woman had made short work of the sixty-seven-year-old man. She then spent the next twenty minutes tearing the entrails out of the man and eating some of them. She had finished eating her fill and was relieving herself on the carpet when she heard a faint call from over near her house. She took a second to finish her business and then stood to charge out the door. She stumbled before she remembered to pull up her Yoga pants. Just as she made it to the front door she saw a shadow walk past the side of the house.

The sight infuriated her for some reason and she charged out the front door. She turned right and ran to the end of the porch, where she hopped up on the railing and looked back along the side of the house. The feral man heard her jumping up on the railing and spun about. He immediately snarled and charged towards her. She waited until he had closed the distance before hurling herself at the man. Although the impact of her body slamming into him slowed him down, the man's greater mass overcame the impact and Justine was slammed to her back. The man falling on top of her and immediately wrapping his hands around her throat.

A series of memories flashed through her mind. Even though her brain was short circuiting, and her thoughts were somewhat incoherent, memories of a self-defense class flashed across her consciousness. The man reared his head back prior to taking a bite out of her cheek and her right hand flashed in front of his face as she both bucked her hips and brought her hand down across both of his wrists. The move collapsed both of his elbows down between them. She then bucked her hips the other way and pushed up with her left hand under his right one, while simultaneously pulling with her own right. The action pulled his right arm in front of his face just as he was snapping his head forward to take a bite.

His face smashed into his own forearm as he found himself rolled onto his side with his right arm extended and her in control of it. The sudden change of events stunned his already muddled mind and he paused to figure out what had happened. Justine gave him no chance to recover and shot to a kneeling position before dropping all of her weight on the back of his elbow. The arm broke with an audible pop, and the pain flooded up his arm. He turned to scream at the source of his pain and got his eyes raked for the trouble. He attempted to roll away from the assault, dragging the broken arm after him. His eyes filled with blood and he lost most of his sight. He didn't see it coming when Justine leaned in and tore out his throat.

After the body stopped twitching, Justine rolled over and lay panting for a while. She had a full stomach so she didn't even chew on the man she had just killed. She didn't move until a noise out on the street caught her attention. She was relatively uninjured but she had overstressed her muscles and they were a little sore. She got slowly to her feet and limped around to the front of the house.

CHAPTER 4

Down in the basement, Barry had climbed out from behind the shelves once the noise stopped. The basement had been divided into two rooms, one for Mrs. Smith's food storage, and a smaller area next to the furnace that held some tools and camping supplies. There was a stairway up to the kitchen next to the dividing wall. Barry immediately went up to the door and gently tried it, trying not to make any noise. The door was locked from the other side. He would have to go outside and come in through one of the ground floor entrances if he wanted anything from up there. Going outside was not something he wanted to do at the moment.

Barry went into the tool area and hit the mother lode. One set of shelves had been devoted to camping equipment. He found two external frame hiking packs which were too big for his still growing frame, and a canvas pack that felt just right. There were gas lanterns and a few flashlights, which he used to augment the feeble light coming through the small side windows. After he got two lanterns going, he used some old shirts he found to cover the windows so nothing could see inside.

Most of the items on the top shelf were out of his view, so he pulled a crate over and was able to take down the items which had previously been out of reach. The first item was an old machete in a green canvas sheath. Although it wasn't the sharpest blade he'd ever seen, it did have a small pouch with a sharpening stone in it. The next two items would also be very handy. The green military sleeping bag and folding shovel were both in good shape.

Further down the shelf was a long leather gun case. Barry pulled the zipper open on the sheepskin lined soft case to reveal a smooth wooden stock. He slid out the Marlin Model 700 and smiled. The .22 caliber rifle was a popular gun at his Boy Scout summer camp, and he was very familiar with it. He verified that the weapon was on safe, then pulled back on the charging handle to verify he had an unloaded weapon. He pushed in on the charging handle, locking the breach open, and set the gun down on one of the lower shelves. He opened the case the rest of the way to find two tiny ten round metal magazines and two really cool plastic ones that were banana shaped and looked kind of like the ones on AK-47s.

He put the case and magazines on the shelf next to the rifle and again stared at the top shelf. He needed ammo now, and hopefully some cleaning gear too. He saw a leather pistol case and a couple of old military ammo cans down at the far end of the shelf. After moving his improvised step stool down a ways, he was able to retrieve the last of the items on the shelf.

The first ammo can held two 500 round bricks of .22LR ammunition and four more of the tiny ten round magazines for the rifle. There was also some fired rifle brass from a bigger caliber gun. The second ammo can had a bunch of cleaning supplies for both rifles and pistols. There were some old t-shirt rags and a military style green canvas holster in there as well. He also found a metal military style canteen with a green canvas cover. It looked like the new fashion for this summer was going to be green canvas.

The Pistol case held the coolest and most frustrating treasure of all. Inside was a Springfield Armory 1911A1 pistol. The weapon was in immaculate condition and had two seven-round and four eight-round magazines with it.

He wasted two hours looking for ammunition for it, but came up empty. Frustration level one.

He spent a good twenty minutes trying to figure out how the pistol worked. Although he had a strong understanding of how semi-automatic firearms operated, this weapon was new to him. He figured out the magazine release right away, even though there wasn't one inserted in the weapon. He also had seen enough movies to understand how the slide worked but he couldn't get it to go to the rear. He finally realized that the safety was preventing him from pulling it to the rear and got it off and the slide locked back. This last done with a great deal of effort, since the springs used to handle the powerful .45 ACP load were substantially stiffer than those of a .22. Frustration level two.

After being very sure that it was unloaded, he spent the next hour getting the feel for the weapon. Although his hands were still a little small for the frame, he could handle the weight no problem. He inserted it into the holster to make sure it was the right one for the gun, then spent another hour trying to practice his quick draw, the flap over the top prevented him from being very fast. Frustration level three.

Having reached the limit of his patience, Barry decided to pack the equipment and get it ready to move to the fort. He was able to fit the cleaning gear into the ammo can with the .22 ammo after discarding the old brass and limiting himself to two rags to wrap the rods and brushes in. There was also a small bottle of solvent and a small bottle of gun oil to squeeze in as well. The good thing was that once everything was in the can, it didn't rattle around and make any noise.

He did have a noise problem with the food however. The preserves and pickled vegetables were in row upon row of mason jars. There were some dry goods, but most of the food was packed in jars that would clink together inside the pack. After some experimentation he found he could eliminate the noise by wrapping each jar in a rag. This cut down on the amount of food he would be able to carry with him back to the fort. This maxed out his frustration level and he sat down with a huff to chill out.

Deciding he needed a brain break, he decided to really explore the basement. There was a chest freezer with a variety frozen food items. After taking stock of the food, equipment and tools. He discovered a PVC pipe with a cap on it. The four-inch diameter tube was the drain cleanout for the house. By opening the recessed cap he had a place to go to the bathroom, which he promptly did, getting most of the stream right down the hole. After putting the cap back on, he went in search of something to drink but came up empty.

Mrs. Smith was known for her lemonade as well as her cooking, and Barry decided he was going to make his way outside and into the main house for something to drink, and to get a better take on what was going on outside. He was still very upset about the loss of his family, but he didn't feel quite so helpless now.

Not knowing if he might have to make a run for it, he only put one jar of Strawberry preserves, one jar of pickles, and a plastic jar of peanut butter in the pack. This on top of the ammo can meant he was going to have limited space to pack additional stuff, but if he had to run away, he wouldn't be empty handed. He put the two flashlights in outside pockets.

He spent several minutes loading up all the magazines for the rifle. This used up two of the small boxes out of a brick. He put one of the big plastic magazines in the rifle and chambered a round. The rest of the magazines were spread throughout his jeans pockets. He suffered a moment of unease as he realized that under normal circumstances, if his father caught him loading a gun inside a house, he would get a whippin' for sure. These, however, were not normal circumstances, and he wasn't going back outside without being prepared.

The machete was on his left hip hanging down past his knee. He re-tied his sneakers, making sure they were double knotted and snug. This was a lesson he had learned from being chased by Will. He was unknowingly recreating the 'Battle Rattle' checks that soldiers had been doing for centuries.

Being as quiet as possible, Barry crept back up the stairs to the outside door. He opened it just a tiny crack and began to peer around the Smith's back yard, craning his head around to see as much as possible. After observing the yard for a few minutes he quietly slipped out and stood next to the back porch. After carefully surveying his surroundings, he crept up the short flight of stairs to the back door.

The screen door opened with only a slight screech of the springs. He then turned the knob on the door, thankful it was unlocked. There was a little resistance but it opened when he bumped it with his hip. He softly stepped into the immaculate kitchen and wrinkled his nose. The stench from the living room had permeated the house over the last several hours, and it was pretty rank.

Barry ignored the stink and went right to the fridge. As he expected there was a large pitcher of lemonade. Barry grabbed a glass from the cupboard, and poured himself a tall glass. He was halfway through it when he realized that it had probably been made with tap water. He let out a mental sigh when he saw the bottled water cooler next to the fridge.

He was halfway through his second glass when he noticed movement outside the kitchen window. He leaned forward and his breathe caught in his throat and he picked his rifle up off the counter when he saw what it was.

After killing the man next to her house, Justine wandered out to the front lawn and looked around. Not seeing anything of interest, and feeling the sun beating down on her, she went back inside her house, knowing that it was her place to sleep. Her full stomach was making her drowsy, and she felt the need to let her sore muscles recuperate.

She collapsed on her couch and dozed off. She had been asleep for a couple of hours when the itching she felt all over her body woke her up. She had dried blood and gore caked all over the front of her and she had dried feces between her legs. She stood up and tore a hole in her yoga pants to scratch at the irritation. Still feeling uncomfortable, a thought flashed through her head that the pool in her back yard offered some relief. She had waded in to her waist and was enjoying the cool water when she heard the noise of the Smith's screen door opening and closing. A series of irrational thoughts flashed through her fevered brain, resulting in her becoming enraged at the thought of something disturbing her bath. She walked out of the pool and headed out her front door.

She went to the body lying between the houses and circled it a few times before leaning over and striking it several times with her fists. The corpse did nothing and she looked around for what could have been the source of the noise.

Barry watched all of this from the kitchen window. He couldn't take his eyes off of the School teacher.

She had a streak of blood and gore down the front of her substantial chest and continuing down her body. The pool water she had splashed on her face had not done much to remove the blood and viscera. Her pants had now been split front to back from the crotch to her backside, revealing both her crotch and butt. What was exposed was the exact opposite of what her bathing suit normally covered and Barry was transfixed by the sight. He couldn't have moved if he wanted to as he watched her bend over the body. The smell was another thing however, it wafted through the partially open window and made him want to gag. The copper scent of blood, the rancid chemical tainted sweat, and the poop that was still on her legs, made him grimace and gag. It took all his self-control to not throw up in the sink.

He didn't move until after she stood up and looked around. It wasn't until she began walking towards the back yard that he realized the back door was unlocked. He scurried over and gently turned the lock button just as he heard footsteps on the porch. He crouched down just as the knob started to turn and didn't look up as the bloody face appeared in the window and looked inside. Not seeing anything that looked like prey or a threat she padded off the porch and continued down along the back yards of her neighbors.

Barry let out a sigh of relief and decided he would hole up in the house for the time being until he could figure on a course of action. He had pretty much decided he was living out a zombie movie and didn't expect any help from the police. He decided he would seal up the house and make do with the supplies on hand. There was enough food here to last for a long time.

That plan lasted until he went into the living room to secure the front of the house. Mrs. Smith lay in the hallway with her head smashed in and lying at an unnatural angle. Her face turned and looking over her right shoulder. Her battered upper torso was on the bottom two risers of the stairs, while her hips were twisted to the side and her legs were scissored open. The visual effect made her looked like she had been twisted like a cork screw.

Mr. Smith lay spread eagled in the living room. His abdominal cavity torn open and entrails pulled out and scattered. Blood was splattered across every wall and piece of furniture. Barry frowned as he noticed that someone had taken a poop right next to his head. The stench was so overwhelming that Barry couldn't even make it across the room to close the open front door. He turned and ran into the bathroom where he closed the door and after spraying some air freshener, took several deep breaths to keep from losing his breakfast.

He sprayed some more of the air freshener onto a hand towel and wrapped it around his face. He went back out and searched around for a while, avoiding going in the front room. He unlocked the cellar door and made several trips from the kitchen and upstairs pantry down to the cellar. On his second trip up he looked at the light switch and figured *What the heck!* And flipped it. The two banks of fluorescent lights down below flickered on. *Got to start using your brain Metzler.*

He hauled 3 five-gallon water jugs down along with the partially full one from the cooler. He eventually brought the cooler down as well, once he found an extension cord. Several more trips emptied the Pantry of everything he wanted. He grabbed a set of silverware from a drawer and called it good.

He ventured as far as the rear portion of the hallway and opened a linen closet. He pulled down some thick quilts and a pillow that he would use for bedding. Unfortunately he failed to notice another pistol case and four boxes of .45 ACP ammo on the top shelf.

He finally decided to just go ahead and live in the basement. He made the decision after searching the garage and finding a couple of bike locks that he could secure the doors with. They were new in the packaging, and he could set his own combinations on them. He grabbed a couple of pieces of scrap wood and some tools to board over the small windows. He didn't want anything to be able to peek through a crack in the blinds and see him.

He made sure that any lights were shut off in the kitchen and hallway (He still wasn't going into the living room), and went down below. After locking the kitchen door behind him, he secured the outside cellar door and began to cover the windows. He had a close call with the last one.

He had been setting the nails through the boards on the floor, using a quilt as a pad to muffle the sound. But there was no escaping the noise when he had to hammer the boards over the windows themselves. He had been careful to make sure there were no visible threats before starting to nail in the boards, but a large dog had heard the noise when he covered the previous window. It had zeroed in on the noise and began to snarl and dig at the window.

Barry peered through a crack and decided to use the noise as cover and banged the rest of the nails in. He had just finished when the noise outside turned into a fight as the dog was attacked by a large man. The two opponents fought until the dog had a broken leg and the man had suffered a torn artery in his arm. They both limped off in different directions where they succumbed to their wounds.

By 7:00 PM Barry was exhausted. He had been running on adrenalin all day long and had kept himself busy so he wouldn't be thinking about his family. He wolfed down a sandwich and finished the last of the lemonade. A quick trip to the sewer pipe and he flopped down on the bed he had made. He left the lights on and curled up on his side. He quickly fell into a deep but troubled sleep, as the nightmares of the day invaded his rest.

CHAPTER 5

Outside, the community and the world fell apart. The toxin had been ingested by humans and animals alike. All high order mammals suffered from the effects. Some people suffered psychotic breaks and just shut down, they fell victim quickly to the ones who became aggressive. The psychosis caused many to ignore the pain receptors in their bodies, and they literally over exerted themselves until their muscles and ligaments tore from their bones and their tendons popped.

Barry spent the next two days holed up and not making a sound. He heard some sporadic gunfire in the distance and there was movement above him in the kitchen several times. The door knob even rattled once, causing him to take up a firing position. But nothing ever got in and he was able to rest up and make a plan.

He knew he wouldn't be able to stay there forever. The water was getting low for one thing, and he wanted to see what was happening. On the third day he removed the towel that he had placed along the floor of the kitchen door to prevent the smell from coming in and stepped into the kitchen. The smell had gotten a thousand times worse, as the bodies in the living room had begun to rot and several of the visitors over the last two days had also relieved themselves in there. He immediately went to the back door and after looking around carefully opened it so that the breeze would help clear some of the horrible stench.

He carefully made his way into the trees, and Squatted down. The woods felt funny now. The slight animals sounds he was used to were absent, but every once in a while there would be some thrashing of the brush as two animals attacked each other. The primitive part of his brain recognized the danger and dumped more adrenaline into his system.

Staying hyper alert, and keeping the rifle at the ready, he slowly made his way back towards his home. Twice he stopped and took cover as bodies crashed through the brush. Once he was deeper in the woods, the undergrowth cleared up and he could see for a distance. He made good time since he could see further, and he didn't have to stop as much. He didn't stop at the fort along the way, he was planning to use it as a waypoint on the way back though.

He planned on raiding his barn for the drinking water that his father kept there. He was going to ferry the cases of water back to the fort and then back to the Smith's basement. His father had a pallet of water delivered every other week so the workers could take them out to the field. Each pallet contained eighty cases of twenty-four half-liter bottles each. There was more than three quarters of a pallet left.

He stopped at his fence and watched the field and barn for movement. The run from the fence to the house would be the longest exposed distance he would cover since the day it all started. There was an unfamiliar SUV parked at the head of the driveway, and several bodies in the yard. He could see several brass shell casings shining on the ground, and he thought maybe the police or someone had imposed some order, but a scream from across the field dashed that hope.

He waited for several minutes after hearing the scream before loping over to the barn in a crouch. He peered through a dirty window, and not seeing any movement crept around to the door. He was going to avoid walking by the truck and what he thought were his father's remains, but he had to look. He approached the truck and crept around to the driver's side slowly. He could see that the body had been gone over by scavengers. The torso had been pulled out from under the dozer bucket. Barry let out a sigh of relief as he realized that the body was that of Chuck, the farm foreman, and not his dad. He went to the barn door, gently lifted the latch and slipped inside.

Everything appeared just as it was when he had gotten the two water bottles out of it three days earlier. The cases of water were undisturbed, and he began stuffing the loose bottles in his pack. He found that he could fit more in his pack if he left the plastic wrap on the cases, and spent several minutes organizing his load. He decided he would leave the ammo can at the fort for the next few trips so he could carry the most water. He put the now very heavy pack on his back, and went back to the door.

He again spent several minutes watching the outside before slipping out and trotting back into the woods. Once in the trees he slowed down and carefully made his way back to the fort. He dropped everything except the rifle and pack and went back for a second trip.

He was startled to see that the Strange SUV was gone. He didn't think that the crazies could drive cars, so that meant that someone had probably been there when he was. The thought gave him both hope and scared him a little since whoever it was could have been the one responsible for all the dead bodies on the front lawn. He wondered if whoever it was had looted his house. He would know soon enough, since he absolutely had to go inside and get some more clothes. The ones he had on smelled pretty bad after three days.

He made his way in through the back door and looked around the kitchen. The smell was horrible and he made his way down the hallway as fast as he could to his room. Again, nothing seemed out of place, and he quickly stripped out of his old clothes and using a bottle of precious water and a washcloth from the bathroom, gave himself a good scrubbing. He wasn't about to wash with the contaminated water, since he didn't know if it could infect him through one of the many cuts and bruises he was currently sporting. His scalp was itching so he went to his Dads room and using more of his precious water and his dad's razor, shaved his head. Finally figuring 'In for a Penny, In for a pound' he brushed his teeth. The tooth brush plus a spare new one went right in one of the outside pockets on his pack.

He felt much better being clean and in clean clothes. He grabbed a full load of underwear and socks. Even though it was summer he opted for two pairs of jeans, since he had been spending a lot of time on his hands and knees crawling through the brush. Two T-shirts, a sweat shirt, and a light jacket were stuffed in the pack. He looked longingly at the bow and arrow set in the corner and then walked out.

He made it halfway down the hall before turning around and grabbing it. He didn't think it was powerful enough to kill an enraged human, but it was quiet. He wasn't going to hunt with it since he didn't want to consume anything that may have been poisoned.

All in all it would take him twenty-five trips to get everything back to the Smith's basement. He had to stop twice in the woods as he saw human figures walking through the trees at a distance. It was becoming apparent that those that had been affected tended to walk with their heads jutting forward and their arms away from their bodies. The posture made them easier to recognize at a distance.

He was back inside the basement organizing the items he had recovered when he heard a clawing at the cellar door. It had happened a few times in the last few days, and he usually just held still and stayed quiet until whatever it was left.

This time however, the scratching became more insistent, and the handles were shaken violently. Barry could hear a person sniffing at the door as he crept up to it with his rifle in his hands. The shaking and pounding continued for almost twenty minutes before it became quiet. Barry was almost positive that it had been two people outside. After the noise stopped he went to the window to peek out but didn't see anything. He made sure the rifle was close at hand when he turned in.

Barry spent the next several days foraging in the surrounding neighborhood. Ms. Allensworth was the only regular feral that he saw, and he kept a wide berth from her.

He watched her successfully defend her territory three times before a large male beat her unconscious. He watched from the woods as the man began to roll her over. He was a higher functioning feral and still had his shorts on. Barry got pretty upset when he saw the man pull down his pants and position himself to rape her.

Without thinking he put the front site on the man's head just in front of the top of his ear. He let his breath out and pressed the trigger. The 40 grain lead bullet left the rifle muzzle and went straight to the man's temple. At first Barry thought he had missed, since the man jerked his head around to look at where the shot came from. Barry was just aiming in on his eye when he fell over. He waited several minutes to see if anything was going to respond to the sound of his shot. After watching for a few minutes he slowly crept down to check on Ms. Allensworth.

Although she was one of the crazies, to his way of thinking, she was 'His' crazy. She was a known quantity in a very uncertain world. He had come to recognize her patterns as she came and went. She still smelled horrible, but after coming across several bodies of other slain ferals, he came to the realization that she was a relative rose garden. She at least bathed (If you could call it that, since her pool was starting to get pretty gross in its own right), and her odor was somewhat bearable until you got too close. Some of the other ferals he had come across were so grime and feces covered that they stank from twenty feet away.

Keeping the rifle pointed at the pair as he approached, he made his way around to the far side of the man. He had to look closely to see the small hole in the man's temple. The hair from his sideburn masked the wound. Using the barrel of the gun he prodded the man and then looked for an exit wound. He finally leaned down, and grimacing from the stench, felt for a pulse. Not finding one, he then was about to check on Ms. Allensworth when she let out a sigh and stirred slightly. This startled him so bad he scooted back on his rump and pointed the rifle at her.

Figuring that she was okay, he made his way back into the woods. They were several houses to the east of the Smith's, so Barry got as far back into the wood line as he could and still see the two bodies lying there. He would keep watch until the sun started to set, then he was out of there. After carefully looking all around to make sure nothing was sneaking up on him, he settled in to wait. It didn't take long as it was only five minutes before Justine rolled over and got slowly to her knees.

Hurt...Bad... the thought was crystal clear in Justine's head. She rolled over and got slowly to her hands and knees. She took another deep breath and paused, as another stream of memories rushed through her head. There was a faint smell that she recognized. Not the musk coming from her attacker, but another clean smell. She had cut a scent cone a few times recently that reminded her of a...a something. It reminded her of her lair. That's where she would catch whiffs of it. Something about it comforted her even as she considered if it might be good to eat. Speaking of which, she looked at the body lying still next to her.

She knew that the male had not wanted to eat her. In fact she knew instinctively that he wanted to mate with her. She on the other hand was not one to waste a meal, and began tearing into his abdomen. Once she came up for air she noticed the hole and small spot of blood on the man's head. She leaned close and sniffed. The faint smell of cordite set off alarms in her primitive brain. Just like some dogs knew that the sound of guns being readied meant danger, even though they had never been shot or even heard gunfire before, she knew that the smell meant danger.

She sat up and began looking around. Suddenly she felt like she was being watched. She peered into the wood line, staring intently at a clump of brush. Nothing moved and she didn't recognize anything, but she knew there was danger there. Looking down at the meal that would surely go to waste, she decided to leave it. She had gotten some protein and she would eat some of the flower petals from a garden across the street, but now she wasn't comfortable with her environment... *"If it looks wrong or feels wrong, it IS wrong"* The thought flashed through her head. Her long ago self-defense instructor's words again penetrating her thought process.

She stood abruptly and began jogging back towards her lair. Behind her, the gun barrel that had been pointing at her from under the clump of brush lowered, and a pair of blue eyes blinked slowly.

Barry's diet had started to decline towards canned goods and other non-perishables. He hadn't had any fresh fruit in over a week. He had gotten some vegetables from various gardens, but being in the open plots exposed him to discovery. Twice resulting in close calls as he was discovered by roaming ferals. The first time it happened he saw the teenager running at him from a block away. He had raised his rifle and fired a round striking the young man in the chest. He stumbled and fell to the ground, but was back up on his feet right away. The next shot missed as Barry aimed for the bobbing head. The round snapped by causing the feral to look to his right as he felt the round pass close by. The third round hit the neck with spectacular results. It clipped the carotid artery and wedged in the back of the throat. The furiously beating heart sent a spray out of the wound that would rival a 'B' horror movie. The body spun to the ground and lay twitching for just a moment before ceasing to move.

The second time was a much closer call. Barry was concentrating on getting a watermelon into his pack when he heard breathing behind him. He had spun about to see a woman standing there staring at him. Her summer dress was ragged and torn, exposing her legs and bare feet. She was emaciated, her skin looked like it had been stretched over her bones, and there was almost no muscle tone. She flinched as Barry spun around, and almost cowered away. Barry made the mistake of looking at his gun before lunging for it. She sensed his vulnerability and dove at him.

Barry managed to get his hands on the rifle and pull it across his body as the girl snarled into his face. He twisted his body from side to side trying to free the rifle, but what little muscle the girl had was wiry, and she maintained her grip. He finally just spun his body all the way around pulling it from her grip. Unfortunately this left him with his back to his opponent. Before he could spin back around she had launched herself onto his back. She caught him as he was half turned around and tried to sink her teeth into his neck. He rammed the barrel of the rifle into her rib cage and pulled the trigger. The bullet travelled between two ribs piercing a lung and then entering the heart. She immediately went stiff and toppled over.

Barry sat down and used his Machete to slice the watermelon up. It had been cracked during the ruckus and he was thirsty anyways now. He spent five minutes eating his fill, while carefully watching his surroundings. He packed the last third of the melon into his pack after wrapping it in a trash bag, then hoofed it home. That had been nine days ago, and he hadn't had any fresh food since.

He also hadn't ventured very far from home. Two days after the incident with the watermelon girl, he had set out from the basement to go forage when he saw a group of four men and two women jogging across the yard of a house down the street. They were jogging in the tell-tale lope that the ferals used. He watched as they spread out and began beating the bushes along a hedgerow. A few seconds later a cat broke from the bushes and tried to cut between two houses. Two men had been waiting around the corner and the cat ran right into them. The small animal was torn apart and the group ate it on the spot.

Barry waited until they were out of sight, before turning around and heading back to the basement. He had some thinking to do. If the ferals were hunting in groups and forming packs, then he would be exposed to a great deal more danger. The chances of an ambush went up and he would have to make sure he wasn't funneled into a trap like the cat. His learning curve just got a lot steeper.

Deciding that he needed to add to his knowledge, he hit the books. During his many scavenging forays into the surrounding neighborhood, he had collected a variety of stuff besides food. Along with various camping supplies and tools he had come across some books on wilderness survival. He wasn't completely in the wilderness, and the power hadn't gone out yet, so he hadn't concerned himself with the basic survival reading. He knew how to make fire, he had matches, Bic lighters, and two sets of Flint and Steel. He had stored almost thirty propane camping bottles, and a ton of batteries for when the power did go out. No what he needed were combat and hunting skills.

While searching a house, he came across some military manuals. Some of them were useless since he didn't have an M-60 machine gun with a tripod and T&E (whatever *that* was). But the FM 7-8 Manual for Basic Infantry, and FM 21-75 Ranger Manual were invaluable. Resigning himself that he was going to have to go back on his vow of not cracking a book during the summertime, he hunkered down and began reading. It took him seven days of study to complete the two books. He only stopped to eat meals and have an occasional video game break. A TV and X-box console had been deemed necessary for survival and were two of the first items he had brought back to the basement.

The first order of business was to get some more supplies. He finally decided to hit the Wal-Mart that was just past the airport on the way into town. He was sure that there would be tons of supplies in there. It was also far enough away from the center of the city that there shouldn't be a *ton* of ferals, he hoped.

The trek was going to be an all-day affair. He would have to leave well before sunrise and probably wouldn't be back till well after sunset. He decided to use the large pack and he would use it to carry a large duffle bag there. He would pack them both and lug the duffle as fast as he could. He would just drop it and abandon it if he had to. But he wanted to at least try to get a major haul out of the trip. He planned on looking in the camping aisle for one of those water bladder packs. He was tired of lugging water bottles around.

After making sure his rifle was clean, he used some duct tape to wrap one of the sling swivels that was starting to rattle. He wiped down and distributed the magazines in his pockets. He still hadn't found a pouch or other carry method that worked for the tiny rectangles. All the various pouches either let them fall out or were too hard to get into in a hurry. The Machete received a couple of swipes with a ceramic knife sharpener. He put new batteries in his two flashlights, and made sure they worked. He was only bringing a little food so he would have room to haul more back. Once everything was packed and ready he set it by the cellar door.

Barry decided to relax and get to bed early since he was planning on waking up at zero dark thirty to head out. He wanted to eat a big breakfast since he wouldn't be eating all day. He limited himself to going through one game of Halo, then turned out the lights. Tomorrow was going to be a big day.

He had no idea how big.

CHAPTER 6

He caught the movement out of the corner of his eye and froze. Turning his head slowly to his left, Barry could make out the flash of brown fur almost a hundred yards away. A second later he saw a black shape move between the trees. The dogs were paralleling him.

That's what you get for being careless Metzler! He had gotten lazy and followed a game trail that was going in the direction he wanted. Not having to duck under branches and having a solid path under his feet, had allowed him to pick up his speed. Carnivores hunted game trails, however, and it seems a pack of dogs was looking at Barry like he might be lunch. He took a knee and pointed his rifle towards the threat. The dogs weren't getting any closer yet. But that could change quickly.

He had just stood up and started to jog towards the road when he heard a *whoomp* off in the distance. The explosion was followed by the crackle of gunfire. Barry didn't pause, figuring it was finally some good guys coming to restore some order. He had only gone another hundred yards when he heard the helicopter, he saw a silhouette flash past through the trees. He picked up the pace.

The pack of dogs picked up on his change of direction. They had shadowed the person trying to determine if he was prey or predator. Several of the dogs had narrowly escaped being eaten by the people they once trusted. Several had also been affected by the toxin and were far more aggressive than they would normally be. The noise in the distance caused some anxiety in them, but the fact that the little human was fleeing set off their predatory instincts. The six dogs turned and began closing the distance on the running boy.

Barry reached the back fence of an auto repair shop before turning and looking over his shoulder. He saw four low slung bodies weaving their way towards him through the trees. The dogs had closed the distance to thirty yards when Barry snapped off three shots with the .22. Only one of them hit a dog, which yelped and turned tail. The others paused at this turn of events, giving Barry enough time to scramble over the fence. He dropped to the other side just as two of the dogs hit the fence where he had been. He tried to get his rifle around to shoot them through the chain links, but they were already bolting along the fence line towards an open gate.

Barry dashed between a row of cars and—spying a work shed—dove into it. He slammed the door and latched it shut. Whenever he left the basement, he took one of the bike locks with him. He did this just as much to have it with him in case he needed it, as he did to prevent someone from locking him out of his redoubt. He used it now to secure the door as the dogs scratched at it and growled just on the other side. Once he was secure, he turned around and took in his surroundings.

The shed was made of corrugated metal and had been attached to the side of one of the garages. Metal shelves held boxes of old automotive parts and tools. An old 55 gallon oil drum took up one corner, and a big drill press took up another. The floor was oil stained and had some trash blown into the corner.

The dogs didn't act like they were going anywhere soon, so Barry pulled a couple of boxes off the metal shelves and pushed them up against the door. He used a rag to wipe down the shelf and then set his pack on it. He then crawled up on it and using the pack as a pillow decided to wait out the dogs. There were a few cracks and holes allowing in enough light that he didn't need a flashlight to see. He would rest up here for a bit and hope the dogs left of their own volition. If not he was going to have to shoot them through the cracks or even the thin tin walls.

As he lay there, he heard several helicopters nearby, and more gunfire. The noise was enough to scare off the dogs. Barry decided he would wait a few more minutes to give the dogs time to get well out of the area before he continued his journey. He lay back and thought how good it would be to finally have someone to talk to. As he was thinking about returning to civilization, he heard the sound of running feet and heavy breathing. Barry thought it might be a feral running from the government troops until he heard a voice.

"They bloody took them all out. I need that extraction!" The man gasped between breaths. "I'm east of the airport at an automobile repair facility. I don't know where those wogs got their intel, but the bloody Americans had full air support, and I think fighters. The air crews reported that they thought the helicopters were shot down by fighters!"

Barry remained perfectly still as the person on the other side of the tin wall whispered fiercely into his radio. The accent made Barry think of the Nazi bad guys he'd always seen in the movies. He was also afraid because the man had said 'Americans' like it was a bad thing. He moved his head very slightly in an effort to see through a seam in the wall but couldn't make anything out. Whoever was on the other end of the conversation must not have had any good news because the man began to blow a gasket.

"I have six bullet holes in me, you ass! I'm not going to make it much further down the Fucking road! I need extraction now!" The man began circling the building, looking for a way in. "I'm going to hole up here. You people figure it out!" He continued around the building until he reached the door which Barry had secured with the simple latch and lock on the door and then barricaded against the dogs. The man pushed on the door firmly but moved on when it didn't budge, not wanting to risk making any noise. He walked across to the building on the other side of the small lot and managed to slip inside one of the vehicle maintenance bays.

Barry had remained still, lying on the shelf as the man tried to get in. Once he was sure the man was walking away, he climbed down and put his eye to one of the seams in the wall. He saw the man, who was wearing a camouflage uniform of some type slip into the building across from the shed. A minute later an Apache helicopter slowly flew over the facility. It made several passes, and once seemed to hover over the parking lot. The helicopter was so close that it rattled the walls to the point that parts were vibrating off the shelves.

He was going around peeking out of the various cracks and holes, when he heard more footsteps outside the shed. He was trying to see who these new people were, when all of a sudden he found himself staring into an eyeball that was looking in at him. The face recoiled at the realization that Barry was looking out at him.

"Holy shit!" The man exclaimed. "There's a little kid in there! Scared the shit out of me!"

Another man put his face to the crack and peered in. He then walked to the door and shook it.

"Hey there, are you all right? I'm from the National Guard and I'm here to help." The man said softly.

Barry moved over to the door and began removing the boxes of parts. He unlocked the door and stepped back into the room. He picked up his rifle but didn't point it at the heavily armed men who surrounded the doorway.

"I'm okay. Are you guys looking for another guy that talks like a Nazi?" Barry asked as he unlatched the door. "Cause he's in the building right over there."

Barry pointed past the troops surrounding the door as he opened it.

"You mean someone with a German accent is in that building?" the man who had lieutenant's bars asked as he followed the pointing finger.

"Yeah, I heard him talking on a radio like you guys have." Barry's eyes were wide staring at all the hardware strapped to the Guardsmen. "He said he has six bullet holes in him."

The lieutenant shot a look at a huge guy with a Green Beret, then stuck his head in the shack to give it a once over.

"Okay, let's get you somewhere safe, then we'll check out this bad guy in the other building."

He gestured everyone back around the corner. A few gestures and the platoon pulled back and began to form a perimeter around the building well out of sight. After a few minutes a Stryker Armored Fighting Vehicle pulled up, causing Barry to crane his neck to look at it as he was led away.

The soldier who had first seen Barry through the wall, introduced himself as Corporal Maggio, and hustled him around the corner of the building and out to the street. As soon as Barry was out of the line of fire, the lieutenant used a bullhorn to hail the building. This was followed shortly by a loud bang, and some shouting. Two minutes later, several soldiers came back around the building dragging the man that Barry had seen earlier. He was semi-conscious, and looked even bloodier than he had before.

"Hey thanks for pointing that guy out for us. He is one of the bad guys."

"Corporal Maggio, are we at war?" Barry asked as they walked towards the AFV.

"Well that guy was one of the people who poisoned our water supply. We're pretty sure he was a mercenary that was working for a terrorist group."

Maggio had to turn and chase after the kid, as he made a beeline towards the man they were strapping to a litter. Maggio grabbed Barry just as he was raising the butt of his rifle to smash the man's face in. Barry managed to get one good strike in to the man's face, fracturing his cheek bone, before Maggio pulled him away.

"You did this!" Barry screamed. "You killed my family! I swear I'll kill you for what you did to my little sister!"

The guy with the Green Beret gently removed the rifle from the Barry's hands as Maggio had to physically lift Barry off his feet and carry him away. They moved him over next to the Stryker and Mag sat down with him as Barry tried to control the tears that were beginning to run down his face. They were the first ones he shed since finding his family dead. He had kept himself busy surviving and had shut off the pain of his loss. But now in the relative safety of these men, and with one of the culprits' right in front of him, the hurt was an iron fist around his heart. The ache was so bad it made the breathe catch in his throat.

"Hey buddy, I promise you we are gonna make these people pay." The giant Green Beret said as he set Barry's rifle down against the side of the tank. Barry noticed it was out of reach. "I'm Master Sergeant Lovell. What's your name?"

"Barry Metzler sir."

"You said your family is dead. Who are you staying with now? And what were you doing in that shed?" Lovell asked as they were joined by the lieutenant.

Barry spent the next ten minutes telling the men about his family and how he had survived. The men were all staring in wonder as he finished. The fact that the twelve-year-old had survived the last few weeks entirely on his own was amazing.

"We have a safe zone established at a hotel south of the lake. We have food and shelter. We'll take you there and keep you safe." Maggio said.

Barry nodded but cast a wary glance at Lovell as he put out his hand for the pistol on Barry's hip. Barry covered it with his hand and scooted back a little. The look in his eyes looked like a cornered animal.

"Master Sergeant, I think the young man can be trusted with his equipment for now," Lieutenant Crowe said. "Barry, you can keep your guns but you can't have them loaded while we're driving, okay?"

"Okay, I don't have any ammunition for my pistol anyways. But my rifle is all I have to protect myself." Barry had relaxed a little.

"Nonsense." Maggio said. "You've got me now. I'll see about getting you some ammo, and some range time. What kind of pistol is it?"

"It's a Springfield Armory 1911A1. It needs .45ACP ammo." Barry said carefully handing over the pistol.

Maggio cleared the weapon, noticing that it was spotless. He showed it to Lovell who just grunted. He handed it back and watched as Barry carefully pointed it in a safe direction before dropping the slide. He then jutted his hip and slowly returned the pistol to the holster, making sure it was never pointed at anyone.

"Who taught you how to handle firearms that?" Lovell asked.

"My range master at Boy Scout camp. He said not to let it point at anything I didn't want to destroy."

"Shit I've seen soldiers who weren't that careful." Crowe said. "Okay Barry, you're good with me, we need to get this show on the road. You want to ride back in the Stryker?"

"That would be cool!"

"Mag, put him up in the gunner's cupola."

"You got it sir!" Maggio was smiling down at Barry. "Come on, I'll show you some awesome stuff."

Maggio took Barry's rifle, and after unloading it, handed it back to him. He took him around to the back of the Armored Fighting Vehicle and began showing him the systems. Barry rode back to the hotel command post riding in the gunner's position in front of Maggio. They spent the trip spinning the turret to lock on to any feral they saw and talking about video games.

They stopped at the airport and the convoy got bigger before continuing the rest of the way to the hotel. Once there Barry was put through a kind of in-processing which came to an abrupt halt when one of the women tried to take Barry's guns away from him. The firm grip and defiant look told her it wasn't going to happen without a fight. Maggio stepped up and defused the situation by saying he would be responsible for the weapons. He held them while Barry's information was recorded and he again related his story. Mag then offered to let Barry room with him. He had a weapons locker in his room, and he promptly gave Barry the combo with the understanding that he didn't touch his military gear, and Mag wouldn't touch Barry's stuff.

Barry spent an hour exploring the hotel before he went down to the courtyard to have dinner with everyone else. He was in line getting food when he heard his name called. Karen Trotter was waving at him from a table. Karen was one of Cammie's friends from high school. He grabbed the rest of his food and made his way over to her table. Most of the kids seated there were older than Barry, but he recognized some of them. They made room for him as he set his tray down.

"Where's Cam?" Karen asked. "How's your family?"

The question was asked in a subdued voice. It was apparent that most of the kids expected the answer he gave them. He spent a few minutes telling his story before they each told similar tales of horror. Karen had just gotten off work at McDonalds when her mother, who had come to pick her up, was attacked and killed right in front of her. She had run back inside but the employees hadn't gotten the doors secured before Allen Drummond had burst through the doors and started attacking more people.

Karen had slipped out the back door and made it to some woods to the south. She had hidden there until a police car had showed up.

The officer had taken her back to the station, but while she was there, one of the officers had turned crazy and had to be gunned down by his fellow officers. Other officers had brought in kids and other victims of attacks, but again the toxin manifested itself and there were more casualties. Finally one of the officers had segregated everyone in cells for twenty-four hours until he could determine who was affected or not. They had eventually been evacuated here by some of the Park Rangers and National Guardsmen who had established this safe zone.

Barry finished his meal after telling everyone of his discovery of Will Petty, and asking if anyone had seen Andrew. No one had, but there was a missing persons board that was posted in what used to be the hotels office. Everyone who had been found alive was listed there. The list included names of families that were known to be okay, but were staying at their houses and any refugees with them.

Barry made his way to the office and checked the lists very carefully. He found the names of several friends and classmates, but no Andy. He wandered back up to his room to find Mag cleaning his gear and getting ready for his watch in a couple of hours. Barry walked over and flopped on his bed with a heavy sigh.

"Hey bud, what's up?"

Barry spent several minutes telling him about meeting his sister's friend and about not being able to find Andy's name on the list.

"Well that just means he hasn't been found yet. Until you see the body don't give up hope." Mag gestured towards his gear. "We find folks every day. Show me where he lived and we'll run a patrol out that way tomorrow when we do a scavenger run. We'll look in the area for him."

"Really?" Barry perked up. "And maybe we could get the rest of my stuff!"

"Sure bud. What stuff do you need?" Mag asked.

"Well I'd like to get my TV and X-box. I have a couple of months' worth of food too. The rest of my gear and clothes…" Barry began to rattle off the litany of things he had back at the basement.

"Whoa, wait a second! Did you say X-box?" Mag was staring intently at his new roommate. "Why do you need a TV? We have one here."

"Yeah but I have a big flat screen plasma. This one is tiny. Halo is much more fun on my big screen."

Mag just stared at the kid with is mouth hanging open.

CHAPTER 7

The two Humvees rolled to a stop in front of the Smiths' house. Maggio climbed out of the passenger seat of the lead Hummer and turned to look at the gunner in the cupola. He racked the slide on the 12 gauge and looked around. Barry climbed out and operated the charging handle of his .22.

"You cover my ass if this doesn't work!" He said, not worrying about being heard since the diesel motors had let everything in a quarter mile know that they were there.

"That's her house." Barry said pointing to Ms. Allensworth's house. "She is usually gone during the day."

"Well let's hope so." Maggio had his head on a swivel as he approached the front door of the Smiths house.

"Come on around back. You don't want to go in that way." Barry was already moving between the houses towards the back yard. Mag and two other guardsmen followed along. Barry checked to see if his tamper indicator had been tripped. The piece of fishing line was still in place. He opened the cellar door and climbed down. He checked to make sure that the door to the kitchen was intact and popped his head back out.

"All clear guys, come on in." And he disappeared back down the stairway.

Maggio left the two other guardsmen outside to guard the door and followed Barry down into his lair. As soon as he got to the bottom of the stairs, he let out a low whistle. He slowly took in the stocks of food and equipment. The aisles between Mrs. Smith's shelves had been crammed with canned goods and other non-perishables. There were shelves with camping gear and other survival gear. There was also a futon couch set in front of a 64 inch flat screen TV. An X-box console and a stack of video games and movies resided on the entertainment center that held the TV. There were glade air fresheners on just about every shelf, but there was still a faint smell of rotting flesh.

"Holy shit! Man you had quite the pad down here. There must be six months' worth of food."

"I have some more sealed stuff upstairs. I don't go up there much because it stinks so badly. The only good thing about it, is that the other ferals stopped coming around once it got really bad." Barry was pointing to the stairway up to the kitchen and the towel laying across the threshold. "I figure there's enough for me for almost a year now."

Maggio walked over and picked up a mason jar of pickles.

"Yeah you can have all of those. I'm pretty tired of pickles."

Maggio barked out a laugh and set the jar back down. He wandered over and checked out the game and movie collection, mumbling his approval at the titles. He finally turned around with his hands on his hips.

"You did all this?" He asked pulling steak out of the freezer. "'Cause I would have paid good money to rent this place before the shit hit the fan. I wish I ate this well too!"

Barry just grinned at him as he began packing up the video games. Maggio stuck his head up the outside door and told the two troops there to call the rest of the guys in for a working party. Pretty soon there was a stream of soldiers carting all the supplies out to the second hummer which was the troop carrier variant. The chest freezer was wrestled up the back stairs and loaded by several sweating and cursing soldiers. After the cargo hummer was full they put a layer of supplies on the floor of the hardback. Maggio stopped the bucket brigade before the Hummer was too full so that they could fit the flat screen in the back on top of the supplies. It was wrapped in heavy quilts and treated like the precious gem it was.

They were latching down the back hatch when one of the troops called out contact. Maggio leaned out from behind the hummer as a scream sounded from up the street. He could see a blonde woman running towards them with a slight limp. The clothing matched what Barry had described but he asked him if it was Ms. Allensworth anyway. Barry confirmed that it was and asked them to not hurt her if it could be avoided.

"Hold your fire unless she gets the jump on me." Maggio said to the gunner in the cupola as he stepped forward with the shotgun. He stayed to the side so the gunner had a clear field of fire.

When the populace had first started to manifest the effects of the toxin, the Guard troops had been issued Crowd Deterrent Munitions. The 12 gauge rounds fired fin stabilized rubber slugs. The rounds were called 'Less than Lethal' but it was only a feel good term for the liability Lawyers. The solid rubber slugs were fully capable of shattering a skull or rupturing internal organs if they hit a person in the right spot. They also caused incredible pain.

There was no 'Cool guy in the movies' racking of the slide, there was already a round chamber. Maggio brought the weapon to his shoulder and dropping his point of aim from the center of mass, fired a round at her legs. The solid rubber slug impacted the front of her thigh with a loud *thwap*. The impact literally threw the leg out from under her, causing her to fall flat on her face and tumble to a stop. The pain was enough to cut through her muddled thoughts and her mind latched on to the idea of danger. She slowly got to her feet and took a step towards the intruders, her instinct to protect her territory conflicting with her survival instinct.

Maggio took a step forward and now racked the action on the shotgun. The visual image and the distinctive noise again making a connection in her brain that she might be in danger. That and the fact that the man who had shot her didn't show any fear, caused her to reconsider attacking the group. She stopped in her tracks and screamed again.

Maggio stepped forward and pointed the shotgun at the ground in front of her and sent a round skipping off the pavement. It bounced up and hit her right on the shin. The impact this time causing her leg to buckle to the outside. She collapsed onto her left side and let out a cry of pain. She was rolling on the ground whining piteously as Maggio stepped a little closer and racked the slide again. It was too much for Justine and she cowered with her hands over her head, still crying in pain.

Maggio stepped back and covered her as the rest of the troops loaded up and the hummers turned around. He watched as Barry ran over to her front porch and left two cans of beef stew that he had opened. He set them down and jogged back to hummers. Justine watched him the entire time. As the convoy left down the street, the gunner saw her get up and stagger to the front porch.

Justine had not had a very good day. She had been scratched up pretty bad by a cat that had leapt off a fence and clawed her upper arm before running away. She hadn't even gotten a meal out of the deal, and now as she was headed back to her lair, she saw a bunch of strangers in front of it.

She screamed at them and rushed to defend her territory when one of them stepped forward and shot her in the leg. The pain was excruciating and the fall flat on her face to the asphalt only added to her misery. Her right quadriceps began to cramp immediately. The injury enraged her further but she was beginning to figure out that she might not be able to handle these ones. She got up though, determined to defend her home. All thoughts of attacking them went out the window when the second shot slapped into her left shin. Her leg let go from under her and she hit the ground again.

She looked up at the man as he approached with the terrible weapon. She could smell that cordite and the danger memory flashed across her thoughts again. In that moment she knew fear again, something she hadn't felt since the toxin took a hold of her. She covered her head and was surprised when the man just backed away. He kept the firestick...*gun*... between them but didn't hurt her again.

She saw a small one run over to her lair, and just as she was getting angry again she realized he had only left something on the porch. She watched him run back to the noisy things that some of the others rode in. She got up and stumbled her way to the two cans of beef stew. They had that faint smell that she recognized as the boys, and she knew deep down that he was supposed to be... *pack member? ...No ...Mate? ...No ...*something.

The smell of the stew she did recognize for exactly what it was. She used her fingers to scoop out the wonderful meal, grunting in pleasure the entire time. The thought crossed her mind that if he could provide such great food she would consider mating with him, even if he was scrawny.

With her stomach full, she staggered to the back yard and walked into her pool. The electricity hadn't gone out yet, so the filter had continued to work. It was past due for a service though and the filter was getting clogged. No pool man had come by to add chlorine, so the water was getting green. It still felt good though so she soaked and wondered about the little guy that she felt she should know.

"Dude, was I imagining that, or was she pretty fuckin' hot?" Maggio asked as they made their way back to the hotel.

"You should see her without the blood and guts all over the front of her." Barry grinned as he kept an eye out his side of the Hummer. "She used to be Miss New York or something, and she was a magazine model before becoming a teacher at our school."

"Gives meaning to "Hot for Teacher" huh?" Maggio and the other soldiers laughed.

"What's that?" Barry asked.

"Van Halen! You've never heard of Van Halen?" Maggio was stunned.

"I've heard of them, I just never heard that song."

"Oh well were gonna fix that!"

"Yeah well we always thought of that song 'Baby's got her blue jeans on' when she walked into town in her Daisy Dukes." Barry was laughing along with everyone else.

"Yeah well if they ever come up with a cure, I'm coming out here and rescuing her so I can marry her!" Polk, the driver said.

"You might have a fight on your hands." Maggio said gesturing over his shoulder at the twelve-year-old in the back seat. "Metzler there would probably kick your ass if you tried."

Barry blushed and had to endure a terrible ribbing the rest of the way back.

CHAPTER 8

Captain Nelson, Lieutenant Crowe, and Master Sergeant Lovell were all impressed at the haul that Barry brought in with him. The kitchen staff appreciated the extra supplies, and Barry's and Maggio's room became the most popular place for off duty troops to hang out. All in all things were looking up until Barry overheard a couple of the women talking about what to do with the kids. They were getting bored and even though there were plenty of chores to go around that only kept them occupied for a portion of their waking hours. The word 'school' was mentioned and Barry immediately became a ghost.

He took to slipping out of the perimeter line and hunting ferals. He had watched them from the rooftop of the hotel, and that coupled with his experience made him a skilled killer. The first time Maggio found out he told him not to get caught. By the end of the week it was a running joke on which patrol would be lucky enough to have Barry covering them. The only hiccup came when Master Sergeant Lovell caught Barry after he slipped back inside the perimeter. He had forgot to put the safety back on his rifle and had just stood up and turned around to see the barrel chested man standing there.

"Uhmm… Hi, Master Sergeant…" Barry started.

"Just what in God's green earth do you think you're doing?" The question thundered out of the monster standing in front of him.

Barry was sure that the master sergeant knew that he'd slipped out, so the question caught him off guard. He stuttered for words for a second.

Lovell didn't let him get his thoughts in order before tearing into him.

"Wha, wha…" He mocked Barry stumbling over his reply. "Answer the question young man! What in the hell do you think you're doing?"

"I, I was just coming back from a …" He stammered.

"I don't care where you're coming from! Why are you walking around my area with a loaded weapon and the safety off?"

Barry sheepishly looked at the red safety indicator clearly visible by the trigger guard. He reached down and placed the weapon on safe and then stood up straight. He looked Lovell right in the eye and grimaced.

"I forgot to…"

"Oh good, you forgot! That tool can kill one of my troops, dammit! If you can't carry it in a safe manner, I just might forget to let you have it!" The man loomed over the boy who was starting to shake. The Green Beret was scary when he was pissed. "How about you unload it properly and get it stored. I'm sure there are some dishes that will need to be done after dinner, and then the trash needs to be collected throughout the entire building. The courtyard needs to be swept too! Get it done now!"

Barry flew up to his room. Captain Nelson stepped over from where he had been watching the encounter.

"Didn't know you were a drill sergeant there, Master Sergeant." He chuckled.

"The kid is smart. I think he'll see that by showing that I was concerned for the safety of the troops, he'll get over it." Lovell said turning around. "The family that came in today said it was Barry that saved them from an attack and led them here."

"Yeah, he is definitely an enigma. What do you suggest we do with him?"

"Well shit sir. He's been surviving out there, no he was *thriving* out there. The guys say he found a copy of FM 7-8 and some other manuals and he read them cover to cover. They also say he moves like a fucking ninja when he's outside the wire."

"I hear ya. The guys on the roof say that they've seen him bag three ferals in the last two days. That doesn't count the ones the guys on patrol have reported." Nelson shook his head. "The kid is definitely on a mission."

"Can you blame him after what happened to his family?"

"Nope, sure can't"

Barry spent the next two days doing chores and keeping a low profile, especially around the command staff. Maggio told him it was just a standard ass chewing and not to worry about it. Barry decided if that was a 'standard' ass chewing, he didn't want to get a 'Non-standard' one. He was able to stay off the radar as the Park rangers had raided a gun store in town and Maggio had gotten some .45 ammo for him.

Yavi was the acting Range Master for the Park Rangers and he and Chris, one of the Bemidji police officers, were in charge of the impromptu shooting range that had been set up. They worked with Barry on his pistol shooting. His small hands posed a minor inconvenience, but his grip strength was excellent. They began with the basics, and worked up through malfunction and reloading drills on the first day. Maggio got permission for him to do Dry Practice on the back side of the hotel, and he spent several hours practicing there. In a few days he was on the firing line with the adult men who had made it in to the complex and needed instruction. He was one of the top shots in no time. He began to slip out again and now every once in a while the roof top watch would hear the .45 barking in the distance.

CHAPTER 9

The Guardsmen and Park Rangers were planning a mission to attack the terrorists that had attacked the US. Barry knew he would never be allowed to go on the mission but Captain Nelson let him go with them to meet the Marines that were flying in. He and Maggio rode in one of the hardback hummers to the improvised airfield they had established south of town. They weren't using the airport because the terrorists might still attack there.

Barry watched at the twin rotor planes swooped in a wide circle before settling to the ground like a helicopter would. They were the coolest planes Barry had ever seen, especially in real life. The ramps finished lowering and a couple of men wearing camouflage uniforms different from the National Guard guys walked down the ramp and headed towards them.

Barry led the procession out to meet them. He marched up to the first man and saluted. To his surprise the man stopped and came to attention.

"Chief Warrant Officer Mark Norris reporting as ordered sir!" The man's voice thundered out as he saluted. Barry was sure the man could give Master Sergeant Lovell a run for his money in the intimidating voice department.

"Welcome Chief Want Officer!" He had no Idea what a Want officer was but he appeared pretty important. "I'm Barry and these are my Army guys!" He said puffing out his chest.

While the big wigs introduced themselves, Barry turned to go look at the awesome planes. He came up short as he almost walked into a wall of camouflage. He stepped back and looked up at a huge Marine who was looking down at him. The man would have been scary if he wasn't grinning. Figuring that the salute thing worked once, Barry tried it again.

"Are you a Chief Want Officer too?" He asked taking another half-step back. The guy really was that BIG.

"It's Warrant Officer there little man, W-A-R-R-A-N-T." The giant said as he squatted down to Barry's level. "And no I'm a sergeant. Where do you think you're headed off to?"

"I was jus' gonna look at that helicopter plane, that's cool!" Barry was stepping to the side to point it out to Jake just in case he had forgotten where it was.

Jake stood back up and kept his body between the inquisitive young man and the Osprey. "That, little guy, is called an MV-22 Osprey. It takes off and lands like a helicopter, but once it's in the air the propellers tilt forward and it flies like an airplane."

"Can I check it out? Please!" Barry was literally dancing from foot to foot. "Dan promised me a ride in the Plane." He gestured at the Park Ranger Cessna Parked at the edge of the field. "But he got shot at the airport and isn't back to flying stats yet."

"He did, did he? Well I think a tour might be in your future but not right now. They have to be refueled and then we're taking them on a mission. After that I'll make sure you get to check it out."

"Aww man! I always get told that!" Barry turned and sulked off towards a Hummer. Corporal Maggio was sitting in the gunners' cupola watching the tree line. Barry was halfway there when he noticed some movement in the brush at the western edge of the field. He slewed the turret around and was dropping the machinegun onto target when Barry's .22 let out two pops and the bushes began to thrash wildly. A third pop and all the movement ceased.

Barry climbed up with Maggio and reloaded his rifle. He then refilled his magazine. He saw Lovell and the sergeant talking about him, but knew a plane ride wasn't in the cards for him today. They watched the wood line until the gear that was staying had been loaded into the vehicles and then headed back to the compound.

On the way back Barry noticed a group of ferals surrounding a house. The troops usually wouldn't fire on them in case there were civilians inside the structure. The pack vanished as soon as they heard the convoy, having already experienced the devastation the metal beasts could put out. Barry made a note of the location and decided he would come back and check it out.

It only took ten minutes to get back and Barry had slipped out five after that. He began jogging back south since the convoy had cleared the route both going out and coming back. Because most of the packs scattered at the sound of the diesel engines, Barry rarely made contact after the Guard or Rangers went by an area. It didn't keep him from having his head on a swivel as he ran though. He went to ground about a hundred yards from the house.

He could see movement in the woods on the other side of the house from the road. He watched as a group of twelve or fifteen ferals eventually came out of the trees and surrounded the house again. He usually wouldn't engage a group this large and was considering slipping away when he heard a young girl scream. As he watched one of the pack members used a piece of iron rebar to pry at the plywood nailed over one of the windows.

Realizing the pack would breach the house, he went to work. He only engaged the targets that were visible on the side of the structure from his position. He didn't want any shots to penetrate the structure and injure someone inside. At this distance, getting a head shot on one of the attackers would be tough. He began shooting them in the legs figuring it would stop their attack, and hopefully slow them down enough to prevent them from swarming him.

There were only three that were clear to engage, and he had hit the first two before the third paused to figure out what was going on. It was the opportunity Barry needed to put a round right through its eye. Another female came around the corner to see why the pack members were howling in pain. When she stopped to look Barry dropped her too. By then the rest of the pack had heard the sound of Barry's rifle. Seven of them rounded the other side of the house and began sprinting towards him. He was only able to get two of them, before the group was between him and the house and he had to stop shooting in fear of hitting the building.

Barry stood up and ran towards another house, the five remaining giving chase but not gaining much as the fleet footed boy took off at a sprint himself. Once he had rounded the corner of a house down the street he ran another fifty yards until he heard the pack rounding the corner behind him. He turned and dropped to a knee and began putting pairs of shots into the torsos of the four opponents in front of him. Unfortunately the .22 is not known as a man-stopper and although two of the ferals fell to the ground, the other two kept coming even after being hit in their abdomens.

It only takes a few seconds to cover fifty yards and Barry only had time to draw the pistol and fire one round before they were on him. The closest one, a woman in her early twenties, pitched forward with her arms wind milling. Fortunately the report startled the male that he didn't shoot and the hesitation allowed Barry to duck to the side. He pivoted on his heel and fired another round as the body went past him. The round slammed into his rib cage at point blank range crushing a rib into his right lung and killing him instantly. The female was down and not moving so he turned his attention back to the other two he had shot.

One of them was struggling to get to his feet while holding a hand over the wound to his abdomen. The other was rolling around, thrashing in agony. Barry fired a round into each of them and called it done. He had put the pistol back in his holster after reloading it, and had picked up his rifle, when a noise caused him to spin around. Another one of the pack had cut around the other side of the house and was trying to jog quietly towards him. It had closed the distance to within thirty feet when Barry turned around and fired four rounds into it. He fired so quickly that all four pieces of brass were in the air at the same time. One of the bullets tore into the ferals diaphragm causing it to stop breathing. It took two more steps and fell on its face.

He jogged back towards the house where he could still hear the sounds of conflict. He 'cut the pie' wide so that he could see what he was getting into. As his view cleared the corner he saw three ferals tearing at another of the boarded up windows. They were having a hard time pulling the plywood off because whoever was inside kept pushing their tools and hands out from under the edge of the board.

He put the front sight on the head of the biggest, most aggressive one and after lining up the sight picture, pressed the trigger. Its head snapped to the side and it dropped like a sack of bricks. Barry began stroking the trigger, and the little .22 sounded like a baby machine gun as he emptied the rest of the magazine into the last two. They both went down, but one was still alive and moving even after being hit repeatedly. Barry changed magazines and put one in its head.

"Hello! Are you Okay in there." He could hear voices talking on the other side of the window. At the sound of his voice (Which was just starting to crack due to puberty), a female voice answered back.

"Yes we're fine. We'll be out in a minute if it's safe."

"Well ma'am, it won't be safe for very long. I made a lot of noise getting rid of that pack." He had his back to the building and was looking around for any more unwanted company.

"Okay, we'll be right out." This time it was a man's voice that answered.

A few seconds later the back door opened and a man stuck his head out. He looked at Barry in surprise and then stepped outside. He was followed by a dark haired woman and a little girl. They all looked around carefully before stepping towards him.

"Are you alone?" He asked incredulously.

"Yes sir."

"What happened to all the crazies?" He was making sure to keep away from the bodies lying on the ground.

"I took care of them sir, but we need to move if we are going to get back to the compound before some more find us." He was pointing in the direction of the hotel.

"We just made our way out of the city, we aren't going back." He said shaking his head.

"The hotel isn't in the city. It's outside, and we have the National Guard there to keep you safe." He was getting nervous being out in the open and in one spot for so long.

"Oh, Okay. I'm Robert, this is my wife Francesca, and this little one is Abilene."

Barry shook all their hands and introduced himself, but urged them to follow quickly. He began giving instructions as they jogged towards the hotel. He always made sure to engage Abilene, and include her in the conversation.

"Stay away from walls and buildings if you don't know what's in them. The ferals will reach through a window and snatch you if they've been holed up in there during the day. They'll also jump off the roof to get to you if they can. That changes in the city where the buildings are close together. Then you stay next to the wall while avoiding the windows..." The Ramos' received a lecture for the whole twenty minutes it took them to get to the hotel. It was only interrupted once as Barry had them hide along a hedgerow to avoid a Gore covered man who saw them anyway. He fired three quick rounds, then took them down a side street to avoid the body. The rooftop watch saw him coming in with survivors and sent out a team to meet them while they were still a half mile out. When the patrol reached the group, Abilene was holding Barry's hand and smiling.

CHAPTER 10

Barry was depressed and bored.

He had gone to an area next to his old neighborhood the day before. He had found the bodies of several of his friends after going to their houses. He was keeping a diary of people he knew that had been killed. He was on his way back, when he came across Andy.

His friend had been hiding in a woodshed and living off of rodents and small reptiles. His diet had exposed him to so much toxin that he had suffered a complete psychotic break. He was naked and scavenging his next meal, looking under logs, when Barry found him.

Barry had been moving through the woods when he saw some movement in front of him. Taking a knee behind a tree, he pulled out some binoculars, and began observing the emaciated form scratching in the loam of a log it had just rolled over. He was behind the poor creature that had a striking resemblance to 'Gollum' from the Lord of the Rings movies. The figure finally turned around and sat on the ground.

"Andy!" Barry exclaimed involuntarily, as he recognized his friend.

Andy's head snapped up, and he almost went belly up in a submissive posture. He had been beaten and raped by several dominant males, but submitting to the abuse had been the only thing keeping him from being eaten on more than one occasion. He saw Barry and realized that that it was only a boy his own age. He snarled and sprang to his feet.

"Andy No! Please!" Barry yelled as his best friend began to run towards him. Barry fired a round into the dirt in front of the charging figure, kicking up a little dirt and leaves. The little .22 just didn't have a loud enough report to scare his friend. Andy screamed and leapt at Barry.

Barry was ready and he had never lost a wrestling match to Andrew. Barry had always been larger and more athletic. This coupled with the fact that Barry was well fed while Andrew hadn't had a good meal in weeks put Andrew at an extreme disadvantage. Barry easily side stepped the attack and delivered a butt-stroke with his rifle as Andrew sailed by.

"Andy! Stop it's me!" Barry backed away a few steps. "Come on man, it's Barry!"

Andrew was slow getting to his feet. The blow to his ribs hadn't broken anything, but the intercostal muscles began to cramp up. He faced Barry with a snarl and took a step forward, yellow streaked saliva hanging from his mouth. The barrel slammed into his solar-plexus causing him to stagger back as his best friend pleaded with him to stop.

"Come on Andy! Please!" Barry had tears running down his face as he came to the realization that his friend was beyond help.

Andy tried to swipe a clawed hand at Barry's face, and Barry easily dodged backwards and followed through with another butt-stroke. The blow sent Andrew spinning to the ground. He quickly rolled under Barry's guard and latched his teeth onto his leg. Barry let out a yell and instinctively smashed the rifle down on Andrew's temple. The blow fractured the temple, sending bone fragments into his brain. Andy collapsed and let out his last shuddering breath while looking up at his best friend. Barry saw a flash of recognition in his eyes just before they closed for the last time.

Barry pulled his leg the rest of the way out of Andrew's mouth and pushed the body away. The padded jeans had prevented the bite from penetrating the skin and kept the toxin away from the mild scrape the bite caused. He fell back on his butt and stared at the body as the tears rolled down his face. After a few minutes he took out his folding shovel and began to dig. Two hours later he walked away from the small grave. He made a wooden cross with the name 'Andrew Petty' and hammered it in place. It was enough to make him give up his jaunts through the woods for a while.

Now he was wandering around the hotel listlessly. Corporal Maggio had the duty, and the other kids his age were all playing kids' games that he found really stupid now. Call of Duty just didn't do it for him anymore, now that he had been out hunting real people, well maybe not people so much, but real Bad guys...things...Whatever. Halo still rocked and he and Maggio played a lot of that.

He wandered up to the roof and talked to Chris and Yavi for a little bit. The bushy eyebrows and comical expressions on Yavi's face always made him smile. He was heading back down stairs when a commotion in the CP caught his attention. He sidled up to the doorway and eaves-dropped as one of the soldiers reported to Captain Nelson that the Mission to New York was returning and would be arriving at the airfield in about forty minutes.

Barry turned and made a Beeline towards his and Maggio's room. He always carried his Machete with him, but got yelled at by Mrs. Waller, one of the school teachers, when she saw him walking around with his .45 on his hip and his .22 rifle slung over his shoulder. So far the soldiers had stuck up for him, but he didn't want to push it. They let him come and go as he pleased now and he didn't want to have that change. He pulled out his 'Hunting Harness', a modified shooting vest that Maggio had helped him make that carried all of his essential stuff. It held all his magazines for the rifle and pistol (he had a bunch of those now, Maggio had gotten them from the gun store they'd raided), a two way radio that the CP monitored all the time, some food (MREs were still cool to him), and a camelback hydration system.

He put the vest on and did his 'Battle Rattle', then he opened up the gear locker and grabbed his pistol. He slipped the belt clip through his belt and made sure the pouches on his belt and vest were all full of loaded magazines. He inserted a Magazine in the rifle, chambered a round, and made sure the safety was on before slinging it over his shoulder. He did not want a repeat of the encounter with Master Sergeant Lovell.

He made his way downstairs and was hiding next to the motor pool looking for a chance to sneak aboard one of the vehicles when he heard footsteps behind him. He had barely turned his head when Lieutenant Crowe picked him up by the back of his harness and without breaking stride continued towards the convoy forming up in the parking lot.

"I wouldn't want someone to think that we left you behind by mistake." He grinned down at the young boy who was walking on his tiptoes as he was being pulled along. "I remember you were promised a ride in an Osprey. Today might be your lucky day."

"Thanks, Lieutenant! I won't get in the way, and I'll scout the edge of the field for ya." Barry straightened his vest as Crowe let him go.

They climbed into the lead hummer, and they let Barry ride in the gunner's copula on the way to the airport. The M240G didn't have the ammo belt fed into it, so Barry was allowed to swing the gun around and practice aiming at whatever caught his fancy. He even pointed out a feral to the gunner in the Hummer behind them. The man was bent over some dead animal, ripping it to shreds and stuffing the bits of flesh into his mouth. The convoy was travelling too fast for the second gunner to get his gun around in time. Barry made a mental note of the location and continued to enjoy the trip.

The returning birds were flying into the airport. The military had killed or captured most of the terrorist network responsible for the attacks. The focus now was going to be on rebuilding. The world was still a very dangerous place, and people would need a lot of help.

The convoy pulled out onto the parking apron and everyone got out and waited. Dan came out and was shooting the shit with Crowe when the Osprey's buzzed the field in formation. They went into the break as their engine nacelles began to rotate into their helicopter mode. After circling the field they settled down on the runway and taxied over to the ramp. The Marines began trooping down the rear ramps to a round of applause by those gathered there.

Barry recognized the big Marine who got off the second plane and walked right up to him. He saluted and said "Hi, Sergeant Derry! I'm here to keep you safe on the way back to our base if you need it. But I'm also ready for that ride too!"

Derry looked down at the kid standing in front of him and grinned.

"Bud, you're gonna hafta talk to the man over there." He said pointing to Mark. Norris and Colonel Neal were talking to one of the pilots. "That shit is above my pay grade."

"Okay." Barry turned and walked over towards the two Marines standing at the rear of the Osprey. One of the crew men walked by and Barry wrinkled his nose at the smell. The Marine had obviously been in very close contact with a feral and smelled to high heaven. The sergeant saw this and scowled at him. Barry didn't say anything since he didn't quite know who was who with the Marines. He was pretty sure that the Warrant officer was pretty important though. He marched right up and did the whole saluting thing again.

"Hi Chief Warrant officer Mark! I'm your scout today. If you need anything let me know. And I can go for a ride whenever you're ready!" He said nodding towards the ramp of the Osprey.

Mark turned and came to the position of attention and rendered a parade ground salute, then reached down and punched Barry lightly in the shoulder.

"You are? Well that's good because I need a good scout. We just got on the ground here bud, but how would you like to go to Virginia with me? The colonel here is going to need a couple bodyguards while we go pick up some important people. Jake and I are pretty tired but I bet you could

cover for us while we're flying and we'll have you back in a day or so."
Mark looked at Crowe, who shrugged. "We have to take them to
Michigan, then Quantico, and then we'll be back here by day after
tomorrow. Is that cool?"

"I'm sure that would be alright," Crowe said.

"This is Colonel Neal, he is the boss of all of us. So you need to make
sure you're on his good side, okay?" Mark indicated a much smaller man.

Barry turned and saluted Neal, who burst out laughing.

"So you're the famous Barry? I heard about you from some of the
National Guard troops." He said returning the salute. "So you think you
can keep me safe for this trip?"

Barry stared at him hard, then not sensing that the colonel was being
patronizing, he nodded his head.

"Yes Mr. Neal, but you have to listen to me when I tell you not to do
something. The crazies are fast and can be very dangerous." He patted his
rifle as he spoke. "You'll need a gun too, because I can only cover one
direction and if Mark and Jake are each covering one then you'll need to
cover as well."

Neal barely kept his mouth from falling open. He listened as the kid
gave him a set of detailed instructions on survival techniques. When he
was done the pilot took him into the cockpit and began showing him
around.

Barry was looking at the mini-gun mounted by the side of the rear ramp
when he heard screaming at the edge of the airfield. Recognizing the
hunting screams of ferals he flopped to his belly on the ramp and began to
fire at a group as it broke cover and attacked two of the security team. The
men had wandered too close to the tree line because one of them needed to
take a piss. Barry grimaced in frustration as his rounds struck several of
the attacking pack but didn't stop them. Gunfire from the Marines and
Soldiers quickly drove the rest back into the woods.

Barry kept a careful eye on the tree line and fired three more times as
he saw pack members creeping back to watch the field. Once he was sure
they were moving on, he stood up and changed magazines in his rifle. He
checked the woods once more and walked over to the command staff.

"They'll head North and East." He said to Mark. "The smell of all this
human activity will draw them from a long ways off. I usually try to thin
the packs out before they get too close to town, but I don't come this far
south. It was the noise from the planes that drew them here."

Barry saw Colonel Neal give Norris a 'WTF' look before turning back
to the conversation. Barry kept an eye on the tree line as some of the
security team went over and put the casualties on stretchers. Barry decided

that it was time for him to move up in caliber. He was training on the AR-15s that had been brought in, but he wasn't confident enough in their use to stake his life on one…yet.

They finished the briefing with Neal asking if they were sure it was okay for Barry to go.

"Yes sir, Colonel. Barry there is his own man but I will let the folks back at the CP know that he's off on a mission of National Security." Crowe was grinning at the young boy. Barry's well-muscled, but skinny chest was puffed out about two miles past his belt line. *National Security,* He thought, *How cool is that!*

Mark checked Barry's gear and walked him over to one of the Osprey's crew members. He instructed the Marine to make sure Barry had a headset during the flight and told him to be ready to go. The Marine showed Barry where he could store his gear if he wanted to and told him not to go anywhere because the flight was leaving in ten minutes. Barry, who never took his gear off when he was outside the compound, declined the offer to stow his gear and took the last seat by the rear ramp and kept his eyes on the woods.

Colonel Neal and CWO Norris finished sorting some material and made their way back onto the command bird. Barry followed Neal up to the cockpit and listened as they went through the last of the pre-flight. Then they went to the back of the plane where Norris had the crew chief, Sergeant Miller, who was now showered and smelled much better, show Barry how to 'sit' the gunners position. He had Barry put on a harness and hooked it to an overhead attachment point. Barry saw some of the pack still in the woods to the north, and Miller got permission to engage.

The high point of Barry's life to that point was reached as he used the Gatling gun to engage the ferals. Miller was surprised at how little coaching it took to get the young man to properly lead the targets. The kid was a natural as he tracked the ferals until the banking airplane took them out of view. Miller showed him how to secure the gun and raised the rear ramp.

Barry made his way over to Jake Derry and began quizzing him on his gear. The Marines had different stuff than his Army guys did and he was curious about it. It turned out that the Marines were part of a 'Special Operations Capable' unit and had equipment that was a bit more advanced than the National guardsmen had back in Bemidji.

CHAPTER 11

The flight passed in short order as they all chatted and exchanged stories of surviving the chemical attacks. Barry was impressed when Jake told him about Colonel Neal getting into a hand to hand fight with a feral that was bigger than Jake.

It stretched the limit of Barry's belief because Jake was HUGE, and Colonel Neal was closer to Barry's size than Jake's. Before they knew it, the back ramp was dropping and the Osprey's were landing at Quantico.

Barry was the first one down the ramp and was looking all around before it was finished lowering. Seeing the crowd waiting to receive them he relaxed a little. He got a few strange looks from the group that came forward to meet them. He watched as boxes of paperwork were loaded into vans. They climbed into a hummer and drove to the base hospital.

Barry, who was taking his bodyguard job very seriously was out of the hummer and looking around before the vehicle even stopped. He opened the door for the colonel and faced towards the closest brush. There was another group here waiting to receive them and they watched the young man with open curiosity. As Neal approached the group, Barry fell in behind him. When Neal saluted one of the men with stars on his collar, Barry followed suit.

"The Marines are recruiting them kind of young these days, Colonel," the Admiral said. The name tape on his camouflage utilities said 'Huff'.

"I think he's a Minnesota National Guardsman actually sir." Neal said as he shook the admiral's hand. "This is Barry, Don't let his size fool you, he is a very capable operator. CWO-3 Norris, and the big one in back is Sergeant Derry. They are also both capable operators."

Neal had gestured at each person in the group. Huff returned all of their salutes, including Barry's, and shook their hands. He looked up at Derry and whistled, not so much at his height as at his overall size. The man had the shoulders of an NFL lineman and the waist of a running back.

"Boy they fed you right when you were little!" He grinned. "I bet Barry here has to climb you like a tree to punch you in the nose!"

Jake just smiled back and said "Yes sir." As Barry got a horrified look on his face at the thought of what would happen to him if he ever tried it. Everyone let out a chuckle.

"This is Anna Napolitano from the CDC, she has been the lead on the scientific side for fighting this thing." Huff said bringing the woman forward then gesturing at the other man standing there. "And this is General Branson, he managed to get caught away from the pentagon when things went crazy. He has been running our logistics."

Barry noticed how the Marines lips became a straight line as they met Branson. The man was dressed in a Class B Army uniform with just four rows of ribbons showing. All three of the Marines were grunts, and recognized the man for the Rear Echelon type that he was. Barry was unaware of this but he picked up on the vibe.

They entered the building with Branson peeling off from the group as they made their way to a conference room. Jake and Barry took up relaxed positions outside the door and waited. A few minutes later Branson appeared carrying a laptop. Jake straightened up and rendered a rifle salute. Barry didn't recognize the gesture so he just stood there. Branson let out a small Harrumph, and went inside.

They stood there chatting amiably for almost three hours before the meeting adjourned. One of the things they talked about was movement and escort formations. Jake drew air sketches and showed Barry a 'tactical walk'. This got them a few strange looks from people passing by. When Barry mentioned this, Jake just laughed.

"Lions don't concern themselves with the opinions of sheep."

Barry thought about that statement a lot in the coming days. Eventually he came to realize that Jake was including him in the warrior brotherhood. He began to feel pride in his abilities and with the work he was doing. By the time they left Virginia, Barry wasn't a boy anymore, he was a young man.

The meeting finally broke up and people began to pour out of the conference room. Both of the general officers and Anna were surprised to see Barry and Jake still outside the doors. Huff stopped and looked at the two of them.

"Have you two had a chow break yet?"

"No sir." Derry said tilting his head towards Norris. "We were waiting for the Gunner, he gets lost easily in unfamiliar places."

"I'm gonna lose you in a minute... Forgive the sergeant, sir. He has an overinflated sense of self-worth." Everyone except Branson was laughing as they began down the hall.

"Do you know where you are sleeping tonight Colonel Neal?" Barry asked from Neal's right flank. "I'd like to check it out before you get there."

"Well I guess we should do as your security specialist suggests." Huff said still chuckling. "We can give you a lift over to the transient barracks."

"Thank you sir. We'd appreciate it." Neal turned towards the two government sedans which Barry was eyeing with some trepidation. He hadn't ridden in a regular car since before the attacks and had seen many victims who had been trapped in their cars. He even avoided riding in the Rangers trucks.

"I'm sure we'll be all right there Bud. We have some firepower to cover us." He said gesturing towards the Hummers in front of and behind the staff cars.

"Ohhh kayyy..." Barry looked at Jake and Mark who both nodded. They all climbed in with Barry riding in the front passenger seat of the Sedan Neal was in. They drove to the barracks with Barry's .22 out the window and Neal still in awe of how focused the young boy was on the surrounding landscape. They managed the three minute drive without incident, and were climbing out of the vehicles when another staff car pulled up. They watched as the attractive lady from CDC climbed out of the car and gathered her things shooting a smile at them as she turned to enter the Hotel like structure that had once been the Transient BOQ. Barry was amazed that she walked around without a gun.

Barry trooped inside with the rest of the group, giving the reception area a good look. He waited patiently as a young Marine issued them room keys and then went upstairs. Colonel Neal had been given a private suite that Barry gave a quick once over. Feeling that the room was safe he took off his equipment harness and collapsed on the couch. Neal went into the bedroom and unpacked his duffle bag. He came out to see Barry hadn't moved an inch.

"Do you want to clean up?" He asked "There's a bucket of water in there." He nodded towards the bathroom.

"No, sir. I like to clean up just before bed so I can sleep clean."

"You are wise beyond your years, young man." Neal grinned "Shall we rustle up some chow?"

"That sounds great, sir. Sergeant Jake and I didn't get to eat during the meeting."

"I didn't either, let's go."

Barry picked up his gear and frowned at the colonel until he put his on. He spent the time mumbling something about biting off more than he could chew.

They went out into the hall where they found Mark talking to Anna. A few moments later Derry came striding down the Hallway. He informed them that there was a top secret place to get the best BBQ around and that a van was leaving shortly from the front of the BOQ to take them there. They all went down to the driveway and were soon driving along streets with woods on both sides of the road. It was one of the most unnerving trips Barry had ever made.

They soon found themselves at one of the mess halls that had been abandoned shortly after the attacks. One of the Marine sergeants had family that owned a BBQ restaurant out in town. Right after things went to shit, he brought them and most of their equipment out to the facility and set up shop. There was a row of smokers set up along one side of the building and the smell of the smoke was causing them to salivate like Pavlov's dog.

"The ferals still make it onto the base and the smell here draws them from miles around." The young lance corporal said when he noticed every one looking.

"You should cover the windows so the light doesn't attract them either." Barry said walking past the young Marine. "The smell only brings them from downwind, the lights will attract them from every direction."

"He does have a point." Jake shrugged as he continued to hold the door for the rest of the party.

They were seated at a big bench table and were introduced to Sergeant Newcomb and his parents. The facility was only about a third full and they had plenty of time to talk about what was going on. A young girl brought out a huge plate of both BBQ beef and Pork ribs. Fresh soft rolls were laid out with butter and a bowl of coleslaw was plopped down in front of them. They tore into the best food any of them had eaten in a long time. Norris and Neal used the time to get a better understanding of the toxin from Anna, While Jake and Barry talked guns, girls (Jake caught Barry checking out the girl who had brought them the food), and video games. The girl part caused Barry to blush as Jake ribbed him mercilessly.

He finally went over to the serving line and was getting a plate for seconds. He fully intended to bring as much of the delicious chow back as he could. He struck up a conversation with one of the boys working the line. Barry asked where the food came from.

"There were several large water towers that weren't polluted during the attacks. The Newcomb's figured out where they were and brought as many cows and pigs into areas where they could be fed and watered without exposure to the toxin. They secured the animals with fences and guards."

Barry nodded his approval and was working on getting a little extra when Mrs. Newcomb caught him sticking cornbread in his pocket. He was startled when he heard her screech.

"That, Young man, is no way to treat my cooking!" She was waving her hands and fit to be tied. "If you are that hungry, then we will make sure you have enough. But you sure aren't going to stuff my cooking into a pocket."

She hustled him to the back and began filling Styrofoam boxes with beef and pork ribs. Big tubs were filled with Coleslaw and Mashed potatoes. Others with gravy, BBQ sauce, and sliced fruit. A bag of fresh rolls was placed on top of the two already stuffed cardboard boxes. He staggered back to the table with a sheepish grin.

Jake let out a loud guffaw when he saw the load Barry was carrying. He didn't bother to help since he was a firm believer in 'what doesn't kill, you makes you stronger'. He did immediately begin the ribbing again.

"Well I guess you were able to charm that little gal out of some more food! Were you able to charm her out of anything else?"

The other conversations at the table stopped and everyone turned to look at the blushing young man. Barry set the boxes down on the table and turned a baleful eye on Jake.

"It wasn't Michelle, it was Mrs. Newcomb!" He stated with a dangerous glint in his eye.

"Oh, Michelle is it? Well at least you got her name! Did you get her digits? Hell, do we even have digits to get anymore?" Jake dramatically grabbed the point of his chin and looked towards the ceiling. "We'll have to work on that."

Barry slugged the Marine on the arm. He wasn't worried about hurting the man so he let it fly. The punch made a solid thud on Derry's shoulder. They were both surprised at the strength of the impact.

"Ow, shit!" Jake recoiled from the blow rubbing his shoulder. "Okay, okay, I give!"

Jake was still grinning, but his respect for the kid went up a notch. Neal and Norris gave Derry a warning look, but that was all. The kid seemed to be holding up on his own.

"At least I'm getting something." Barry retorted. "I think the girls you prefer are out back in the pen, or wait, maybe they were on the menu!"

"Hey don't Judge!" Derry cried in mock outrage.

The table burst out in laughter, including Jake. The colonel and Norris added in a few jabs at Jake as well until everyone was out of breath. The atmosphere and mood was infectious, and the group had been under so much stress that it felt good to relax and blow off some steam. The group spent another twenty minutes enjoying the experience before the driver told them that the kitchen was closing and he wanted to bring back food to the night guard while it was hot. He also had several cardboard boxes he had to carry out to the van.

Barry slung his .22 over his shoulder and began his own juggling act, trying to carry the boxes and open the door for the colonel and be alert. Jake took pity on him and carried the boxes under one arm as they made their way out to the van. Once everything had been loaded, everyone climbed in. It was then that Barry noticed that everyone was relaxed and smiling. It was the first time he had seen any of these people in such a state, and the realization hit him pretty hard. *We needed this.*

The world came crashing back in on them on the drive back to the BOQ. Twice Barry saw bodies running off into the woods. The mild adrenaline surge put his mind back on the situation. *Time to get your head in the game Metzler.*

They pulled up to the BOQ and helped the driver pass out the food to the guards on duty. They put the rest of the food in their refrigerator. Barry went back out and grabbed his two boxes and was following the group into the stairwell when he passed General Branson going the opposite direction. The man had a scowl on his face as he went storming into the lobby. He paused though as the smell wafting from the boxes Barry was carrying brought him up short. He turned towards the young man, but Barry smiled, turned up his nose, and was in the stairwell before he could say anything.

The next day when the conference broke for lunch, Branson noticed that only a few people went to the cafeteria. He knew this because he always hustled to get there ahead of the crowd. It wasn't like the Pentagon where there was a dining room for general officers, and he hated to wait behind his subordinates. He was astonished when he returned to the conference room to see what looked like the leftovers from a catered lunch. The room smelled of BBQ and fresh bread. Paper plates and wrappers were being picked up by the big Marine sergeant and the young man. Admiral Huff was leaning back, working vigorously on something stuck in his teeth with a toothpick.

"I didn't know you had lunch planned here sir." He said.

"I didn't Carl. Barry here was nice enough to share his with us." He gestured at the last remains that were being cleared. "And I must say it was quite a feast."

"I see."

Branson had to sit through the rest of the afternoon smelling the BBQ and listening to his stomach rumble. The intestinal signals did not go unnoticed by others in the room. Those others included Barry and Jake, who had been told by Admiral Huff to grab chairs by the door. They could serve as guardians if someone tried to get in, but didn't need to be on their feet all day.

The meeting ended in the early afternoon and Barry went out to do a little hunting. He also wanted to practice his new Land Navigation skills. He had learned to use a basic map and compass in the boy scouts, but the lessons were rudimentary. Lately he had been learning how to use terrain association, and the military grid system. He had a radio on him and Colonel Neal said he was going to be staying in the room. Jake was also going to be nearby.

Barry hit the wood line and began paralleling the road towards the Newcomb's BBQ house. He made it halfway there when he noticed a figure moving towards him through the trees. He quickly scanned the area and took a knee, keeping his rifle pointed towards the approaching figure put not at it. The teenager stopped when he saw the weapon and began to moan. He definitely looked feral. His clothes were tattered and there were bloodstains on his chest and what was left of his shirt. He slowly put up his hands though, so Barry didn't fire.

"Are you okay?" Barry asked.

"Ahh uhhmmm" The young man began to rock back and forth, then pointed off towards the west. "Ahh Hummme."

"Home?"

The teenager nodded his head. He had twigs and leaves stuck in a mop of dark brown hair that kept falling in front of his eyes. This caused him to constantly brush it aside and flip his head. It was a fruitless gesture as the matted hair just kept falling right back down. The feral sat down cross-legged and continued to rock his body. Barry could see what looked like a series of small bullet wounds on his legs. It took him a moment to realize that the small black and blue bruises with the circular wounds in the center were from shotgun pellets.

"Do you want to go home? Who shot you?"

The man nodded his head yes, then shook it vigorously no. Then he pointed at Barry.

"Hurrt."

"I didn't shoot you, but yes guns do hurt." He said lifting the rifle.

The feral cringed back and almost bolted. Barry lowered his rifle but still kept it pointed in the general direction of the man. He wasn't about to take any chances. The ferals had been getting smarter recently, to the point of using tools. If this was a trick...Barry stood a little straighter and began looking around in case this guy was a decoy so others could surround him. He didn't see anything but made sure to be extra vigilant. He pulled out his radio.

"Jake this is Barry." He spoke quietly into the handset.

"Go ahead." The voice crackled back.

"I have a wounded teenager in the woods next to Lyman road." Barry said. "He's been hit with a shotgun."

"Copy that, I'll notify emergency services. Can you get him to the road?" Jake asked as he walked over to Norris' room.

"I don't know, I kind of have him at gun point. He's feral."

"What? Why didn't you just shoot him?" Norris opened his door and Jake brought him up to speed on what was going on.

"Barry, this is Mark. Are you able to communicate with him?" Norris asked taking the radio from Jake and gesturing for him to gear up.

"Yes sir. He's trying to talk, but he's kind of in one of those catamoronic states."

Mark let out a bark of laughter at the statement.

"You mean 'catatonic'."

"Yes sir." Mark could imagine Barry rolling his eyes, which is exactly what he was doing. This caused him to laugh again as Jake walked back in the door strapping on his vest. He gave Mark a 'What's up?' look. Norris just shook his head and grabbed his own vest while they went out to the hallway. They stopped at Anna's door and knocked quietly on it.

"Well try to get him to the road. But do not let him get close to you! They can still spread the toxin in their saliva. If he won't go with you don't force it. If he places you in danger kill him son." Mark finished as Anna opened the door.

"Copy that sir."

"Anna, Barry has captured slash made friends with a feral teenage boy out in the woods. We are going to go out and recover them if you would like to come along." Mark said as he handed the radio back to Jake and finished strapping on his own gear. "Jake get us a car would you please."

"Aye, aye sir!" And he was off striding towards the stairwell.

Mark brought Anna up to speed as she gathered a medical bag and hustled out of the room. They went out front where the same white van was being pulled up. They piled in as Jake got an update from Barry.

"He keeps trying to talk to me, but he makes the words slow and drawn out. He keeps telling me his home is over by the enlisted housing."

"Okay, we're coming up on Lyman road now. How far out are you?"

"I'm only about twenty-five yards from the road. What are you driving?" Barry asked as he gestured for the young man to come towards him.

"We're in the same white van we used the other night." Jake was driving slowly along the tree lined road.

"I've got him coming towards me but I don't think I'll be able to guide him with my gun on him, and he's a bit bigger than me." Barry said as the feral approached him slowly.

"Well just slug him like you did me last night." Derry's wisecrack earned him a frown from Mark and Anna.

"I can hear a car...I've got you in sight. Come forward another fifty yards... Okay stop. We're in the woods off to your left." Barry was looking back and forth between the van and the teenager.

The young feral had stopped at the sound of the van and moved closer to a tree. This also put it behind cover from Barry's rifle. He let out a growl when he saw Mark and Jake climb out of the van in their full cammies and gear. He crouched down and looked back and forth between them and Barry.

"Hold your position." Barry called out putting the radio away. "You're scaring him!"

"Yeah well I'm glad because these fuckers scare the hell out of me!" Jake shouted back.

The feral caught a glimpse of Anna through the trees and immediately stuck his head out further. He also stopped growling. Barry made a soothing gesture with his left hand. The others approached more slowly and soon were alongside Barry. Anna began to step forward when Mark put a hand on her arm to stop her.

"Not happening. He could still have a psychotic break and we cannot afford to lose you." Mark had let his rifle dangle by its sling, Jake on the other hand had his up with the red dot in his sight centered right on the feral. All the activity was beginning to agitate the young man and he kept looking behind himself like he was going to bolt.

"Hey, hey there." Anna said in a soothing voice. "We're here to help you."

"Huuurrrtt." The word was a plea for relief.

"I can see you're hurt. If I try to help you, are you going to bite me?"

The question caused a series of thoughts to flash through the man's mind. His logic told him that he was hungry and he should eat her, but the survival instinct told him to bond in a pack and work cooperatively. This resulted in a confused look on his face.

"I'm gonna take that as a yes." Jake said.

"Hunngreee." The word was easily recognizable.

"Hold on." Barry said.

He took out a power bar from a pouch on his harness. He opened it and stepped forward a few feet. He set it on the ground and backed away.

"Go on eat. It's okay." Barry gestured towards the food.

They watched as the feral boy slowly approached and picked up the bar. He sniffed it once before tearing into it. He chewed the sticky goodness for several minutes, grunting with pleasure the whole time. When he was done, he looked at them and grunted.

"Muh?"

Everyone except Jake laughed. Barry made a shooing gesture as he pulled out a packet of MRE cheese and a pack of crackers. The feral got a hurt look on his face but backed off. Barry tore the foil packets open and approached the same spot. He set the packets on the ground and backed off again. The teen again approached and sniffed the food. He immediately put the cheese packet to his mouth and sucked the entire pack into his mouth. He then looked up at them and smiled.

The sight caused everyone to grimace. The cheese was oozing between his teeth and there were still chunks of the power bar and other unidentifiable things mixed in it. He began stuffing the crackers in his mouth and chewing them into the paste which was already there. Crumbs and drops of the goop fell down onto his chest as he continued to grunt in pleasure. He nonchalantly picked up the droppings and stuck them in his mouth, ignoring the leaves and other detritus that the globs had picked up when they hit the ground. When he was done he looked around and then pointed to his mouth.

"Creek." He concentrated for a minute and then a light bulb went off in his head. "Thirssey."

"I bet." Barry laughed. "Scoot back again."

He shooed the feral away again and went forward. He opened the foil packet the cheese had been in, then bent over and squeezed the valve on the tube connected to his hydration pack. Water flowed in to the foil packet. He set the packet against the tree and retreated again. It wasn't even enough to rinse the glop out of his mouth and they had to repeat the action several times before the young man sat back with a satisfied grin on his face.

"What's your name?" Anna finally asked him.

"Nuhhmm?" His face took on a frustrated look. After a minute he said clear as day "Bill."

They all looked at each other in shock.

"Bill is your name?" Anna asked him to confirm.

"Bill" he said again and this time started laughing. "I ayumm Bill!"

"Christ, he's like a three year old." Jake said.

Bill stopped laughing and stared at Jake. It was obvious that Jake was Bill's least favorite person in the group. Jake was cool with that since the feeling was mutual. Finally Bill pointed at his own chest.

"Fifeeen" a pause then "Fifteen!"

"You're fifteen and your name is Bill." Anna smiled at him then pointed at her own chest. "I'm Anna."

"Annna!" Another grin.

"I'm Barry."

This time Bill began bobbing his head as his brain began to function like it used to.

"Baarreee...friend!" Another smile. At least this one had less debris stuck in the teeth.

"I'm Mark buddy." Norris said.

"Markbuddee." Bill said with a confused look on his face.

"No just Mark." He said laughing.

Bill laughed too then turned to look at Jake.

"I am the fucking God of fear, pain, death, and destruction." He said with a straight face.

"Come on Jake! He's trying to be our friend." Barry said shooting a stern glance at the Marine.

"Yeah well the jury is still out on that kid." Jake said still with his rifle pointed at the ground between them and Bill. Bill just gave him a quizzical look and sat down. He started scratching at a scab on one of the pellet wounds. He looked up again with a pleading look.

"Hurt still."

"We'll help you, but you can't bite us." Anna said.

"No bite." Bill acknowledged, bobbing his head up and down then covering his mouth with his hand.

Anna started to step forward but was again brought up short when Mark stopped her.

"Still can't let you near him. You're too valuable." He said gesturing for Jake to move forward. "Let us secure him and then you can treat him."

"He's not gonna like that." Barry said as Bill tensed up at the approach of the big Marine. He didn't run but he did cringe away.

"I'm not gonna hurt you there guy, as long as you don't go crazy on me." Jake said pulling a set of flex cuffs from his vest. He slowly made his way behind Bill who stayed sitting down. Jake showed him the cuffs and pantomimed putting his hands behind his back.

Bill looked at the others with a pleading expression on his face and made a keening sound. He kept his hands in his lap and began rocking back and forth faster.

"No Hurt. Pleassse." He moaned.

"It's okay Bill. We don't want to hurt you, but you have been poisoned. We can't risk getting it too." Anna explained.

"Poisoned?" Bill stopped rocking and put his hands behind his back. Jake applied the cuffs gently but firmly.

Anna had to wait while Mark moved up and got control of Bills other arm. Once they were sure he couldn't break loose, she was allowed to come forward and look at his wounds. Barry stood watch as they began to treat him. All in all he had seven pellets of #4 shot in him. It was obvious from the pattern and depth of the shot that he had been hit at the extreme range of the shotgun. It had been a few days at least since he had been shot, the bruising was turning from dark purple to yellowish green. Anna wiped down the area but said she'd rather have the wounds treated by a medical doctor.

"Can we take you to a hospital Bill?" She asked.

"Osspital." His voice, which was raw from screaming and lack of use, cracked as he responded. He swallowed again. "Thank you."

"All right, let's go." Mark said as they stood Bill up and walked him back to the van. Jake and Mark each holding an arm while Barry led the way. They were just coming out of the woods when a Military Police hummer pulled up next to the van. Mark explained what had happened, and asked the MP's to follow them back to Base medical.

Once there, Bill was put in a bite mask, and taken into surgery. Anna made sure she was present and as soon as Bill was sedated she began collecting various samples from him. All of his clothes were cut off and bagged. She swabbed his mouth and the wounds on his legs. She also insisted on a fresh blood sample. The staff finally told her to take a hike so they could clean him up. She took her samples and went over to the lab to study them.

Barry asked for and received permission to stay and see how things turned out. The procedure to remove the shotgun pellets only took forty minutes after he was x-rayed. It took another hour before Bill regained consciousness. He was in restraints and a bite mask, but they weren't tight and they allowed him some movement. Anna and Barry were both there along with a staff psychiatrist. After an hour, Bill's speech had improved to a third grade level. He still showed signs of anxiety and displayed nervous muscular twitching. He was able to tell them that he was a dependent of a Marine who lived on the base and his address. They promised to look for his family.

Barry made it back to the BOQ and told Colonel Neal about the whole thing.

"Barry, you are going to change the world someday. I swear." Neal laughed. "I need you to be a little more careful though. I promised to bring you back to Minnesota."

"Yes sir"

"Get some sleep. We head back tomorrow."

CHAPTER 12

Northeast of Bemidji, MN

Barry was having the time of his life as the Osprey began its descent towards the airport. It was shortly after takeoff and right before landing that the crew chief lowered the tail ramp and allowed Barry to man the mini-gun. The young man was holding on to the guns handles and leaning out almost into the slipstream. They were approaching the Bemidji airport from the northeast when Barry leaned way out and started gesturing for Sergeant Miller to look down.

Miller grabbed the overhead attachment point and leaned out to see what the kid was pointing at. Down below a group of survivors had pulled several vehicles into a knot on a road. They were surrounded by an overwhelming crowd of ferals that were circling them, and throwing rocks and sticks.

Miller told the pilot to inform the other aircraft in formation and they began a descending turn to get closer. As soon as the surrounded group saw the approaching aircraft a white sheet with 'SOS' on it was displayed. The other Crew member had Neal and Mark put on headsets and informed them of the situation.

"Well let's go sort this out." Neal said into the intercom.

"Aye aye sir!" The pilot banked the tilt-rotor into a steep descending turn after telling the other aircraft in the formation what they were doing. The Marines and Barry all got their gear ready while Miller took over the mini-gun.

The Ospreys circled to the right to give the gunners the easiest field of fire. Short bursts from the mini-guns began to chew up the attackers on the ground. The planes didn't even get to circle the fight once before the attackers broke and ran for the surrounding woods. The three MV-22's set down 100 yards from the vehicles. Mark, Jake, Neal, and Barry all walked down the ramp and waited for someone from the cars to approach. It took a few seconds before a large bearded man stepped out from between two cars and approached. He stopped about twenty yards away when he noticed that not all of the guns were pointed at the ground.

"You all from the government?" He asked keeping his eye on Miller, who was not doing anything to hide the fact that the mini-gun was now pointed towards him and the vehicles behind him.

"We're from several different branches, yes, except for Barry here, which makes him the only honest one among us." Neal gestured at the young man standing next to him.

This brought a chuckle from the man who seemed to relax.

"Well thank you very much for your assistance, we probably would have been able to hold them off but it would have cost us some ammo and maybe even a casualty. Something we can Ill afford until we get to Bemidji." The man stepped forward and stuck out a hand the size of a baseball mitt. "Name's Seth Adams."

"As in 'Grizzly Adams'?" Barry asked, stepping forward with Neal.

This time Seth broke out into a full blown guffaw as he shook first Neal's hand, then Barry's.

"Yeah, I've been told that a time or two!"

They finished making introductions as more members of the convoy came over to meet their saviors. Once everyone was comfortable with each other Neal and Mark pulled Seth aside and asked him a few questions.

"What do you need in Bemidji?"

"Well, first of all we heard that the medical center there had been recovered and we have several pregnant women with us that we would like cared for. Secondly we had heard that the National Guard had re-established an operating base there and I was going to see if I could get in touch with the CDC. I used to work for them and I have a few ideas about this toxin."

"Well you heard correctly. The National Guard has been clearing and securing the city. We have one of the CDC's top scientists with us." Neal gestured at the Parked Osprey. He was about to walk Adams over to the plane when Barry grabbed his arm.

"Colonel, we need to get a move on. The Ferals are regrouping in the tree line and I don't want them damaging one of the planes if they attack with rocks and spears." Barry was gesturing towards the tree line.

"Miller!" Mark yelled at the crewman leaning on his mini-gun. "Movement in the tree line!"

Miller, who had been eyeing several of the women that had come out from behind the cars, snapped back to awareness and swiveled his gun towards the tree line. He saw the movement that Barry pointed out and sent a stream of rounds across a fifty yard section of woods. He was rewarded with several screams and some violent shaking of the underbrush. A second burst and all movement stopped.

"Perceptive young man there." Seth said in admiration.

"Yeah, he keeps us safe." Mark said in a very serious tone.

"How about we take your folks that are in need of medical attention with us. We'll leave a few of our shooters with you and have a gunship come out and fly cover for you the rest of the way." Neal suggested, getting the conversation back on track.

"Wow! That would be great!" Seth said. "I'll get my people ready. And the sooner I can get with that CDC scientist the better."

Barry rode the rest of the way back to Bemidji with the convoy. Seth had grudgingly turned over command of the convoy to Barry. At first he had taken the suggestion as a joke, but after a few words from Neal and Norris, he relinquished control. Barry, for his part, had to be convinced as well. He didn't like the idea of leaving 'his' people before the mission was complete.

He relented at the colonel's insistence, and made sure the convoy arrived safe. The driver of the jeep he rode in arrived with a lot of survival information crammed into his brain by the time the convoy made it back to the hotel.

Upon arrival, Barry noticed a somber mood among the people. Barry immediately recognized the behavior and wondered who the victim was. He was finally approached by Dan Preston and Lieutenant Crowe. They took him inside and told him that Corporal Maggio had been killed the day before trying to rescue some people.

Barry just sat there stunned. The first real friend he'd had since the whole thing started was dead. A sense of crushing guilt came over him as he convinced himself that if he had been there he could have prevented it. Most of the people were subdued in welcoming him back, knowing how close Barry and Mag had been. He went straight up to his room.

He pushed open his door and walked over to the weapons locker out of habit. He put his rifle away and then stood there staring at Mag's stuff.

Mag's rifle and Tac vest were missing, but most of the rest of his gear was still there. He leaned in and pulled out a calendar that they both kept.

There were notes about significant things that had happened recently as well as little reminders of everyone's birthdays. He flopped down on his bed and flipped back two months. He had been reading the informal diary for about ten minutes when there was a knock on the door. He set the calendar on his nightstand and opened the door to see Jake standing there with two beers in his hand. Barry smiled and stepped back.

"I know you're a little young for a beer, but in my book, you sure as hell have earned the right to toast your friend with one." Jake said handing him one of the cold bottles as he walked over to the small table in the corner. "I didn't know your buddy, but I heard good things about him."

Barry took the beer and eyed it for a second before taking a sip. Jake almost choked on the face he made at the taste.

"Yeah, it's an acquired taste."

"Why in the hell do you guys drink this stuff? My dad gave me a shot of Brandy once, it was worse than this." He said lifting up the bottle.

"Like I said, you get used to it." Jake raised his bottle and an eyebrow. "You want to say something about your buddy?"

Barry raised his bottle and sighed.

"He was like my older brother, but way cooler and nicer than my real one. He was awesome at Halo…" He gestured with the bottle towards a game console next to the TV. "And he was always teaching me about his guns and stuff. But he made sure I knew all about my guns first. And he stuck up for me when the other adults tried to get me to stay back here with the little kids." He looked Jake in the eye. "He knew I could take care of myself, and I can!"

With that he tilted the beer to his lips and took a big swallow. He put the bottle on the table and put his head in his hands with his elbows on his knees. He sat there for a few minutes before looking up at Jake.

"My dad and brother are missing, I'm almost positive they're dead. My mom ATE my sisters and my dog."

He shook his head. "I killed my best friend from school and his entire family is dead, and now Mag is gone too. I don't think I like this place anymore, but I don't know where to go."

"Yeah you've caught some shitty breaks. I lost my folks in a car accident when I was just a little older than you. Had to live with my Aunt and Uncle until I was seventeen and joined the Corps. Found a family here though."

Jake leaned back and took another pull as he eyed the kid in front of him. "I know I can't replace your friend, I suck at video games. But I promise you, if you want to learn how to shoot, I'll teach you everything I know."

"Thanks Jake." Barry got up and flopped on his bed. "I would like to learn how to shoot an M4 better, but the women around here keep trying to get me to go to these tutoring classes. I was going to go loot an AR-15 from one of the sporting goods stores. I can scrounge up Magazines and ammo."

"Don't worry about that little man, I'll make sure you get the proper gear."

They sat and talked until Barry's eyes started getting heavy, and soon he had nodded off.

Jake picked up the calendar and looked through it. When he flipped to the current month of August he saw that Barry's birthday had been that day.

The following morning when Barry finished brushing his teeth, he walked downstairs to the operations center. It was oddly quiet with just the on-duty communications officer there. He nodded at Barry and told him that there had been some survivors brought into the courtyard, which was where everyone was. Barry figured them to be the group from the previous day, so he took his time going down there. He wandered by the kitchen first and grabbed a muffin and carton of milk. Next he went to the drying racks where some venison jerky was being dried. He pulled a strip off the rack and headed to the courtyard.

A sheet had been hung over the breezeway, obscuring his view of the courtyard. The sound of whispered voices could just be heard coming from the courtyard. He started to get an uneasy feeling, and was reaching for the pistol at his side when Jake stuck his head around the sheet.

"There you are!" He gestured the young boy forward. "The colonel has some questions for you."

"Uhh... okay," Barry said, and stepped into the courtyard.

"HAPPY BIRTHDAY!" Almost every person in the community was there. The entire place was strung with birthday banners, and presents were overflowing and stacked around one of the tables. Newly promoted Captain Crowe, Colonel Neal, Mark Norris, and a large contingent of the National Guard troops were standing off to the side. Barry just stood there, frozen in place, staring at all the smiling faces.

"Come on son! Let's get this party started!" Crowe walked over and took him by the arm. A cake was brought out and candles were lit. The whole crowd began loudly singing 'Happy Birthday'. The cake was huge and the candles were spread around the outside. It took him several puffs to blow them all out amidst the catcalls and hootin' and hollerin' going on. The kitchen crew began cooking breakfast and pretty soon an all-out party was going on.

Barry was led over and parked in front of the table with the presents on it. The gifts varied from military gear which included a brand spanking new M4 with a scope and tac-lite, to a homemade Popsicle stick man made by Abilene, the girl whose family he had saved and led back to the compound. Homemade cards matched the store 'looted' cards in number. Almost everyone recounted how Barry had come to their rescue or aid in some way.

The young man stood there and gazed around at all the people laughing and smiling at him. He was speechless as he picked up the little Popsicle stick man and turned it over in his hand. The figure had been painted green and had little bobble eyes and a plastic gun glued to its hand. On the back was written 'Barry- our hero'. He stared at the small piece of wood and plastic as a tear rolled down his cheek. He looked up to see little Abilene Ramos staring at him.

"Do you like it? I know it's not cool like the other stuff, but I wanted to make you something to say thanks." She looked down at her shoes bashfully.

"This is my absolute favorite thing ever!" Barry said hugging the girl. He struggled to keep the tears in check as he was reminded of KK, his little sister.

Jake caught on to the scene and stepped up.

"How cool is that!" He exclaimed looking at the little figurine. "Hey Gunner! Check this out! Barry has his own Army man named after him!"

Mark and several others gathered around and began to fuss over the present. Abilene was taken aback by all the attention and huddled next to Barry. He smiled at her and made a production of threading a piece of para-cord through the figure and wearing it around his neck. Abilene smiled and ran back to her mother who mouthed 'Thank you' to Barry.

The party lasted more than two hours, with Crowe finally calling a halt to the festivities so they could get the Marines back home. Barry took his new equipment and secured it in his room. After the hustle and bustle of the morning he took a little while to himself so he could set up his new vest and gear. He thought about the morning's events and how he had been feeling since he returned from the east coast. The convoy to the airport was loading up when Barry walked out of the hotel with a duffle bag and all of his gear.

He marched up to the Truck that Jake was standing next to and tossed the bag in the bed. He then turned and faced the giant man in front of him.

"I need you to keep your promise and teach me how to shoot. Like you. With this." He said hoisting the M4 on its sling.

"Oh Christ!" Jake said realizing what was happening. "Uhh, you may have to wait a little on that bud. I have to get back to California. Things are going better here but San Diego is a lot bigger, and LA is a huge mess. I have to go back and help out…"

"I know." The direct stare made Derry more uncomfortable than being chewed out by a Drill Instructor. "I'm going with you. I can be more help there."

"Ahh shit!" Jake looked around hopelessly. His eyes finally settling on the group of officers by the front of the hotel. "Uhm, I would have to have permission, and the colonel would…"

Jake stopped talking to Barry's back as the young man marched up to the other group of men. He jogged over and the group of men turned to face the young man who had come to a halt a few feet short of them.

"Hey Barry. Are you coming to the airport with us?" Colonel Neal asked, taking in his rifle and tactical gear.

"Colonel Neal, I would like to go with you to California, sir!"

Neal looked at Crowe, who looked at Norris, who looked at Derry, who just shrugged.

"Uhh, sir…" Derry began. He fumbled with words for a second before standing up straight and looking the officers in the eyes. "I promised Barry I'd teach him how to shoot. I didn't think about how soon we'd be leaving, and he, well he would like to come out to California and help."

"What about your friends here?" Norris was aware that Barry had no family left.

"I'll be back, sir." The young man met everyone's eyes, one at a time. "Jake promised I could get trained and that's what I want."

"Why do I have the feeling I've had this conversation before?" Mark asked looking at Jake.

"Because he's just like Jim." Jake said referring to Mark's son.

"I'm just asking for a ride." Barry said surprising them all. "I have a compass and can walk, it would just take me a long time."

Neal's mouth dropped open for a second as he realized the kid probably could make the trip. He pulled his mouth closed into a grimace and turned to Crowe.

"Well it looks like he may be riding with us some more."

"We did say he is his own man." Crowe agreed.

"Gunner?"

"I have some rules that my kids have to live by, do you think you can abide by them?" Norris asked returning the young man's stare.

"Yup." The grim determination on the boy's face was the portrait of a warrior.

"Where's your gear?" Neal asked.

"In the truck sir."

Anna, Seth, and Lovell came out to the vehicles. The burly Green Beret had his arms full of luggage, which he easily tossed into the bed of the truck. He took in the serious looks on everyone's face and frowned.

"What's going on, Captain?" he asked Crowe.

"Mr. Metzler here is going to California apparently." Crowe answered.

Lovell looked down at Barry and smiled.

"Well they probably need him more than us, now."

Barry turned a smug look at the Marines as if it was the final word and marched back to the truck. Derry looked at the colonel who nodded, then followed him. A few minutes later the convoy rolled down the street headed to the airport.

CHAPTER 13

Over the Pacific Ocean

The Ospreys flew out over the Pacific Ocean and made a descending left hand turn. The Navy ships that were supplying power and water to the base were anchored in an even line to the southwest as the late afternoon sun cast a gold and red sunset against a few high level clouds. The planes in the formation peeled off one by one and landed. The lead bird parking closest to the base operations building.

A small crowd was gathered behind a set of barricades. As The Marines began to troop down the ramp, a cry of 'Daddy!' was heard. Neal's head snapped up and he looked around as a young woman ducked under a saw horse and sprinted towards him. Neal picked his twenty-year-old daughter up in his arms and spun around with her.

"Cori! Oh my God Honey! We went to your Dorm and looked for you! I thought you were gone!" Neal had tears running down his face.

"I went to Blake's house..." The colonel walked off with his daughter under his arm.

"Dad! Jake!" A teenage girl was waving as everyone ignored the barricades and pushed out onto the field. A group rushed out to swarm Mark. They began to include Jake in the hugs when the youngest girl in the group stopped and stared at Barry standing off to one side.

"Who's that?" she asked in a quiet voice, suddenly becoming quite shy.

"Mel, this is Barry." Mark gestured for the young man to come forward. "He's going to be staying with us for a while."

Barry, who had not taken his eyes off of Mel since the second he saw her stepped forward and mumbled "Hi".

"Oh My God!" The older girl exclaimed. "He is sooo cute! Can we keep him?"

"He's not some puppy, Terry!" Mel snarled over her shoulder at her sister, before turning back to Barry. "Don't let her bug you, she's a butthead!"

"Uhmm Okay." Barry still could not take his eyes off Mel. She was just starting to blossom into a woman and it was very apparent to Barry that she would be more beautiful than Ms. Allensworth.

Mel grabbed his hand and led him over to where the gear was going to be dropped off from the flight. She had to slap away Terry's hand as she made a fuss over Barry.

"Ohh, he's just like a little Army Man!" She exclaimed as she tried to pinch his cheek. "I bet this is what Jake looked like when he was little!"

"You're an idiot! You know that!" Mel was on her like a momma bear protecting her cubs. "He hasn't even gotten to know us and I bet he wants to go back to wherever he came from." She turned to Barry, and in a much more civil tongue asked. "Uhm, where are you from?"

"Bemidji, Minnesota."

"And he talks cute too!" Terry, who never lost an opportunity to exact revenge on her sister, was all about teasing Mel over what had to be love at first sight. "When you guys have kids, I hope they talk like that!"

She had to dance away as Mel took a swing at her.

"Daaad! Can you please get her to stop! Sheesh!"

"Tone it down a little Terry." Mark was a firm believer in rank having its privileges' among his children, and Mel got Terry in trouble on a regular enough basis to warrant a little grief.

They waited as the duffle bags and other gear were dropped out of the back of a truck. Barry was introduced to a huge group of survivors and other military personnel. As he was standing there, Jim, Marks son walked up and shook his hand. He eyed the gear he was carrying and nodded appreciatively.

"Nice pistol." He said gesturing at the absurdly large gun hanging from the younger man's hip. The eighteen-year-old had a scarred face that was slightly asymmetrical. It was evident that he had suffered some form of trauma that required surgery to fix. His slightly lopsided grin took the edge away from the somewhat fierce countenance. The family resemblance to Mark was unmistakable. The tone of voice was only a little sarcastic.

"He knows how to use it too, Jim." Jake said, ending any thought Jim might have of poking fun at the new kid. "Barry has saved more lives than anyone on this base. He survived on his own, right at the center of the outbreak, by himself."

"Wow!" Jim's respect for Barry went up several notches. Jake didn't hand out compliments easily.

"I didn't use it that much, I only killed twenty or so ferals with it." He said shrugging. He pointed at the case tied to his duffle bag. "I mostly used my Marlin .22. I just got my M4 and haven't used it in the field yet"

"You survived using just a .22 and a .45?" Jim asked with even more awe in his voice. "How many did you get with the .22?"

Mark frowned at the question but didn't interfere with the conversation. He was not one to talk about the number of people he had killed. He was interested in how Barry would answer.

"I honestly don't know." Barry shrugged. "I only engaged them when I had to. I don't think more than a couple hundred. I was usually trying to get people back to the compound, the only ones I went after were the Alphas."

"What do you mean 'Went after'?" Jim asked, as a look of astonishment crept across his face. "We used .22s at our house from a barricade to defend against the packs, and we had this one alpha that really went after Jake, but we never left the house unless we were armed to the teeth." Jim rubbed the scar on the side of his face at the memory.

"Yeah, the packs will form around those ferals that are the most successful. That usually means the ones that hunt and kill us normal folks. A pack that gets bigger than five or six individuals will start to cause problems, so I would take out the alpha's…leaders, in the area around our command post. It keeps the area a lot safer."

All three of Mark's kids looked at Jake who just nodded and raised an eyebrow.

"Wow." Terry's friend Tia said. "Talk about a 'Green Ball'!"

The kids all laughed at what had to be a private joke.

"Uhmm, I don't know what that means." Barry said with a bewildered look on his face. This just caused everyone to laugh louder.

"Come on," Mark said as they grabbed their bags and began walking towards a bright orange truck in the parking lot. "I'll explain it to you on the way home."

CHAPTER 14

"Uhmm I don't know, Mel. Your dad wouldn't be comfortable with this." Barry protested as he was drug by the hand out onto the sand. The sound of the waves crashing against the rocks in front of the Hotel Del Coronado was drowned out by laughter as Melanie Norris continued to tug on his hand, only pausing long enough to pull off her sandals.

"Oh come on! If there is one person who my dad would trust with my well-being, it's you!" She said over her shoulder as she finally let go of his hand and ran towards the pile of rocks. Although he was wearing his pistol, and Coronado was considered to be a 'Safe' area, Barry disliked being out in the open without his rifle. The vast openness of the sandy beach made him uneasy, and the immensity of the ocean definitely put him on edge. Two months ago, the largest body of water he had ever seen was Lake Bemidji, and you could see across that. The late October sun had burned off the marine layer, and the breeze was just cool enough to keep their jackets on.

"Come back! Jeez Mel, I don't want your dad mad at me the week before I start CCTC!" Barry picked up the pace and easily caught up with girl as she skipped through the sand towards the jumble of rocks. "Mel! Darn it!"

Since that was the extent of Barry's swearing, Mel knew that he was getting upset. She slowed and took his hand again. The two of them had grown very close over the last few weeks. Mark had Barry and Jim bunking together at the house, but Barry and Mel spent almost all of their free time together. The Norris residence had become an impromptu way station for gathering survivors at the beginning of the outbreak. It still served that purpose in a somewhat diminished capacity now that there were 'Societal Stabilization Programs' being employed.

"It really is okay." Mel said stepping up on one of the granite boulders. "I'm not going to jump in and we'll stay away from the surf."

"'Stay away from the surf' is exactly what we are going to do!" Barry exclaimed. "You know I don't like this. And we're way out in the open too."

"Barry Metzler! You know well and good that we are perfectly safe here!" Mel had her hands on her hips and was looking down on him from another rock. "Geez, for such a tough guy, you sure are a ninny!"

Barry realized she was right, and he probably would have jumped off the tallest rock right into the pounding surf if she asked. He sprang to the rock she was standing on and swept her up over his shoulder with ease.

"Ninny huh?" He said carrying her over to the edge and holding her out over the bubbling white water. "How's this for a Ninny?"

Mel screamed the scream that all girls did when they were being tortured by their men, half mock terror and half laugh. Barry made sure to dangle her low enough that she got splashed repeatedly. He made sure to add in a few tickles for good measure, before carrying her back down to the sand. They both flopped down still laughing. Jim and his friend David walked up to them as they lay there panting.

"Hey you guys, Dad says to be cleaned up and ready for dinner in twenty Mikes." Jim said looking down at them.

"Twenty Mikes!" Mel mimicked in a serious tone. "How many Melvins is that? How about we be there in seven and a half Ruperts?"

Barry gave her an elbow, and sat up.

"Sorry Jim, you know how she is—" he started.

"Dude, you don't have to make any excuses for her. I've been living with it all her life."

They all made their way back to their rooms and got cleaned up for dinner. Mel holding Barry's hand the whole way until she had to peel off and go to her own room. She boldly pecked him on the cheek before darting into her room.

"You know, I think I'm supposed to kick his ass to defend my sister's honor or something." Jim joked to David as he slugged Barry in the shoulder. The punch was hard enough to send Barry bouncing off the far wall of the corridor. Barry slugged Jim in the thigh hard enough to give him a 'Dead leg' and dashed past heading towards their room.

"You have to catch me first you big goof!"

"You little..." Jim hobbled after the fleeing felon.

Barry made it to the door first and was trying to get in when Jim Freight-trained into him. The two wound up wrestling in the hall with Jim eventually on top, holding Barry's wrists, making him hit his own face with his hands. Although Jim outweighed Barry by forty pounds, it still took him a lot of effort to overpower the smaller boy.

"Ooh, why you want to hit yourself!" He said as they laughed. "Oh ho! What's that? A little thunder! Huh? A little lightning!" They laughed at the lines from a movie they had watched the night before.

David was standing over the shenanigans when his father Cliff stuck his head out to see what the ruckus was. He took one look at the kids on the floor, then looked at his son who just tilted his head and shrugged.

"Alright you clowns!" He had to raise his voice to be heard. "Knock it off before I whip all three of you!"

"What the hell did I do?" David turned an indignant look on his father.

"You're a passive participant! And even if you didn't do anything this time, I'm sure there's something you guys did that would deserve it!"

David really couldn't find fault in his logic, since it was 100% true. He reached down and pulled Jim off of Barry. They both got up grinning and marched into the room. They really had to clean up now, since they had broken a sweat and the sand was really stuck to them. They took turns jumping in and out of the shower and were in the hall a few minutes later. The group all streamed down into one of the ballrooms for a nice sit down dinner.

The island of Coronado had fared much better during the outbreak, than the city of San Diego surrounding it. Home to two naval bases, it had plenty of military personnel on hand to deal with the crisis. Naval Amphibious Base Coronado was the home to Naval Special Warfare. The SEALs and members of the Special Boat Squadrons were highly trained operators with the combat skills to fend of attacks from the mainland. The Marine Corps also had their Basic Recon Course collocated at the base, adding to the pool of talent.

Naval Air Station North Island, was home to several aircraft carriers whose ability to supply power from their nuclear generators, and their ability to purify salt water, enabled the island to be used as a safe haven for the people fleeing the violence that engulfed the city across the bay. It also had runways capable of handling aircraft of all sizes. It was home to several naval helicopter squadrons that were capable of conducting search and rescue missions.

The Hotel Del Coronado was the historical icon of the island. The management had made the hotels' facilities available 'For the duration', and it was one of the few areas in the country where there was virtually no risk of the ferals attacking. Coronado had originally been two islands, forming San Diego harbor. When the harbor was dredged to accommodate naval shipping, the material dredged was used to fill the channel between the two Islands making them one. They still had more dredging to do so they wound up connecting the island to the mainland to the south (Technically making it a peninsula).

The primary means of access to the island had originally been a ferry, until the Coronado Bay Bridge was constructed. The bridge was an engineering marvel that set several records for its construction. The military personnel had been able to secure both access points to the island. This made it the one of the only truly safe areas as the world went down in flames.

Colonel Neal and Mark had to come down for a meeting, so they decided to bring their families for two days of relaxation. Neal still lived on Camp Pendleton, and even though the base had been recovered, it was such a large area that ferals were still found on a regular basis. Sometimes they were discovered after someone was attacked. This made it dangerous to be outside alone.

Mark lived in Rancho Bernardo, a suburb in north San Diego. His neighborhood had suffered horribly during the collapse. The neighborhood was adjacent Lake Hodges, one of the reservoirs that had been targeted by the terrorists dropping the chemical weapons. There were still packs of feral humans as well as affected animals all around his home. This meant that the people staying there had to be on full alert all the time. The location however, was halfway between San Diego and Camp Pendleton. It made a great collection point for people who were then evacuated to Camp Pendleton.

Neal and some of the other surviving Marine staff were coordinating recovery efforts with the Navy, while Mark was meeting with some of the instructors at Naval Special Warfare to begin setting up a training curriculum for survivors. The curriculum was to train them to exist in this new world that they faced, so that they could go out and rebuild without getting eaten. MCRD San Diego was just across the Bay from Coronado, but had suffered 99% percent casualties during the initial outbreak of violence. The recruits and Drill Instructors were given city water to drink out of their canteens, and they were all poisoned. Everyone on the base who wasn't poisoned was killed. This virtually eliminated the Instructor base for the Marine Corps on the west coast. MCRD Parris Island on the east coast, had fared much better.

The families had been staying at the Hotel Del and enjoying the beach. Mark brought his two dogs, Buster and Thor, who were trying to make up for two months of being cooped up. The kids exercised them twice a day at the house, but they were not allowed to run off leash. Coronado had a dog area on the beach where the two animals could frolic in the waves and burn off some energy.

Barry missed Bert and had spent a lot of time playing with and getting to know Buster and Thor. He and Mel had grown close while spending time caring for and walking the dogs. There wasn't much else for Barry to do since Jake was busy and the formal training for civilians hadn't been set up yet. He had been debriefed by several Marine Corps staff about his experiences. He was allowed to keep his weapons and gear, and trained with them as much as he could. Jake taught him a lot, but he was constantly going off on missions.

Jim had taken Barry under his wing like the little brother he didn't have. He began showing Barry shooting drills that his father had taught him, and they worked out together. Barry had an inherent toughness that showed as he struggled to keep up with Jim who was five years his senior, and forty pounds bigger.

The only real disagreement they had was video games. Jim still loved them and Barry had outgrown them. That didn't keep the occasional all-nighter from happening, Barry still had skills.

The families finished their mini vacation and went back to work. For Barry and Jim, who would be in the first class of the training program, they would have a final week to prepare. The students would live in barracks on the base at Pendleton. Mel was already making plans to stay with Jen, Marks girlfriend who was living on base and working at the hospital. She wasn't planning on letting her man out of sight for long.

CHAPTER 15

"The weapon you see before you is the M4 carbine! It is a shoulder fired, air cooled, gas operated, 5.56 Millimeter rifle with a cyclic rate of fire of 600 rounds per minute!" The instructor's voice boomed across the classroom. "It has a maximum effective range of 550 meters for a point target and 800 meters for an area target! Normally when training recruits you would not fire this weapon until you had completed the first phase of Boot Camp. Due to the current circumstances however you will begin immediately learning to operate and defend yourself with this weapon!

"You will learn to do so in a safe and efficient manner! DO NOT be a safety violator! If I or my staff catch you operating MY rifle in an unsafe manner you will wish you were eaten by a pack of ferals! You have been issued one of the Marine Corps rifles, therefore you have been issued one of MY rifles. You will take care of MY rifle as if it were your own. Some of you have personal weapons as well." This last was accompanied by a glare at Barry, Jim, and the few others who already had them before the class began. "You will be issued ammunition ..."

The first true day of class was actually their third since arriving at the base. The first two were spent getting checked out by base medical and updating their shots. Then they stood in unending lines to get issued their basic clothing and equipment allowance. Then they were assigned to living quarters. The first class consisted of 200 students. They took up only a small portion of the barracks space that had formerly been for students at the school of infantry. The students were assigned rooms and were given instruction on where everything was to be stored and how. They lost the first of many classmates on the first day, when she refused to accept all the 'bossing around' and dropped voluntarily.

It was day three and the 197 students were sitting in an auditorium style lecture hall as a Marine instructor began teaching them how to tear down, clean, and reassemble the M16/M4 weapons system. The class took several hours with the instructors moving up and down through the aisles assisting the students. Although the course was being run in a military manner, it was not Boot Camp, so the instructors were very approachable and the exchange of information was free flowing. The instructors also gave the trainees tips and short cuts to cleaning the weapons.

After the students had lunch, they went directly to the range for Weapons handling drills. The first day consisted of proper carry and presentation of the weapon. The students drilled all afternoon on how to access and get the weapon aimed in on the target from anyone of its carrying positions. The repeated drills were designed to install 'muscle memory' so that the students would be able to instinctively defend themselves. Because of the threats present in the environment, the students would carry their loaded weapons on them at all times during their training.

Day four started out with a morning workout that consisted of the 'daily seven' Calisthenics and a short two mile run. After cleaning up and getting breakfast, they were back in the classroom again for more classes. After lunch they were on the firing line learning how to clear Malfunctions.

Sergeant Derry was the instructor and Barry was amazed at the skill the man displayed. The man was able to manipulate the rifle as if it was an extension of his body.

"This period of instruction will cover Immediate Action Drills! An Immediate Action Drill is The Unhesitating Application of a probable remedy to a weapons malfunction. The key word here is Unhesitating! If you hesitate in a fight, you will lose! You will practice these drills until they are so ingrained in you, that your children will have them genetically imprinted on their brains when born! You will do them till your fingers bleed! Shit I may have you do them till your fingers fall off! Don't worry, I will make you amphibious and they will grow back just like a salamanders tail!

"There are three types of Malfunctions! They are called: Type one, Type two, and Type three! Are you with me?" His question was answered by the required 'Argh'. "A Type one malfunction means you didn't chamber a round! Now this could be caused by several factors! All of the factors are caused by YOU being stupid! Either you forgot to chamber the round, you forgot to seat the magazine properly, or you are using damaged and unserviceable equipment and the bolt could not pick up the round from the magazine! Lastly you may have properly chambered a round, but the weapon was non-functional or it was a dud round, creating a misfire! In 99% of the Type one malfunctions, it is operator error that causes these things! Do not be the operator who is in error during a fight! You will lose!

"The Immediate Action Drill for a Type one and a Type two malfunction is performed in the following manner: You will maintain a firing grip with you strong hand on the pistol grip of the weapon. You will firmly smack the bottom of the magazine with your weak hand to ensure that the magazine is seated properly. You will then tilt the rifle to the right, this will point the ejection port towards the ground and allow any dud rounds or debris to fall out freely. You will then operate the charging handle like so!" He demonstrated by using his left hand to cycle the action on his weapon. "Completely cycling the bolt through its full range of travel. While doing this you should observe anything that falls out of the ejection port. If it is gun parts and not ammo or dirt, you are fucked! Drop the rifle and go to your secondary, Got it?"

"Argh"

"Good! I will now demonstrate using dud rounds only in MY rifle."

The students watched as Jake set up the malfunction then inserted a magazine loaded with the inert rounds. He pointed at a target on the side wall of the lecture area. He nodded at one of the other instructors who had a shot timer used by competitive shooters. He pushed a button and the small box made a beep. It took Jake all of .6 seconds to complete the drill. Most of the students were still looking at the instructor holding the shot timer and never saw it.

"Did anyone NOT see what I just did?"

Half of the students raised their hands.

"Why the hell not?" The question was rhetorical and they set it up again. And again he finished so fast that the motion was just a blur. "Did you get it that time?"

Several of the students were too shy to admit that they had missed it. Jim picked up on this and decided to be the sacrificial goat.

"Could you please demonstrate the process one more time slowly please, Sergeant?"

Jake, who knew full well that Jim could probably do it almost as fast as him, let him have a little ribbing.

"Okay, for all you students who have slow eyes, I will do it one more time and then you are going to do it."

He sent a mock glare at Jim. "Alright, Stevie Wonder, follow along closely…"

They finished the first week with 195 students.

CHAPTER 16

The students of CCTC-1 started their second month with 182 students. After spending the first month concentrating on weapons handling for the rifle, pistol, and shotgun. They were now going into wilderness survival. They first learned how to acquire and purify water in the wilderness. This included making filters from natural materials. A cotton rope was used to transfer water from container to container to filter out turbidity. They spent extra time learning to distil the water if it tested positive for the toxin.

The next subject was shelter. They spent endless hours building various structures that did everything from keep them warm in the winter to sunshades for the desert. They made Tee-pees and log houses, tents and lean-tos. They learned a thousand and one ways to use 550 paracord. They lost a student who fell out of a tree he had slung his hammock in. He fell twenty feet and broke a leg and an arm.

Next was fire. How to build one using a lighter took a few minutes. Learning to use materials found only in the desert took a bit longer. Bow and drill, Ferro rod and steel, magnifying glass, all of it. They added things to their packs so that they always had at least three ways to start one. Cotton balls with Vaseline and Magnesium rod shavings mixed into them for starting wet wood. They made miniature alcohol stoves from aluminum cans and other containers. They learned how to use butane torches to solder tin.

Month three was field craft. They had to take what they had learned and apply those survival techniques in the bush. They learned how to track both man and beast (They would joke about the fact that they were one and the same now), and how to avoid being tracked. Traps and snares took up two weeks of classroom and field time.

Next was Land Navigation. The GPS satellite system was still up and running so they learned to use hand held units. The majority of the time however was spent with a Map and Compass. The students studied terrain association, intersection, resection, and modified resection. The outer edge of the map was no longer a jumble of weird symbols, but a source of valuable information. Once they were competent during the day, they did it all again at night. Barry got teased about his pace count changing because he was growing taller by the day.

Next was tactics. They learned how to be 'Force Multipliers'. The Special Operations instructors included former Army Green Berets, SEALS, and Force Recon Marines. They studied small unit tactics and learned how to train others to protect themselves. This time the traps and snares were aimed at people. They studied IEDs and how to make them for use in a defensive perimeter or to deter someone pursuing them. This led to how to recognize and avoid or disable them.

They finished their fifth month with 135 students in the class. They were halfway there.

CHAPTER 17

The students of CCTC-1 began the second half of their training learning how to grow vegetables.

Until the country's infra-structure came back on line, food was going to be a real problem. The bulk of America's food came from the central states. California did have a huge agricultural base, but without proper irrigation, the crops were drying up in the fields. The students were taken to several of the farm sites that were established on the base and given instruction on soil preparation and cultivation of various crops. Barry, who had grown up on a farm, wound up teaching several of the instructors some of the techniques his father used. One of the instructors almost got punched in the nose for suggesting that Barry stay and help in the fields.

The students still had to maintain their combat proficiency, and the physical training had advanced to long road marches with packs and gear. The students would often hike ten or more miles to a training area (that was only four or five miles away), and then have to hike back a few days later. They also had to continue to demonstrate woodcraft and survival skills. They were now able to adapt and survive with almost nothing.

They started their final month back in the classroom.

Psychiatrists and Psychologists were brought in to discuss what kind of effect, the attacks had had on people. The various psychosis that had been discovered to date, as well as dealing with people who had taken advantage of the lack of Law Enforcement. Feral humans were not the only humans that you had to watch out for. The students were subjected to a mini prisoner exercise adopted from the Navy and Marine Corps SERE School.

They entered 'Hell Week' with 104 students, the final exercise ending in a four day survival scenario where the students were tested to their limits. The exercise culminated in a twenty-three mile forced road march back to the school house. The 82 who completed it were now ready to go out into the world and help get society back on its feet.

CHAPTER 18

The graduation party was in full swing as Jake walked up to the club with his date on his arm. Nicole was a stunning 5'11" dark haired beauty who had been a lifeguard before the attacks. She had survived the initial outbreak in Encinitas, by taking shelter in the back of liquor store and barricading the doors. She waited out the first week, hoping that some form of order would be restored. She had been lucky enough to be picked up by a group of several Marines who were fighting their way back to the base.

They walked into the foyer and were greeted by Tia and Terry who were scoping out the guests as they arrived. They took in Nicole's good looks with more than a little jealousy but were friendly to her as they pointed the couple in the direction of their family's table. They wandered over and said hi to Mark and Jen.

"Where are the two graduates?" Jake asked after introducing Nicole. "I thought they'd be here by now."

"I think Barry is getting a last minute briefing from his commander regarding tonight's activity. She won't let him out of her sight for very long." Jen said gesturing to an area between two decorative pillars. They all turned to see Barry with his back to a pillar, while Mel spoke earnestly to him.

"Looks like he needs a QRF to bail him out Gunner." Derry said with a grin.

"Why don't you go do that Derry, she hasn't seen you in a while." Mark said while turning to Nicole. "Can I get you a drink Nicole?"

"Please, it's Nikki, and I'm fine. I'm going to hit the powder room and I'll grab one on the way back." She asked if anyone else wanted something and made her way back out to the foyer and the restrooms.

Mel was straightening Barry's shirt and going on about how he had been mentioned as one of the honor graduates that afternoon at the graduation ceremony, when she saw Jake approaching. She squealed and jumped up into his arms for a hug. Jake winked over her shoulder at Barry who was letting out a sigh of relief at being rescued.

"Jake! Where have you been? I heard you got back from LA last week but we haven't seen you."

"I had to do some work over at the pool. One of the water survival instructors had an accident and I had to cover. Then I met a gal, and I've been hanging out with her for a bit." Jake said setting the young teenager back down. He held her at arm's length and spun her around. "Wow Mel! You look stunning!"

Mel blushed at the compliment as she smoothed the blue dress back down along her slender frame. The dress had actually belonged to her older sister Terry, who had never worn it. A multi-colored opal necklace and matching bracelet perfectly accented the blue dress and Mel's long dark hair. Before Barry had come along, Mel had had a crush on Jake, and she still got twitterpated when he was around.

"How you doing, Bud?" Jake asked as they all began back towards the table.

"I'm doing okay. Gonna rest up till Monday before I see what they're going to do with us." Barry had some bruises and his feet were still aching from all the hiking they had done during their final week. "I'm probably going back out into town to help at the Gunner's house."

They were all getting ready to sit down when Terry and Tia came hustling through the crowd and whispered into Mark's ear. Mark looked at Jake and shifted his eyes towards the bar. Jake caught the look and stood back up. The two of them were making their way to the bar when the sound of breaking glass caused them to break into a jog. They stepped into the bar to see Nikki holding her arm and Lieutenant Colonel Barrent, the Provost Marshall bent over in front of her holding his face in his hands.

As they approached he looked up at Nikki and snarled. It was the wrong thing to do.

Kirk Barrent was standing at the end of the bar, and immediately noticed the attractive brunette when she walked into bar area. Almost every male in the bar noticed as she walked over and waited to be served by the busy bartender. Barrent took two steps and leaned in close. Nikki felt his breath on her shoulder and glanced in his direction. She was startled to see a face leaning over her shoulder, she was even more shocked when she realized the man was staring down towards her chest.

"Excuse me!" She said as she flinched away, but was brought up short by the man's hand holding onto her arm right above the elbow. Nikki was in great shape, with muscular arms, but Barrent maintained his grip by squeezing her arm even harder. Terry and Tia had just walked into the bar area and saw what was going on. They immediately went to get Mark and Jake.

"Oh! I'm sorry." Barrent slowly released her arm once she was no longer moving away from him. "I'm the base Provost Marshall and I was wondering if I could buy you a drink."

"I don't think so!" the disdain evident in her voice. "I'm here with a gentleman, someone with manners, not some pig!"

"I would be careful how you speak to me. This is my base and I could make things very difficult for you. What's your name?" He put a stern look on his face. Two of the Enlisted Marines at the bar took a few steps back. Nikki noticed this and began to get concerned that the man might really be in charge of the base.

"I'm here with Sergeant Derry." She finally said as she caught the smell of whiskey coming from his breath.

Barrent let out a laugh. "A sergeant! I'm a colonel in the Marine Corps!" his voice went up in volume enough to cause a few stares.

He stepped forward and again gripped her arm just above the elbow. Nikki swung her glass with her other hand, smashing it into the side of Barrent's face. The glass broke and the piece that was left in Nikki's hand slashed across Barrent's nose, cutting it wide open. He immediately covered the wound with his hands. After feeling the cut, he looked up and snarled at the now terrified girl. He began to take a step towards her when he caught movement out of the corner of his eye. He turned just as Jake landed a right cross to his cheek. The blow drove him to his knees as his body fell against the bar.

"Are you alright?" Jake asked turning towards Nikki.

"Yeah, he just grabbed my arm..." She had to stop speaking as Jake gently moved her aside with one hand while he squared off with Barrent who was surging to his feet. Jake, who was never one to take his eye off an opponent until he was sure they were either dead or secured, was ready as

Barrent attempted to rush him. The attack was thwarted when Mark reached out and took Barrent by the throat, digging his fingers in around the Adams apple. Jake also threw a snap kick to Barrent's mid-section, stopping his forward momentum, and knocking the breath out of him. Mark continued to wrap his arm around the man's neck and began pulling him towards the side door to the bar.

"Excuse us for just a second." Jake said over his shoulder as he followed the now feebly struggling Barrent and Mark out the door. Once outside Mark and Jake pushed the lieutenant colonel up against the wall. Mark released his grip on the man's neck and stepped back as Jake leaned in to get in the man's face.

"What in the hell was that, you piece of shit?" The statement hissed through Derry's teeth.

"Jake! At Ease!" Mark barked out.

Derry was too disciplined to not immediately follow an order and stepped back, placing his hands in the small of his back. He stood up straight but kept his eyes on Barrent as he recovered himself.

"You're both under arrest!" Barrent gasped out as he attempted to get into a fighting stance. "I'll have you both Court Martialed for striking a superior officer!"

"Oh well then I'm gonna earn my brig time then, you fuck!" Derry said and snapped a punch into the side of his head. Barrent, who considered himself a martial artist attempted to block the blow but was only partially effective. Derry's fist still slammed into the side of his head which then bounced off the wall. The blow turned Barrent's knees to water and he slid down the wall.

"Jake! Dammit, that's enough!" Mark put a firm, but gentle, hand on Jake's shoulder to stop him from continuing the beating. Several Marines had followed the men outside and were standing there with stunned expressions on their faces. Barrent was trying to get to his feet and shaking his head.

"You're done, Colonel. Stay down." Mark's firm tone and pointed finger should have been a discouragement, but Barrent's ego wouldn't let it go. He pushed himself upright using one hand on the wall while the other was pressed to the rapidly growing mouse over his left eye.

"You don't give the orders around here! I do!" Barrent grinned as two Military Police officers jogged up. "You two arrest these men right now!"

The two MP's looked back and forth between the Provost Marshall and Jake. No one with a survival instinct was going to set a hand on Jake unless they knew what they were doing. And even then the survival part wasn't a sure thing. The corporal, who was the senior of the two, stepped up and set his hand on Jake's arm.

"Can I talk to you a moment sir?"

Jake spun on the poor man easily pulling his nineteen-inch bicep out of the man's grip.

"You touch me again and I'll fucking destroy you in place! Do you understand me, you fucking pogie? And I'm a sergeant of Marines. Don't call me sir!"

The MP took a step back and made a soothing gesture with his hands.

"I said I need to talk to you, Sergeant." The corporal's tone took on a firm edge. "Now no matter what, that's going to happen. Let's do it without any trouble."

The lance corporal who was with him had turned to cover his partner when a loud voice bellowed "That's enough! Lieutenant Colonel Barrent, you are way out of line! Compose yourself... Now!"

Everyone turned to see Colonel Neal standing at the top of the stairs. He was shooting laser beams at Barrent.

"I don't work for you anymore! General Moore is back on active duty. That means I'm back in charge of the base, sir!" The last was thrown in with a sneer.

"Yes I am, and you can consider yourself relieved of duty." Barrent looked around to see the general standing behind him in the small crowd that had gathered.

"Gentlemen," he said, looking at the two MP's. "Lieutenant Colonel Barrent is hereby relieved as the Provost Marshall. He is to be escorted to the brig and secured there until I sort this whole mess out. Take him by medical first and have him patched up."

"Aye, aye sir!" They both said in unison coming to attention. They immediately turned and began securing Barrent as he spluttered about being the victim.

"But sir! These two non-rates attacked me! I want to press charges!"

"Corporal, is the watch commander on the way?" General Moore asked as he looked Derry up and down.

"Yes sir. Staff Sergeant Milner is en route, she should be here any second."

"Very well, secure your prisoner and put something on his face to stop the bleeding." Moore turned back to Derry. "Are you Sergeant Derry?"

"Yes sir!" Jake's body was locked in a perfect position of attention.

"Did you strike the lieutenant colonel?"

"Sir, yes sir!"

"I see. Very well you will report to my office at 08:00 tomorrow morning for office hours do you understand me?" Moore was looking up at Derry. His stoic expression could have been carved out of granite for all the emotion it showed.

"Aye, aye sir!"

"You are dismissed, Sergeant."

"Aye, aye sir!" Derry did a parade ground about face and stepped away.

"Sir, if I could have a word..." Mark began.

"I'll see you in my office at 07:30, Gunner," Moore said as he shooed every one back inside. Nodding at Neal as he did so. Barrent began swearing at Derry, Mark, and the two MP's who were leading him away. Derry remained at a position of Parade rest until the crowd dispersed. He let out a sigh and turned to face Mark.

"Shit Gunner, I'm sorry. I really fucked that one up." Jake was shaking his head and looking at his feet. "I guess I'll be giving my stripe back."

"Don't worry about it, I gave a couple of mine back one time as well." Mark laughed at the startled look on Jake's face. "Come on there's nothing we can do about it until tomorrow morning. Might as well have a good time tonight."

The rest of the party went well, with the MP watch commander discreetly pulling a few people aside for their statements. Nikki spent a good ten minutes with her and several witnesses at the bar corroborated her version of events. The only other time a fight almost broke out, was when Barry asked Nikki to dance. Mel started shooting laser beams at his back until Jake laughingly scooped her up in his arms and took her out to dance next to them on the floor.

Jake and Mark arrived at the commanding general's office at 07:15. They were both dressed in their 'Alphas', their Gabardine coats displaying their ribbons and shooting badges. Mark had eight even rows over his three shooting badges. Jake had six rows plus two more on top over his two expert (rifle and pistol) badges. They reported into the admin at the CO's office and stood around waiting, they did not sit down in order to avoid wrinkling their uniforms.

Colonel Neal stepped outside and motioned Mark in a few minutes later. Mark turned towards Derry and gave him a thumbs up.

"Fuck it, don't mean nuthin'" he grunted.

"Drive on!" Derry gave the grunts reply to the time honored saying the Marines used when they were about to get screwed by the Corps.

Mark marched into the general's office and the door was closed behind him. Jake stood there for a few more minutes before going to the head and carefully cleaning his face with a damp towel. He was beginning to sweat in the uniform and the one thing he was not going to let the general see was him looking nervous. He walked back down the hall and only had to wait for a few minutes when Colonel Neal stuck his head outside the door and motioned Jake in.

Jake strode through the door and marched right up to the general's desk. He came to a position of attention centered and eighteen inches from the edge of the desk and stared at a point above the general seated in front of him. Marines do not salute when inside a building and uncovered, unless they are under arms.

"Sergeant Derry reporting as ordered sir!"

"Sergeant Derry, you are here because you are accused of striking an officer. I have read the Military Police report and witness statements from last night, I was also a witness to the event. This is a non-judicial proceeding, if you are not satisfied with my decision in this proceeding you may request mast following it. Do you understand?"

"Yes sir!"

"Good. I want you to think long and hard before you do such a thing since there are only two figures of authority higher than me in your chain of command. I am going to ask you a few questions, the Gunner here told me to make them simple yes or no questions so your grunt brain can answer them without any problem. Do you understand?"

Jake's eyes shifted to the side momentarily to see Norris and Neal staring at him.

"Yes sir!"

"Sergeant, did you strike Lieutenant Colonel Barrent last night?"

"Yes sir!"

"Once outside, did you strike him again and make the statement, and I quote 'I'm going to earn my brig time then, you fuck'?"

"Yes sir!"

"Are you aware that striking an officer is a crime?"

"Yes sir!"

"And are you aware that swearing at an officer could be considered as conduct unbecoming a Marine?"

"Yes sir!"

"Very well then, I am hereby going to render my judgment with Colonel Neal and Chief Warrant Officer Norris present as my witness. My sentence will be carried out in two parts: loss of pay, and incarceration." Moore said with a slight frown on his face.

Jake started to get a queasy feeling in his gut. He would rather lose a stripe than do time in the brig.

"Due to the heinous nature of striking an asshole without waiting for me to be there to see it, I hereby order that $100.00 be deducted from your pay, because that's how much I would have paid on the spot to see it. As for incarceration, I hereby restrict you to quarters for ninety-six hours. The quarters will be those that I designate. In this case it will be the MWR Beach cottages at Del Mar beach. During the time of this confinement you will have no more than 200 visitors, do you understand me?"

Jake was still trying to assimilate the punishment when the light bulb went off in his head. Since the initial outbreaks, there had been no payroll or other services as everyone tried to survive. Jake hadn't received a paycheck in almost a year. The corner of his mouth curled up a quarter of an inch as he fought to control his smile.

"The general asked you a question!" Mark barked out.

"Sir, yes sir! I understand completely!"

"Do you wish to dispute my findings in the matter, Sergeant?"

"No, sir!"

"Very well then. Sentence to be carried out at 16:00 today. You are dismissed!"

"Aye, aye sir!" Jake took one step back, executed an about-face and marched out the door.

Moore leaned back and looked at both Neal and Norris. He let out a long sigh and got to his feet.

"Well shall we deal with our wayward child?" He asked as he went to the side door of his office. He leaned out the door and nodded at the two MP's there. They led in a very battered looking Kirk Barrent. He had been given a clean uniform from his room at the BOQ. His nose had been stitched up at the hospital, but the entire left side of his face was black and blue, and his throat had red marks from Mark's fingers that were also starting to darken into an ugly shade of purple. Barrent looked around the room and watched as the general sat down. Realizing what was about to happen, he sighed and then presented himself at the desk.

"Lieutenant Colonel Barrent reporting as ordered sir!"

"Mr. Barrent, at ease." Moore said. "You are here today to answer for your behavior over the last few weeks, especially last night. I have read the fitness report Colonel Neal submitted regarding your behavior prior to the outbreak and immediately following it while he was in command. I have received several other reports from other commands regarding their interaction with your command, and I have read the report generated by your own watch commander, Staff Sergeant Milner."

Moore leaned back and gestured at several file folders on his desk. "I have also just completed office hours on that sergeant you were involved in an altercation with. Although it was against my true feelings in the matter, I had to punish him with loss of pay and confinement. As much as I'm sure you deserved it, his striking you the second time was conduct unbecoming and he had to be disciplined."

Barrent took this in and glanced over at Mark who was watching the proceedings with a neutral expression on his face. Barrent did a poor job of concealing the sneer that crept over his face at the news that the enlisted Marine had been punished. Although the general was obviously pissed at him, it appeared that he was at least maintaining his loyalty to his fellow officer and not towards the enlisted Marine. He wanted to hear what he was going to do to Norris, a Warrant Officer being only slightly above enlisted personnel in his mind. He wiped the smirk off his face and turned back towards the general.

"Yes, sir." Barrent was beginning to see light at the end of the tunnel. Sergeant Milner had always been pretty squared away. He hadn't had any issues with her, although she wasn't his type, she was built a little too square to the ground and lacked the curves he found appealing. He had signed off on her fitness reports, which had always been favorable. A little loyalty towards her chain of command was to be expected.

"Now as far as your performance in your command goes..." Moore began.

"Excuse me sir." Barrent made the fatal sin of interrupting the general. "What about Warrant Officer Norris? He was involved in the altercation and assaulted me."

It took every ounce of self-control for Moore not to come unglued at the temerity of the man standing before him. The general took a deep breath and leaned back in his chair. He stared at Barrent for almost a full minute before speaking.

"I was going to address that in a moment."

Moore raised an eyebrow, and Barrent took the hint. He closed his mouth and stood a little straighter.

"Now, as I was saying. I have received several reports on your interaction with other commands, both prior to and after the attacks. It is very disconcerting to see a command that has so little faith in its Marines that they cannot be trusted to keep and maintain their own gear. This was done to the point of micro-management. The result of this was almost a complete breakdown of the PM's office and their ability to respond to the crisis in an effective manner.

"Colonel Neal made mention of this in his report. He also commended your response after you made it back to base." Moore nodded towards the colonel standing off to the side. Barrent was unaware of the report and was starting to regret his snide remark to the colonel. He nodded with a sickly smile towards Colonel Neal. At least he was seeing some support from his fellow officers. This might not turn out as bad as he thought it would.

"That report is what kept me from relieving you on the spot once I was out of Sick Bay. Now as to the incident last night, I have five witnesses who have made sworn statements that you assaulted a Miss Nicole Palmer in the bar. I am very aware of your behavior prior to your divorce, and your reputation as a 'swordsman' precedes you. This combined, with the highest request for transfer rate by female Marines in your command tells me that you have an impulse control issue."

"Sir, I admit I had a little too much to drink, and I apologize if I seemed forward. I only ever touched her on the arm, and that was to help her maintain her balance. She seemed a little wobbly in her heels." Kirk was not feeling the love here and he was beginning to feel the strain of maintaining his stance. "The issue of my ex-wife should not be a factor since she left me months before our divorce and I was essentially single, sir. As far as the female requests for transfer, the job of the Military Police on an infantry base can be rough, and the occupational field has one of the highest RFT (Request for Transfer) rates for women Marines anyways."

"But not as high as that experienced during your command." Moore said.

Barrent just shrugged as if it weren't that big of an issue.

"As for the matter with your wife, you were seen out in town by several other field grade officers at various restaurants with various women, this was prior to your divorce, and in fact it was during your wife's pregnancy." Moore had no respect for the man in front of him and it was becoming apparent in his tone. "Any one of these things, while they may be cause for concern, does not bear sufficient weight to justify removing you from your command. But when taken as a whole, your performance and behavior indicate that you are not fit for it.

"Now as for the matter of Chief Warrant Officer Norris, after reading the report from your staff sergeant, including the witness statements, I am firmly of the belief that: (A) Your conduct was unbecoming of an officer in the United States Marine Corps, and (B) Gunner Norris acted in a manner necessary to prevent further injury to Miss Palmer and yourself.

Although you seem to have tempted fate, challenging Sergeant Derry to a fight."

Moore shook his head again. "Gunner Norris' actions were commensurate with those of a person attempting to prevent further violence from taking place. The witness statements all support his claim. You however have a severe credibility problem. Something no Marine Officer should *ever* have. We don't have time for a general court martial, nor do we have the energy and assets to spare. I am hereby reducing you in rank to first lieutenant, and ordering you to be confined for ninety days. During that ninety days, you will report for supervised working party details each and every day. I am fining you one month's pay to replace the broken glassware and to reimburse Miss Palmer for the dress she was wearing. It was stained in the incident. Due to the nature of our circumstances I will not be considering your request for Mast until such time as there is some form of legal system restored to deal with you. Do you understand my decision?"

Barrent just stood there with his mouth open.

"The general asked you a question, Lieutenant!" Colonel Neal barked.

"Uh, yes sir!" Barrent stood up straighter and began to glare around at the others in the office.

The two MPs that had led him in, stepped up next to him. Each took hold of an arm, and they led him out of the office.

Barrent shot them both a look but didn't say anything as he was taken away.

After the door closed, General Moore leaned back in his chair and blew out a long slow whistle. He looked at Norris and Neal before asking "Well, how much trouble do you think he's going to be now?"

"Ah hell sir, I don't think we're done with him yet." Neal said. "Some of his troops stated that he could carry a grudge."

"Don't know the man myself except by reputation sir." Mark was nodding in agreement with Neal's statement. "But men like that don't make those kinds of threats in jest. I think he'll be a real pain in your side if he isn't monitored."

"Yeah, we're going to have to keep an eye on him." Moore nodded at Neal.

"Yes sir." Neal replied.

"Gunner, please apologize to Sergeant Derry for the goat rope I put him through, I know waiting for office hours can be a little stressful." Moore said, rising from his chair.

"Shit sir, that kid's bullet-proof. He'll be all right." Mark was grinning as he stood also.

"I bet he's bullet-proof!" Moore shook his head. "He looks like he could eat a locomotive for breakfast."

"Yeah, he's getting to the point where I have to pay attention in the combat pit." Mark shrugged. "One of these days, he's going to get ahold of me and it's gonna hurt."

"Holy shit!" Neal said busting out laughing. "Well I was wondering what I was going to do with my daughter who has asked about him every day since she met him at the airfield. Now I'll just have you straighten him out!"

"Yes sir. I have the same problem with my girls, all of them, including Jen!" Mark was chuckling and shaking his head. "They all worship the ground he walks on and follow him like a bunch of ducklings when he's around."

"We're done here gentlemen." Moore said stepping towards the door. "I'll see you at the meeting on Monday and we'll go over what's happening in LA."

The mention of the city sobered everyone right up. There had been progress made in securing the vital areas needed to restore some of the infra-structure, but the sheer number of ferals was preventing most efforts to reclaim residential structures. It just wasn't safe for people unless they were in large, well-armed groups. The Marines were having to fight for every square inch, sometimes more than once for the same square inch. This had a negative effect on morale, as men were lost retaking an area they had secured the week before.

"Aye, aye sir!" They both said in unison, and left.

CHAPTER 19

Jake leaned back in his lounge chair and looked out towards the Pacific Ocean. Barry and Mel were splashing in the waves with Buster and Thor, while Jen and Mark looked on. Nikki walked out from inside the cottage and set her glass of Rum punch down on the small table that was between the two lounge chairs. After straightening her towel, she plopped down next to him and raised her glass.

"If I'd have known that this was what jail was like, I would have taken up a life of crime much earlier in my life." She raised her glass and clinked it against his Corona bottle. They both took a sip, and stared out at the group of people on the beach. Since beginning his 'Confinement' yesterday, there had been a steady stream of visitors and well-wishers coming by to shake Jake's hand and drink a beer. The BBQ last night had turned into a full on bash, when LCpl Sullivan had pulled up his car and began playing music out of what had to be the world's loudest automotive stereo system.

In order to maintain compliance with Jake's 'Jail time' a green military log book had been set up as a sign in journal on a pedestal by the front door to the cottage. Everyone coming to visit had signed in on it. Some of the comments were derogatory, some to the point of being pornographic, the latter including some reference to Barrent. Both Mickey Mouse and Donald Duck apparently had come by several times. Other celebrities in attendance included Godzilla (whose handwriting looked suspiciously like Sergeant Sanchez's), Batman, Poison Ivy, and SpongeBob SquarePecker.

The Norris clan had shown up with steaks, burgers, and beer. Mark had reserved the cottage next to Jake's while setting up his 'Punishment'. All the Marines, along with most of the students from the training class had come by to haze Jake about his being in 'jail'. The flow of guests had been non-stop and had resulted in the MPs coming by to police up the passed out bodies off the beach. It was still too dangerous to be sleeping out of doors. The occasional feral still popped up in the area.

Buster and Thor came trotting up from the beach followed by Barry and Mel. Jake let out a little sigh at being reminded that he was no longer the apple of her eye. Nikki noticed this and smiled at the big softy sitting next to her. For such a fierce man, he had a boyish side that was so endearing that she wanted to cuddle him like a Teddy Bear. The fact that he was as handsome as a Roman God and built like a stallion didn't hurt either.

Buster went straight up to Jake, stuck his sandy face right on his arm, leaving a streak of sand and dog slobber on his sleeve. The boxer's jowls having a built in, extra capacity, slobber holder. Thor marched right up between his legs and shook sand and salt water all over everything in a five foot radius.

"Gahhh!" Jake yelled as he tried to push the 130 pound dog away. "You dumb dog! Get off of me!"

Nikki had rolled away from the coming onslaught and was standing just outside the damage radius holding her drink above her head to keep it safe from the dog debris being flung about. She was joined in her laughter by Mark and Jen, as Mel and Barry pulled the two dogs towards the hose. Jake stood with his arms outspread with sand and slobber covering every exposed inch. He looked at Nikki and Jen then scooped them up, one over each shoulder and took off towards the waves with both women screaming like little girls.

Mark looked over at Barry, who was staring in awe at how the man could run across soft sand with two women over his shoulders and still make it look easy. Barry finally looked over at Mark and made the Bull horns sign on his forehead. Mark let out a loud guffaw and returned the gesture. The gesture came from Mark's father who had always used the saying 'Mess with the Bull, You get the horns!' Mark fully believed in this, and had taken to making the sign whenever one of the kids had come to him complaining about some injustice inflicted upon them by one of their siblings. Knowing full well that they tortured and annoyed each other, Mark would send them on their way with the gesture.

Mel poked Barry in the side and handed him Thor's leash. They began to lead the dogs back over to the Norris cottage.

"Make sure you dry them both off!" Mark yelled after them. "Especially Thor! Otherwise the whole place is gonna smell like wet dog!"

"Okay, Dad."

"Yes sir!" They shouted back over their shoulders.

Mark turned back to watch Jake and the girls splashing in the surf, and was considering joining them when his cell phone chirped. He went over and looked at the screen. Seeing that it was the operations center number, he slid his finger across the screen to answer it.

"Norris"

"Hello Gunner, this is Staff Sergeant Lyle, sir. I have the duty and just received word from a Scott Preston from Benji Minnesota?" The staff sergeant stumbled over the city name.

"He would like you to get in touch with him sir, regarding a Barry Metzler. He said it was a family issue and said you would know where to find the kid."

"He's blow drying my dog as we speak, Staff Sergeant. Thanks for the call, I'll get a hold of Lieutenant Preston right away."

"You got it, sir. Have a nice day."

"Ooh rah."

CHAPTER 20

Bemidji, MN

Dan Preston banked the Cessna Skymaster around to the right so his brother could see the flaming structure three thousand feet below them. There was still frantic activity on the ground, as the pack of feral humans that had attacked the survivor refuge chased down the last of the people attempting to flee the slaughter. The old motel had served as a gathering point for survivors of the collapse. Located about forty miles south of the city of Bemidji, the motel lacked the defensibility that some of the other refuges could provide. Still, several families had been able to secure the structure and make it into a reasonably safe habitat for themselves. It was safe until it had come under attack by a huge pack of ferals.

As the collapse continued, Darwinism began to weed out the weak and the slow at first. Mankind had spent millennia using opposable thumbs and a larger brain to develop tool use and construct a society around himself. When that was stripped away, the naked hairless monkey that was man, became ill suited to stay at the top of the food chain for long. But mankind is anything if not resilient and adaptable. The ferals soon adopted tool use again, and even though they were essentially suffering from a constant psychotic breakdown, they began to cooperate with each other as their survival instincts overcame their desire to kill everything around them.

These new 'Super Packs' were forming with the most intelligent and cunning Alphas directing them. These packs were arming themselves with pry bars and shovels. They began to set traps and became very effective ambush predators. They also began to attack the less fortified hideouts that people had gathered in for protection. They would overwhelm small farmsteads and devour everyone there.

The motel that was burning below them had been a redoubt for people in the area who couldn't fortify their own homes or had lost them to various circumstances. The National Guard command post that had been set up in Bemidji had been in radio contact with the folks below and they had sent out a plea for help when they had come under attack. Dan and Scott had already been airborne in the Park service's Cessna and had immediately headed down while a relief column was organized and dispatched. It was evident now that the column would get there too late to have any real chance of preventing a major loss of life, but they would come and hopefully find survivors hiding out who had escaped the violence.

Dan circled lower as Scott took pictures with a digital SLR camera with a telephoto lens. Several of the attackers looked up from the victims they were consuming to snarl at the plane. Scott got as many facial shots as he could, they had begun to do this back in Bemidji, and when warnings had been posted about the ferals, a surprising amount of survivors had identified neighbors, relatives, and friends from the photos. This resulted in small parties going out to recapture their relatives so that they could be brought back and begin the detox protocol that had been set up at the hospital. The ward currently had seventeen occupants restrained and getting treatment.

The relief column was four miles away when Dan turned to head back to Bemidji due to fuel constraints. Scott had kept up a running commentary to the column so they knew what to expect when they got there. They buzzed the chain of vehicles as they travelled north back to the airfield, getting a wave from a couple of the guardsmen who were riding in the gunners copulas. With a final rocking of the wings, Dan climbed back up to his cruising altitude of seven thousand feet and flew straight back to the field.

Once they had landed the plane and tied it down they walked over to the operations center for the northern half of the state. The Hotel was still being used as a shelter, but after battling to recover the airfield twice from attempts by the terrorists to use it for further spreading the toxin around the country, they had moved the command post to the airfield. The fact that the BCA (Bureau of Criminal Apprehension) building was directly adjacent to the terminal was an added plus.

After checking in, they made their way to the BCA building where they both had offices. As soon as Scott walked in, Kate Barry, rushed up to him and handed him a standard message slip used around the office. He looked at it, then did a double take and read it again.

"What's up?" Dan asked trying to read over his brother's shoulder.

Scott frowned at him in annoyance, shrugging him off until he had read it through.

"It's about Barry, His half-brother managed to send us an inquiry about him from Texas." Kate volunteered as Scott finally handed Dan the slip to read.

"Holeee shit!" Dan Exclaimed. "Man I thought we had recovered and buried all of his family except his father."

"His half-brother is a lot older and was living somewhere down south, Minneapolis I think. But now he's in Amarillo for some reason, but he was able to post this to the missing family web-site. I'll get in touch with Mark right away and see if we can get them re-united." Scott went over to his desk and picked up the phone. "I bet by now Barry has cleaned up half the state of California..."

Barry had just finished cleaning up his half of the room he was again sharing with Jim over in the cottage. After washing the sand off the dogs, he went inside to shower. Thor's ability to generate copious amounts of hair was amazing. They had gone through several towels and then used a blow dryer for five minutes to get the dog into a state where the public would be safe from the menace of dog water being flung on them. He threw on some shorts and walked out to the living room.

"Hey Barry." Mel said over her shoulder when she noticed him.

"Yeah? What's up?" He said hopping up onto a stool next to her at the breakfast bar. It was her usual spot when acting as the "Communication Coordinator" for the house. She had a tablet laid out in front of her and the cordless phone set right beside it.

"Dad said he just got a call from base ops about you. He wants us to stay here. He'll be right over."

"Huh? Well should we call back to base ops? I think if it's about me I can answer their questions."

"Well here he comes." Mel gestured at Mark who had just closed the short patio gate behind him. They waited as he knocked some sand off with a towel before coming through the sliding glass door.

"Hey bud." Mark said gesturing towards the phone. "The comm center just called and said Scott Preston had called looking for you. I figured it would be a little quieter over here to call back." Mark gestured at some of the horseplay going on in front of Jake's cottage.

"Yes sir."

They gathered around as Jake called the communications center and was eventually patched through to the BCA building next to the Bemidji airport. After a few more minutes, Mark was speaking with Scott. A few seconds later he said "Well I'll let you tell him, he's right here." Mark held the phone out towards Barry.

"Hello?"

"Hey Barry! How have you been?" Scott asked.

"I've been well sir."

"Barry, I've got some news about your older brother and father. It seems that your brother had come up here from Minneapolis right at the start of the outbreak. He went to your house but, after finding your mother and sisters dead, he left to go back and look for his girlfriend. I guess just recently he posted his information on a lost family blog, and was contacted by a man who says he is caring for your father." Barry sat on the barstool with a stunned look on his face as Scott continued. "Your brother went to Oklahoma city to try and connect with them. I've sent the link to Marks e-mail. You can start trying to re-establish contact with your family there."

Barry just sat there stunned.

"Hello?"

"Oh uh, yes sir." Barry shook himself out of his reverie. "Thank you so much Mr. Preston, I really appreciate this!"

"I'm just passing it along. It was someone back at the hotel looking out for you that brought it to my attention." Scott chuckled. "They all miss you around here and not a day goes by that I don't hear someone mention your name son."

Barry flushed at the praise.

"Yeah I miss you folks too. But I'll be headed that way as soon as I can." Barry noticed the startled look on Mel's face. "I need to get some stuff squared away here and I'll be in touch sir."

"They're in Texas I believe, Barry. Look at the blog and get in touch with them before heading out."

"Yes sir, thank you sir!" Barry's excitement was beginning to show.

"Now you're starting to talk like a Marine!" Scott was still chuckling. "Be safe getting back out here."

"Yes sir, goodbye." Barry hung up the phone and looked at Mark who was already calling up his e-mail. He turned and looked at Mel, who had an unreadable expression on her face.

"They found my brother and dad..." He was cut off by Mel grabbing him and squeezing him. He hugged her back before holding her at arm's length and staring into her eyes. Tears were starting to roll down both their cheeks, as they smiled at each other.

"Oh Barry, I'm so happy for you..." Mel started but was cut off by her father.

"Here it is." He said turning the tablet towards Barry.

Mark had opened the e-mail and then opened the embedded link. A few taps later and they were looking at a message string, posted by Barry's older brother Henry.

Metzler Family and Friends, Bemidji Minn.

To anyone reading this, this is Henry Metzler. I can confirm the death of my step-mother; Cassy-Louise Metzler, and my sisters; Camille and Kristin Metzler. I was at my house the morning of the outbreak of violence. I was not able to locate my father Dale or my younger brother Barry. If anyone has seen them please post their information or location here. Thanks Hank.

Hank, your brother Barry survived and was in Bemidji at the refugee center as of a few months ago. My daughter saw him there and he was well. No word on your father sorry. Dave Goodell

Dave, Thanks! I will try to contact someone there. Hank

Contacted Bemidji, someone said he went to California? With the Marines? If anyone knows anything about this please contact me. I left a message there for him.

Mr. Metzler, My name is Colton Fuller. I have taken in a man who was poisoned by the toxin. He has been undergoing the detoxification program here in Amarillo. He has stated his name is Dale Metzler from Bemidji. If this is a relative of yours, you can contact him through the hospital.

I have contacted the hospital in Amarillo and am on my way there. If anyone knows where Barry is please direct him to this site.

Barry clicked on the script box and began typing.

Hank! I just found out about this site. I see you went to get Dad last week. I am on my way to Amarillo now. I will update you on an ETA! I am coming! -Barry

Barry turned from the computer and looked at Mark.

"I need to go find my dad and my brother sir. Could I maybe ride shotgun on a convoy heading east or something?" Barry was already making plans, and going over his equipment lists in his head.

"Let me check with Colonel Neal and base ops. Let's see if we can get you a flight over there. It would be a little quicker than walking don't you think?" Mark was looking at him with a raised eyebrow.

"Yes sir!" Barry's excitement was showing. "That would be awesome!"

CHAPTER 21

Colonel Neal was just walking out of General Moore's office when he saw Barry walking down the hall towards him followed by Mark. Neal had to do a double take because the slender young man looked like a Marine going into battle. He had a slung M4, and his ever present .45 on his hip. He was wearing a tactical vest and had a three day pack with water bladder on his back. He moved with the ease of someone whose gear was an extension of their body. Other than the slight swish of fabric nothing rattled or made any noise.

"Hey Barry, how are you?"

"I'm fine sir. I was coming over here to see if there was any way I could catch a ride east towards Texas. My brother and dad are there." The excitement oozed from Barry's pores. "My dad is being treated in a hospital in Amarillo, and my brother is on his way there."

"Oh wow! Okay that's great news! I know you thought they were lost. If you can give me five minutes to take care of something, I'll walk you over to flight ops and see what we can come up with." Neal waved the folder in his hand at them before leading them back down the corridor to his office.

Mark and Barry waited in the hallway until Neal came back out and they all went outside to get into a Hummer for the short trip to the airfield. Once there Neal led them into the Air Ops planning office. Neal asked to see the major in charge and they were escorted into an office.

"How can I help you today, Colonel?" Major Burns was the air operations boss for the airfield.

"Major, this is Barry Metzler. He's from Minnesota. We've just received word that his father and brother survived the outbreak and are in Amarillo, Texas. He just graduated from the new training course, and he is ready to head back home."

Neal put his hand on Barry's shoulder edging him forward. "Is there a way we can get him on whatever transport is heading east so he can be reunited with his family?"

"Pleased to meet you," Burns said—shaking the young man's hand. He noticed the strength of the handshake and his eyebrow went up. "I'm sure we can find something heading east. I'll give him over to one of the air ops planners and they can cobble together an itinerary for you. When will you be ready to leave?"

"Right now sir." Barry shrugged and lifted his gear. "I can leave anytime."

"Well Okay then. Let's get you over to planning." They followed the major down a corridor to another office where they were handed off to a young Marine who went through the flight manifests.

"Well we have a flight on a C-130 out to 29 Palms in two hours. Then you'll have to stay overnight and we can get him on another flight to Dallas. I'll see if we can get him a bird back over to Amarillo from there." He flipped through a folder, looking at a few more pages. "Yeah that will probably get you guys there the fastest."

"It will be just me travelling." Barry said.

"Only one of you?" The Marine looked slightly startled when he realized it would just be Barry travelling.

"Yup, can you make something happen quicker?" Mark asked looking at the flight roster. He pointed at a line and lifted an eyebrow. "Barry has this letter from General Moore here, asking that he be rendered any and all assistance possible…"

The young Marine looked up and grinned.

"Well in that case…"

CHAPTER 22

Barry staggered into the pilot locker room at 29 Palms. His gear plus the G-suit he was wearing only contributed slightly to the instability in his step. The majority of his imbalance came from the thirty minute flight he had just completed from San Diego to 29 Palms. The flight was made in a two seat F-18 fighter, which had been piloted by Satan himself.

After receiving a safety briefing and getting fitted for a G-suit (Pilots tended to be on the smaller side and it was no trouble finding one that fit), he was given a crash course in parachute operation, then stuffed into the back seat of the fighter. As soon as the plane taxied out to the runway, the fun stopped. Some invisible giant shoved Barry back into his seat and the next thing he knew he was looking straight up at the clear blue sky. Twenty seconds of trying to breathe later and he found himself floating as the pilot pushed the plane over through negative G's to level off. He had to swallow hard to keep his guts from floating out of his mouth.

"Look down there! You can still see San Diego is trashed" And with that the plane flipped on its back and Barry was trying to keep his guts in his body again. They flew upside down for several minutes before the pilot righted the aircraft. "You ready to turn and burn?"

That was the beginning of his damnation. The other plane in the two plane section moved off to their left by about a mile and flew straight and level. Barry's plane however, apparently was incapable of doing the same thing as it went through a series of high G maneuvers that left Barry grunting into his face mask. Only the lack of contents kept him from emptying his stomach all over the cockpit. He did keep the issued barf bag close though, just in case. With a final loop, the plane leveled out and made its approach to 'The Stumps' as Twenty Nine Palms is not so affectionately known by the troops stationed there. The first leg was done.

After turning in his gear, Barry was met by a Marine who took him to the small hotel on the base. He was issued a room and given directions to the chow hall. Barry needed a few minutes before he was going to attempt to eat anything so he decided on a quick dip in the pool. An hour later he realized he was getting burned, so he toweled off and went in search of food.

He was used to Marine Corps chow halls by this time, and the food was hot and filling even if it wasn't five-star cuisine. He wolfed down two trays worth and made his way over to the PX.

Colonel Neal had made sure he had plenty of money on him and a letter for places that weren't back on currency yet. He found a few items for his pack and killed a few more hours watching a movie at the base theater. He finally went back to his room and after 'Field stripping' his new purchases and fitting them into his pack, crashed out.

The following day's flight was far less harrowing, C-130s being somewhat less acrobatic than F-18s. He was packed and waiting outside the hotel when the car came to get him. He was seated at the front of the cargo area with the few other passengers who were crammed in front of the plane's cargo. Barry spent the flight looking at pictures of him and Mel on his tablet. Although she had been happy for him, she had definitely not liked him going off on his own. She had gone so far as to suggest that her father and Jake escort him the whole way. Jake had laughed it off and told her they would just slow him down.

After reaching Dallas, Barry had to wait another day to catch a ride in a helicopter going back towards Amarillo. Finally after three days of travel, Barry found himself standing in the Airport terminal in Amarillo. The airport was on the east side of town and the hospital was less than two miles away. The city had made it through the attacks relatively unharmed, being too small of a population center for the water supply to be attacked directly. Oklahoma City to the east however had been hit pretty hard and feral people and animals had made their way west.

Barry did his 'Battle Rattle' check and adjusted the carbine on its sling. He set off and made it to the hospital without incident. He noticed crews of workers welding and installing bars on the ground floor windows of some of the buildings at the edge of the medical center. The Main hospital had obviously had them installed a while ago. It was common practice to fortify buildings as the populace began to reclaim structures.

Barry was sent to three different wards looking for his father before he was told that he was no longer there. A clerk finally told him that his father had made pretty good progress and that Hank had checked him out. The last anyone had heard was that they were in a convoy that was heading to Oklahoma City and then they were headed north. It had left almost a week before.

Barry used the hospitals Wi-Fi to send an e-mail to Mark and to check on the web site to see if Hank had responded to his post. He hadn't, so Barry decided to head towards Oklahoma. He hiked back out to the airport and was told that there was nothing headed to Oklahoma City in the near future. His best bet was to get on with a convoy heading that way. He was given warning that the highways were relatively safe from Ferals, but bands of robbers were notorious for robbing solo travelers. Since most of the landscape was arid plains between the two cities Barry decided to follow the advice. The going would be pretty slow if he had to low crawl to Oklahoma City.

He checked in with the Air Force captain that was in charge of the Military operations at the airfield. The captain had been briefed by the helicopter pilot when they had arrived, but he didn't know he was going to have to take care of a kid. Barry overheard him calling back to Pendleton to ask what was going on. When the captain used the word 'babysit', Barry got a little pissed. He gathered his gear and made his way up onto the roof. After checking the perimeter and access points, he was able to string his hammock between some AC units and set out some warning devices. He crawled into his 'Ranger Roll' and was asleep in seconds.

CHAPTER 23

Barry's Journal

Sept. 9 — They told us to keep a journal out in the field, so here it goes. I finally got onto a convoy as part of the security team. Not sure if I like having to follow all their rules. The team leader, Mitch is an okay guy, so things aren't too bad. We left out of Amarillo this morning. We are delivering supplies to towns along the way. The briefing before we left said that we should be more concerned about 'brigands' (Who uses that word now a days?), until just outside OKC (Oklahoma City), where the ferals are pretty bad from what I hear. I'm kind of concerned that my Dad and Hank are going into such a dense population of ferals. The bigger cities have had it really rough.

We spent the day moving really slow on the I-40 heading east. We didn't have any problems until we were leaving McLean, our first stop. Just to the east of the city we came upon a road block made up of some junk and old cars piled up on the highway. The people who put it there took off when they saw the size of our convoy. We had to dismount and set up a perimeter while the trucks pulled the wreckage out of the way. I was on the south side of the highway when we started taking fire from the north. All we had were little commercial handheld radios and some of the guys were relatively untrained. The radios filled up with chatter pretty quick, but some of the guys with military experience got them settled down after a minute or two. They returned fire and the brigands fled. We were back on the road after ten minutes.

We saw one of the trucks that fled the road block in Shamrock (the next city east) and reported the vehicle to the local police. They were familiar with the guys and would make an arrest now that they had been identified.

We're in a small town called Beckham for the night. Tomorrow we are going to bypass Elk City and push on to OKC.

Sept. 10 — We had a rough day today. The abandoned vehicles on the highway kept us at a really slow pace. This allowed the ferals to get close and pelt us with rocks. The landscape is arid and there aren't many trees unless we are near a creek bed. But they manage to hide in among the cars and other stuff on the road.

I wound up shooting more than a dozen of them, which finally earned me a little respect from the others. The guys on the security team are nowhere near as competent as the Marines or National Guard. I wound up having to tell some of the older guys what to do. If we hadn't been getting attacked I don't think they would have listened to me.

Took us forever to get here and come to find out Dad and Hank have already headed up north towards home. I'm going to have to catch them on the road along the way, or else I guess I'll see them there. At least the lady at the hospital knew they were going to Wichita. I was able to use the internet and send a progress report to Mark and a message to Mel. Been thinking about her a lot during my downtime.

I'm going to see if I can get on with a convoy headed north tomorrow.

CHAPTER 24

The figure moved quietly along the side of the building at the edge of the industrial park. The sun had dropped behind the horizon a few minutes before and the sky was still a reddish pink panorama with a few small wisps of clouds for texture. The reddish hue turned the buildings a pale pink with its reflection, the muted tan and brown of Barry's clothing and gear seemed to absorb the color and blend right in.

After failing to get on board a convoy in a timely manner, Barry had set out on his own to head north to Wichita. He had been told of a group that left regularly out of Edmond which was to the north of OKC. He had been able to top off his supplies and started to make his way north. He had run into a few ferals since the city was still rife with them. The packs were not that large in the city, since they tended to hunt out the urban areas quickly, but he had run into one pack that caused him to hole up in an abandoned warehouse.

After thinning out the pack, he waited for them to drag their dead away for consumption, then slipped away. A few hours later he found himself looking across a parking lot at the last of the buildings before he had to strike out across country. He took a knee and watched the open space for a while. He wasn't fond of open spaces, they allowed bad things to see you from a distance. He couldn't wait all day though, so with a final sweep of his eyes to his rear he set off.

He moved at a ground eating lope that covered the distance to the brush line quickly. His eyes never stopped scanning his surroundings until he was in some brush off of the highway. He spun around and took a knee. He watched his back trail for a minute and seeing no movement, slithered out of sight.

He had considered heading to Tinker Air Force Base to the southeast, but if he couldn't get transportation there, he would lose two days of travel. So now he was paralleling the I-35 north to get to the east side of Edmond. The going was relatively easy at first, but he was soon coming into the suburbs near Edmond, and the area was packed with mid-sized residential communities. These areas had produced the largest concentrations of affected people and domestic animals. This demographic also suffered the highest casualty rates during the initial outbreaks of violence.

As he ventured further north, he wound up having to hide more often to avoid contact. The ferals he saw were for the most part loners and he avoided or dispatched them easily. When he finally ran into a pack it was a small one and he saw it coming from a distance. He avoided it by hiding in some brush on the east side of the highway. He didn't have any back-up or a safe place to hole up, so he slogged on, making very poor time. He made it into Edmond having expended twenty-two rounds of his 5.56 ammunition for the carbine.

The staging area for convoys heading north was a facility on the southeast corner of the intersection of the I-35 and the 66. Barry crossed a small creek and after pushing through a last little bit of brush was looking up at a huge white cross. There was a reinforced chain link fence around the entire facility with lights mounted on tall poles. Barry could see an armed patrol moving in his direction but on the other side of the fence. He was also very aware of the machine gun pointed in his direction from the gun pit next to the vehicle gate.

Lowering his rifle until it dangled by its sling, he raised his now empty hands and stepped clear of the brush. One of the security guards standing on the inside of the fence waved him forward. He kept his hands at shoulder level and approached the gate. After a mild interrogation, he was admitted to the compound and taken to see the officer in charge of the Army detachment that had a presence there. A quick radio call verified his status, but there weren't any convoys leaving for at least another four days. He decided to spend the night and he would head out on his own in the morning. He did get a hot meal, a warm bed, and his ammo replaced, plus a little extra, so he went to bed happy.

CHAPTER 25

The North West School varsity football team had decided to do their summer practice the day after the terror attacks on the United States. Although the population was outraged at the events of the previous day, and a small plane had even crashed into a railroad bridge bringing the events closer to home. The community had rebounded and was determined to go on with the American way of life. And football was a big part of life in Wichita.

The plane had passed over the northwest edge of the city, dropping brown packets into the water before heading off to kamikaze into a bridge. The toxin began to spread through the city's water supply, leaching outward from the reservoir.

The August sun was brutal and the coach had the team drinking lots of water during the three hour practice. The young athletes dehydrated bodies began absorbing the toxin at an accelerated rate. By the end of practice they were all starting to show flushed skin and were running slight fevers. This went mostly unnoticed as this was normal after such a strenuous workout. Most of the team hit the showers at the school and then made their way to a popular burger joint to eat, while others slipped off to acquire some beer. There was going to be a gathering in a cornfield tonight.

Most of the team members wore their jerseys to show school pride while others wore Red, White, and Blue in an extra burst of patriotism. The pick-ups were circled around a small bonfire and the music was blasting from the back of one of the trucks. The party came to a screeching halt, literally, when a scream cut through the music. Everyone looked over at Laney Smith as she staggered out of the cab of her boyfriend's truck with her hand covering a bite wound on her neck. She was not doing a very good job of slowing the blood flow, as it was pumping between her fingers as she stumbled into the center of the fire circle and collapsed.

Brad Rogers, her boyfriend, stepped into the circle after her and looked around at the other kids. Most were staring in shock at the feebly writhing girl on the ground, but some were just staring with blank looks on their faces. This included Darby Connor who was a manager for the team and was showing skin flushed bright red from her jaw down across her chest, and all along the inner side of her arms.

Brad tilted his head back and screamed into the night. Most of the others gathered around followed suit and answered. Darby leapt on Laney's back and, after pulling her head back by the hair, darted her head forward to rip a bite out of her neck. While some of the students screamed and tried to run away, the affected ones who were all wearing their jerseys fell on them.

The North West High School football team formed the first hunting pack in the Wichita area. The pack quickly expanded to over fifty members and began hunting the northern edge of the city. They would terrorize the population for the four months, killing hundreds of people.

The reign of terror came to an end when Sheriff Jesse Lansdowne was able to trap a majority of them in an industrial building. By funneling the trapped teenagers out through a single door, he was able to secure them and bring them in for detox treatment. They had been restrained and undergoing treatment for four months with varying results when it all came apart.

Dale Metzler had been found in a ditch after being caught and beaten by a group of men who then left him for dead. The beating had broken several bones and ruptured internal organs. This coupled with the condition his body had been in from the trials it had been put through since he fled his home, left him a physical wreck.

Dale had slowly worked his way south from Bemidji after succumbing to the toxin, successfully hunting along the way. He had avoided most of the populated areas, and his body did a good job of ejecting the toxin as he consumed more and more untainted water. He did however get exposed to the toxin on several more occasions, causing severe psychotic breaks. A year later found him hunting along a creek in north Texas.

He was spotted by a group of Good old boys who had been fishing downstream from him. They had used their Pickup to run him down, and once he was caught, they spent twenty minutes beating him until they thought he was dead. They left him lying there and drove off. Although close to death, Dale had managed to crawl a few yards before losing consciousness. He was found there by a kindly old man who wrapped him in a blanket and took him to the medical center in Amarillo.

He had been undergoing treatment there for three months when Hank walked onto the floor and went to his bed. He was still under bite protocol so there was a mask over his face, and his forearms were encompassed by leather wrist restraints that prevented his hands from coming together. Hank stopped and looked down on the man who had raised him. A lump formed in his throat as he bent over and hugged his father. He held him as sobs shuddered through them both. After spending a bit of time just being with his father, the doctor caught Hank's eye from the doorway and gestured for him to come out into the hall.

"Mr. Metzler, they told me you were asking about your father's treatment. What can I do for you?"

"I just wanted to know his general condition and if he can travel. And if so is there anything I need in the way of special instructions."

"Well we've treated him for the physical injuries to the extent we can. Those will just require time now. The toxin however is another story. He still has occasional fugue states and becomes violent with the staff. This is usually when he first wakes up, he struggles for a bit with his restraints but calms down eventually." The nameplate on the doctor's smock was Halstrom, and he absently fingered it as he spoke. "He has been taking in enough water to flush the toxin at a pretty good rate, and his body fat percentile is very low, so there isn't much being stored there. His leg and arm are out of the casts as you can see. He just needs to continue the detox and be monitored."

"Thank you sir, and when can he travel?"

"Oh yes, sorry." Halstrom peered back in at Dale. "There really isn't anything preventing him from travelling, but he is still feral. His body is still secreting the toxin into his saliva, so he does still pose a threat to those around him, especially when he first wakes up. That is when he is still suffering from the psychotic breaks and the serum content in his saliva is the most concentrated. He would need some pretty strict security protocols, and I wouldn't suggest travelling alone with him. We won't stop you though, we need the beds."

"When I talk to him, he seems okay. He twitches a lot." Hank sighed and dropped his head. "He says the word 'Home' a lot too."

"His periods of lucidity will increase, and he should gain back most of his cognitive functions over the next few weeks." Halstrom gripped Hank by the upper arm. "Be thankful he survived, there's a lot of folks who lost loved ones. Some of them even killed their own family members before we knew that people could recover. And even so, we don't know if they will recover fully."

"Oh we lost family all right. I found my step-mother and two younger half-sisters, my brother is still missing I think he's okay. So if I use your bite protocol and make sure he's restrained, I can take him home?"

"I'll get the paperwork started…"

CHAPTER 26

Hank pulled his blue Durango into the parking lot of the Wichita Medical Center. They were getting in later than expected, because they'd had to wait almost two hours to get fuel. The government was releasing some of the petroleum reserves, and some fuel was starting to make its way into the inner states but they were still on severe rationing.

It had been a week since Dale had been discharged and they had only made it this far. It was unsafe to travel in a lone vehicle so they had to wait and join up with convoys. The logistics were slowing them down more than anything else. Fuel being the precious commodity that it was.

Hank walked around the front of the SUV and helped his father out of the car. It was time for a general check-up. They had been successful so far in the move as far as Dale's condition went. They had agreed that he would sleep in a bite mask and restrained, but he was coherent during most of his waking hours. He became agitated if his senses became overloaded, they had kept to themselves while traveling, having to haul extra cargo in the convoys to avoid having additional passengers in the Durango.

They were going through the check-in process when a disturbance broke out in the treatment area adjacent to the lobby. Hank had just handed the man behind the counter his dad's medical file when they heard screaming coming from down a hallway. The man behind the counter spun around and started through the door when he was slammed back through it by the solidly built teenager who was pummeling his face and head. They both slammed into the counter, sending paperwork flying, before crashing to the floor.

Hank leaned over the counter to see what was happening. The teenager, who was obviously feral, had his teeth embedded in the man's face. The teen was in a hospital gown which was no longer secured in the back and the blood that had already soaked into it was weighing it down, causing it to fall forward on top of the man who was now feebly struggling against his attacker. There were still noises of a fight coming from down the hall.

Hank pawed at the pistol on his hip and tried to get a shot at the feral. It only took him a second since they weren't thrashing around and he was able to adjust his aim to get a better angle. He fired one round from his Springfield XD. The 9mm bullet plowing into the ferals spine and punching into its lung before shattering a rib under his nipple. The body collapsed as Hank turned towards the hallway where a vicious fight was visible through the small window in the door.

He turned and began hustling his father towards the front door. They stumbled down the front steps and Hank shoved his father into the Durango. He ran around the front of the car in time to have it between him and the front door as several more teenagers spilled out into the lot. One saw them and charged straight at the Dodge as Hank started it up and dropped it into gear. The young girl slammed into the side of the SUV and slapped her palms on the passenger window, snarling at Dale. He met her gaze and snarled right back at her. The response startled her and she recoiled as the blue SUV shot out of the parking lot.

Brad Rogers, Darby Connor, and Kevin Lusk had all been captured at the warehouse by the Sheriff. They had been caged like dogs and driven to the medical center to begin the detoxification protocol. Thirteen of their classmates had been brought in with them and kept in the same wing. They were treated in the high security area until they started to show signs of recovery. Unfortunately as Brad and Darby became more lucid, the only thing that improved was their ability to think and reason, the psychopathy that they were under was still affecting their thoughts, thoughts that would make Hannibal Lecter blush.

Kevin had been trying for a week to get loose when his chance finally came. One of the orderlies failed to put his wrist restraints on properly, and he managed to work his hand free. Waiting until there were no staff in the room he quickly freed himself and the others. This included all of the people undergoing treatment. Everything was going well, when one of the

'Non-pack' people who was almost clean of the toxin began to scream. It was a stupid and futile move on her part as it only got her killed. Darby, who was four months pregnant from rutting with almost every male in the pack, leapt to the side of the bed and clamped a hand onto the woman's neck. She lifted up on the bite mask to expose the throat. Opening her mouth so wide she looked like a snake dislocating its jaws, she darted her head forward and bit down on the throat. Working her jaws back and forth to saw through the cartilage, she crushed her victim's windpipe. With an explosive sigh that threw blood all over Darby's hospital gown, her body went limp.

The screaming did not go unnoticed, and an orderly shoved his way through the door. He was brought up short by the sight of half the ward out of their beds. Kevin was waiting behind the door and shoved it closed as soon as the orderly was clear of its arc. He then used a piece of a tray stand that he had broken up to stab down into the orderly's back. The jagged metal ripped through his shirt and skin, finally stopping as it slammed against a rib. The orderly arched his back in a natural reaction to get away from the pain that exploded across his back, twisting and reaching around to the site of the wound. He screamed at the pain and tried to rush at his attacker.

As soon as he turned around, Brad jumped on his back and rode him to the ground, biting into his upper neck. His teeth skid against the poor man's skull as he chewed at the flesh. As the blood soaked orderly was going down, Kevin stabbed out again with the jagged piece of metal in his hand, this time sending it ripping through the abdomen and into the small intestine. Brad drove the man's head into the floor and the body went limp. He stood up and looked behind him at the room full of newly freed hunters. Several began moving towards the two bodies to feed, but a commotion in the hallway focused their attention on the door.

Brad yanked the door open and rushed out into the hall followed closely by the rest of the pack. He grabbed the closest person he could, a nurse who had been rushing to help, and began pummeling her to the floor. Kevin turned right and rushed to the end of the hallway, and burst into the emergency room lobby. As the rest of the pack flooded the hall and continued to attack both patients and staff, they heard a gunshot from the lobby. Darby immediately stood up from the nurse she and Brad had killed, and went running towards the noise. She was followed by several others, and they burst into the lobby in time to see Hank hustling his father out through the door. Glancing down at Kevin's still form, she let out a scream and charged after the retreating figures.

Brad and several other pack members heard a sound further in the hospital and wound up chasing several survivors through the corridors until they were cornered in a restricted treatment area. The area was used to treat burn victims and was full of oxygen tents and other specialty equipment. Three of the people who had been run to ground were armed, when Brad burst through the door they all fired. Brad was struck by three bullets which stopped him in his tracks. He was still standing there as the flash fire from the oxygen soaked textiles in the room ignited into flames that sucked the air out of the room and sent an orange ball of fire rolling along the ceiling of the hallway outside. The fire quickly spread throughout the wing, killing another member of the pack and two staff that were hiding in a closet.

As both staff and ferals spilled out of the building chaos ensued. Most people were armed these days, but the chaos prevented anyone from getting a firm grasp on the situation. As the survivors got organized, they began to engage the ferals who continued attacking people. The ferals that ran away, were not engaged, since the shooters couldn't tell if they were feral or a patient trying to get away. Darby and three others who had followed her outside when she chased Hank and Dale to their car, managed to slip away in the chaos.

The call went out for the fire department, but a third of the facility was a total loss by the time they got there. The staff began moving patients and equipment to a nearby warehouse to continue service. The bodies were identified to the best of the police's somewhat limited ability. There were several that were burned beyond any hope of recognition.

CHAPTER 27

Barry's Journal

Sept. 13, 07:30 — Made it onto a crew today going all the way to Wichita. I should be able to make it to there by 20:00. We leave in twenty minutes so I am updating this and sending out e-mails to Mel and her dad. Still nothing on the website from Hank or my dad. I hope they are doing all right. I hope to know in a few hours!

The convoy rolled into McConnell Air Force base after a relatively quiet trip. After dismounting and checking in, Barry was offered a ride into town which he gladly accepted from one of the families that he had escorted. They were stopped at the entrance to the medical center by a volunteer militiaman who informed them of the incident at the hospital which had occurred the day before. Barry, with the help of his letter, was allowed to approach the scene on foot. After talking to one of the guards at the entrance to the building he was finally escorted to a harried man who was sitting in a pickup with one leg on the ground going through some notes. He looked up as Barry approached and got a nod from the guard.

"What can I do for you young man?" Sheriff Lansdowne asked taking in the easy manner in which the young man carried himself and his gear. "You look ready to go into battle."

"I'm always ready for battle sir." Barry said looking him in the eye with an intense gaze that Lansdowne found just a little unsettling. "I am looking for my brother and father. They were supposed to have arrived or come through here in the last few days. My brother's name is Hank Metzler, my father's is Dale Metzler and my name is Barry. The Guard CP in OKC said that this was their next destination. Can I ask what happened here sir?"

The sheriff finally broke eye contact and set the file he was going through on the dash. He stepped out of the car and stretched, the audible cracking and popping causing Barry to wince in sympathy. Jesse grunted at this and gestured for Barry to follow him towards what used to be the emergency room entrance.

"We had a pack made up of one of the High School football teams. We managed to trap them in a warehouse, and capture them. They were undergoing treatment here when somehow they got loose." Jesse gestured at the wreckage in the lobby as they walked through the door. "What was your father in here for?"

There was a pregnant pause before Barry answered.

"My father was poisoned and went feral sir, my brother was taking him home after receiving treatment in Amarillo."

Jesse turned and looked at Barry, a sympathetic look on his face.

"Well if he was ever exposed to the toxin, then he would have been treated in this ward. I'm sorry but there were pretty severe casualties in here. We took photos of the people we buried, but there was a fire and we do have a couple of unidentified bodies that were burned beyond all recognition." They began walking towards the hallway leading further back into the hospital. Barry, who kept his head on a swivel always, glanced behind the counter as they walked around it. His eye picked up a blood smeared patient file lying on the ground at his feet.

The picture staring up at him from the ground was that of his father's gaunt face.

CHAPTER 28

Hank was startled by his father's yell as they pulled away from the chaos. He hesitated to put his seatbelt on in case he had to un-ass the vehicle. Dale continued to scream at the young female as they bounced out on to the street nearly colliding with another car. *Great, six cars left in this town and I nearly have an accident with this one!*

Hank split his attention between the road and his father. Dale had turned back around in his seat and was facing forward again. He was breathing heavy and staring out the front windshield.

"You okay, Dad?" Hank was hesitant to ask, he didn't want his dad to come unglued on him.

Dale slowly turned to face his son, and fixed him with a look that had reminded Hank of when he got in trouble as a kid. "I'm fine. Did you see the look on that bitch's face when I screamed back at her?"

Hank almost wrecked the Durango a second time as he just stared at his father. Then they both burst out laughing. The laughter was the catharsis needed to finally breakdown the last barrier of awkwardness between them. They both opened up about what had happened with Dale telling his son about his incomplete memories of what had led him to be found in a ditch. Hank told his father about the days immediately following the attacks and how he had found the family at the house.

"Was it me?" Dale finally asked, his voice hitching in his throat.

"No pop. I'm positive it was Cassy and Cammie. I never found Barry, and then I heard he had gone to California with some Marines. I've been leaving messages on a 'Find your Family' website, but I haven't heard from him. I haven't checked it in a while though."

"So he survived though?"

"That was the last word I got from the survivor compound back home."

"Well we should check the website." Dale's voice sounded hopeful after hearing some good news.

They had already left town headed north and did not want to backtrack to get access to the internet. They had enough gas to make it to Topeka, so they decided to push on through. The drive to the northeast would have taken them a third of the time two years before, but now even though the wrecks had been for the most part cleared, there were still obstructions and the roads were in poor shape after almost two years of no maintenance. The 145 mile journey would put them in Topeka after 2:00 AM.

CHAPTER 29

Barry collected the rest of the paperwork in the area and separated out anything pertaining to his father. The file was mostly intact, and it only took him a minute to put it back together. Figuring out what had happened was a different matter entirely. The witness reports of what had happened were incomplete and contradictory. Two of the incinerated bodies were the right height for his father, but none matched Hanks taller frame. This gave Barry a little hope, and his spirits were lifted further when one of the Security Staff mentioned seeing two new arrivals fleeing in a Blue SUV.

Barry checked the website but didn't leave a message. He then sent updates to Mark in California and Scott in Bemidji. Figuring that Hank and his dad might still be in town, he wasted the rest of the day checking the various hotels that were still in operation and some restaurants. After exhausting himself walking around town, he ate, then got a room for the night. After taking a sinfully long shower, he hit the rack.

Hank checked the website an hour after Barry did, he and Dale saw the message from Barry's earlier post and got very excited. They decided they would wait another day where they were and drive back to OKC if they had to. After leaving a message on the site telling him they were in Topeka, they went to bed as well.

The following morning had Barry looking for a ride north. If Hank and his dad had survived, he figured they were heading north for home. He finally got a ride with a trucker who was returning to Kansas City after delivering a load of produce down to Oklahoma. The next logical place for

Hank to go was Kansas City if he was following the roads north back towards Bemidji. Oscar, the truck driver was ready to go, so Barry didn't get a chance to check the website before he left. He threw his backpack up in the cab and settled in for the trip. They were on the road by 10:00 AM and made it in to the Kansas City freight terminal by 5:30.

Hank and Dale checked the website throughout the day to no avail. They decided to head back to Oklahoma City, stopping back in Wichita to see if they could recover some of Dale's medical file. They updated the site, telling him they were headed back to Oklahoma City, and letting him know what Hotel they would be staying in. After they packed up and waited in a ridiculously long line again for fuel, they began retracing their route back to Wichita.

Barry was able to check the website at 9:00 PM, and nearly crawled out of his skin he was so mad. *Well that's what you get for being an idiot and not leaving a message last time, Metzler!* He shook his head trying to clear it of the self-recrimination, then started typing:

Hank, I made it to Kansas City looking for you guys. I will stay here for the next 24 hours. If I have not heard from you guys, I will head back to OKC and meet you at the hotel. Do not leave there! I will meet you guys there as soon as I can. Barry

Hank and Dale pulled up to the front of the medical center and looked at the damage. Shaking his head at the waste, Hank got out of the car and again approached one of the volunteer security staff, he was relieved to see it was one of the same staff members from the last time they were there. As Hank walked towards the man, he got a strange look on his face and raised a radio to his lips. Just as Hank reached him, he held up a hand as he received a reply into his earpiece.

"Are you Mr. Metzler?" he asked when the transmission ended.

"Yes, I'm Hank Metzler." Hank had a puzzled look on his face, he didn't recall exchanging names the last time he was here.

"You have a brother in the Marine Corps right?"

"Huh?" Hank was caught off guard. "Um no, my brother is twelve or thirteen years old now. Why do you ask?"

"Well a young guy with orders from the Marine Corps came through here yesterday looking for his father and brother. Found some paperwork inside in all the mess, claimed it was his father's medical record. Guy was 5'10", looked like he knew what he was doing, carried his M4 like he was born with it. If he was twelve years old, I'll eat my socks."

The man had gestured for Hank to follow him, which he did. "The sheriff will be able to tell you more."

Hank was beginning to feel like he was in the twilight zone. There was no way Barry was a Marine, and having not seen Barry in almost three years, the image in his head was of a skinny grade school kid who hadn't hit puberty and sure as hell wasn't 5'10". Hank was led to the same pickup parked almost in the same spot where Barry had met the sheriff.

"Jesse, this is Hank Metzler." The guard said and left Hank there.

"Hey Hank, Jesse Lansdowne." Jesse said stepping out of the truck and pumping his hand. "Your younger brother was here day before yesterday looking for you guys. We had no Idea where you went. He spent the day out in town looking for ya. Where did you all go after the mess here?"

"Well first off I'm not sure this guy is my brother." Hank was still feeling confused. "Barry would only be…" Hank paused and thought about it. "Well shit! I guess he'd be fourteen now. I heard he went to a Marine Base, but your officer said the guy who was here said he was older?"

"Well he sure wasn't some twelve year old. He spoke like a Marine, and he seemed like he knew his stuff. Had a request for assistance letter from the Corps. The National Guard guys at the airfield even verified it."

"Wow, well we got a message from him on the family finder website, saying he was in Oklahoma City and we were heading back down there to meet him, but if he's here…"Hank trailed off.

"Well he took your medical record with him. I know he was going to head over to the freight terminal to see about catching a ride. Did you want to check the website to see if he has left an update?"

"Thank you that would be great." Hank went back to the Dodge and got his dad. They all went inside and got on the computer.

"Well shit! Looks like he went right by you!" Jesse said after reading the post. "Damn, and now he's heading back towards Oklahoma City. Boy you guys are running a Chinese fire drill!"

"He has to come back through here though right?" Dale asked. "Let's let him know we're here. If we don't get a response we'll head back. Hopefully it will save us a trip."

"Ya'll ought to go put a sign up on the highway too. If he's moving through here, he might see it on the road." Jesse suggested. "I have a professional sign maker at home that would love to help you out."

"Really?" Dale asked.

"Oh yeah, wait till you meet her…"

They left a message on the board and then followed the sheriff to his house, where they met the artiste. Tricia Lansdowne was a nine year old, precocious ball of energy who took to the task with such enthusiasm, it left Hank and Dale speechless. In short order they found themselves being bossed around like minions. Whereas they had thought that a simple 'Barry Metzler-We are here' message in black and white would be sufficient, they were promptly informed of their misguided thoughts and were corrected appropriately.

Three sheets of butcher paper were laid out for adornment, while Jesse was sent to get some lumber. Tricia informed the two men in front of her who were obviously creatively challenged, that no one would pay any attention to a blah sign written in black and white. A paint set was brought out and three very colorful messages were made up. Dale had to excuse himself halfway through the process to go outside and get his emotions under control as the memories of his youngest daughter got the better of him. An hour later, Jesse returned with some plywood and good news. He handed them a printout from the website. It said simply:

Stay there! On my way!

CHAPTER 30

Barry was excited as he headed back over to the freight terminal. Going to the dispatch office he was surprised to see Oscar there.

"Hey amigo! I thought you were heading further north? Couldn't you get a ride?"

"My dad and brother are back in Wichita! I need to head back that way."

"Well shit! You're in luck then. I'm headed back that way in a couple of hours."

"Really? Mr. Melendez If I could get a ride back with you that would be super." The look on Barry's face caused the old trucker to smile on the inside, but his face took on a grim countenance. "Sorry, ain't gonna happen with the way things are."

"What?" Barry was shocked. "Why not? What's wrong?"

"I told you, my name is Oscar, and as long as you keep trying to make me feel old I got no room for ya." He stood there shaking his head.

Barry broke out into a smile and slugged the man on the shoulder.

"Well Oscaaar!" he said, dragging out the man's name. "What can I do to help you get ready?"

They went to the truck where Barry put his pack and rifle in the cab. He then spent the next twenty minutes watching the loading process and getting a tutorial in weight and balance of loads, and other subjects relevant to the task at hand. They were on the road in half an hour, Barry almost squirming in anticipation. The ride down was uneventful for the first half of the journey, but that's where their luck ran out.

Bill Wellington and Cliff Bluefeather were trouble, always had been. When the world went to hell in a hand basket, they immediately took advantage of the lack of Law Enforcement, and let their bad sides come all the way out. Cliff drank and Bill did whatever chemical he could smoke, snort, or otherwise ingest into his body. They had become fairly successful at highway robbery, working the stretch of I-35 between Topeka and Wichita. Along with two other friends Greg and Dave, they had made some pretty good scores, both in terms of loot and women. They had taken over a farm that was over twenty miles from the Interstate, and no one had ventured that far looking for them to date.

Their usual scam was to fake a broke down car and ambush people when they stopped. Billy's boyish face usually set people at ease, and made it easy for them when victims let down their guard. Their last score had kept them fat and happy for a couple of weeks. A husband and wife had been driving a delivery van full of supplies for their small store up in Topeka.

Mike Evans and his wife Lisa Marie had fallen for the broken down car bit and stopped as Billy shot them one of his smiles. Mike had his pistol tucked into his belt as he got out of the truck but it didn't help him. Cliff saw it and shot him from cover with his deer rifle. Lisa struggled but the four men were able to tackle the feisty woman and tie her up. They had killed her when she had finally had enough of the abuse and sexual assaults and attacked Dave. She had nearly put his eye out, and he still had the open cuts to show for it.

Being inherent cowards, they never tried to attack anyone that appeared well armed or more than two vehicles. They set up their trap this day by parking one of their pickups at an angle across the road and removing one of the good front tires and then laying a spare rim with a shredded tire down next to the front hub. They then lowered the front end so that the wheel hub and disc were sitting on the ground.

Dave and Cliff hid off to the side of the road while Billy and Greg waited in the cab of the truck. It was an Indian summer and hot as hell. They had a cooler in the back with some beer and were keeping cool by draping wet towels over their heads. The grumbling had reached a new high before Cliff gave them the signal that a car was coming. They put down the towels, and climbed out of the cab. They moved to the center of the road and watched as a Semi crested the slight rise to the north. Billy shot a nervous glance at Greg when he saw a second figure in the cab.

Oscar brought the rig to a stop a little closer to the truck than Barry would have liked. Oscar finished setting the break before turning to Barry.

"Come on, time to earn some Karma." He grinned.

"My Karma bucket is full." Barry mumbled as he grabbed his rifle and hopped down from the cab. He left his pack in the truck, but he lived in his tac-vest. He was clipping his rifle to the lanyard that was attached to his vest, and turning towards the front of the vehicle when he pulled up short. From his position he could see partway into the bed of the pickup's bed. He noticed a two-ton floor jack sitting in the bed. He looked at the pick-up sitting on its hub and started to get a tingle. *If it looks wrong or feels wrong, it is wrong! Listen to your gut!* The words from one of his instructors echoed through his head.

Barry brought his rifle to the low ready and began slicing the pie around the front of the truck, he saw Oscar's arm over the front of the trucks curved hood as he raised his hands. He saw one of the men still in the process of drawing a revolver and snapped the rifle up and sent two rounds into his chest. He took a knee as there was a loud boom from the other side of the truck. He leaned out and snapped a round at the leg of the fat boyish faced man as a round spanged off the grill of the truck next to his head. The fat man fell over screaming as Barry spun around to face the direction the last round had come from. A voice called out from the ditch as Oscar's body hit the ground.

"Drop it asshole! We have you surrounded from a position of cover!"

Barry dropped and rolled under the front bumper. The asphalt was still uncomfortably hot. That combined with the heat radiating from the engine above him caused him to rethink his choice of location. He was scrambling towards the driver's side when another round skipped off the pavement right in front of his nose. He looked right and saw the fat guy trying to bring his pistol bear. Tears were forced from his eyes as he squinted over the sights. Barry continued rolling towards the set of double axels, having to move in fits and starts because of the rifle and the tight quarters. Another round cracked by his head, making him halt his scramble.

"This is your very last fucking chance!" The voice said again. "I have had you in my sights the whole time. Now stop moving unless it's to push that rifle out from under there! Anything else and I'm going to put one through your legs!"

Barry hesitated for a split second, weighing his options. He looked around and saw two guns pointed at him, and he didn't know where the third shooter was exactly. He slowly placed his rifle on the pavement and pushed it out from under the truck.

"Glad to see you're finally coming around. Now crawl out from under there slowly."

Barry did as he was told and found himself tied up and sitting on the running board to the truck as the three surviving bandits discussed what to do with him while they bandaged Billy's leg. The fourth bandit wasn't going to be joining anymore conversations…ever.

"I say we just Kill 'em and be done with it." Dave said.

"Well you sure are some kind of soldier boy, ain't ya?" Cliff asked as he went through Barry's pack. They had stripped him down to his T-shirt, and searched his pants turning out all his pockets. The scene had been almost comical as they kept finding things in the various pockets of his pants. It had reminded Billy of the scene where Bugs Bunny was spanking the baby gangster and all kinds of weapons fall out of his diaper. His comment to that effect causing the three of them to laugh out loud.

Barry just sat and stared at them as they finished looking through the cab. Cliff began moving them along in case someone else showed up. Oscar and Greg's body were tossed into the ditch without a second thought and the tire replaced back on the front hub. They shoved Barry into the cab of the pickup between Billy and Dave while Cliff drove the semi behind them. Billy spent the entire trip jabbing the barrel of his pistol into Barry's ribs, and threatening him with all sorts of unimaginative tortures. 'I'm going to cut off your balls and feed them to you' being the most common. The moments when he wasn't threatening Barry were spent telling Dave to go easy on the bumps and complaining about the hole in his leg.

Barry took very careful note of the route they took. The terrain was Kansas flat and there were few landmarks. The good thing was that the roads, even the dirt ones, were long and straight. They drove east into Chase county and eventually pulled up to a small farm with three buildings clustered around a circular driveway. The Main house was just starting to show signs of neglect, and the few pieces of Machinery visible had weeds growing around them, showing their lack of use.

Barry was hauled out of the cab and shoved none too gently into the barn where he had handcuffs put on his wrists which were then padlocked to a chain looped around a pillar. After giving them and extra squeeze to make sure they were uncomfortably tight, Dave grabbed a pair of bolt cutters off the wall and went outside to break into the trailer.

Barry looked around for any surveillance devices, spending the better part of the next two hours peering into the most likely places a camera could be set up. The three idiots outside didn't strike him as technologically savvy, but he wasn't about to risk exposing his abilities. Once he was sure he wasn't under observation, he used a thin strip of flexible metal that was concealed in one of his belt loops to release the tension on the cuffs to a comfortable setting and then replaced the loid back in the belt loop. He wasn't about to attempt an escape during daylight hours with no gear. He was going to wait until night time when hopefully he would just have to deal with one guard.

Outside, Cliff and crew were having a grand old time looking through the spoils of their efforts. The truck had been carrying groceries and some tools. There were several cases of beer and wine that were immediately opened. The majority of the booze was brought into the barn and stacked along one wall. His captors wandering over and checking on him every time they entered the barn. Barry just stared at them as they taunted him.

The sun was finally getting low in the sky and the barn was getting dim when Barry heard another vehicle pull up outside. There was a sound of raised voices and then the door was opened and a woman and two kids were drug in by a man Barry hadn't seen before. They were taken over to a work bench and had cables put around the kids necks before being chained up next to Barry and left there.

"Hey guys, are you okay?" Barry asked as the two frightened kids huddled in their mother's arms. The young girl was crying and complaining that the cable lock around her neck was choking her. The children's wrists were too small to be handcuffed, so their captor had put small cables around the kid's necks and crimped them closed with metal clamps. The kids went quiet and huddled closer to their mother when Barry spoke.

"Who are you?" The woman asked turning the kid's bodies away in a protective gesture.

"My name is Barry Metzler ma'am."

"What have they been doing out here? Have you seen anyone else?" She shot a frightened look at the door as what was obviously a party was getting underway outside.

"They aren't going to do anything if I can help it." Barry said. The note of confidence in his voice causing the woman to stare at him. "Just try to make the kids comfortable and we'll be fine."

"How are we going to be fine?" The woman's voice was rising towards hysteria. "That's Cliff Bluefeather out there. He's been trouble in these parts since I was a little girl. The same goes for the rest of them. Dave has been suspected in half a dozen sexual assaults, and Brian spent more time in jail than out of it before the world went to hell."

"How many were with you when you came in, and how many others did you see out there?" Even though Barry was trying to stay relaxed and conserve his energy, it was still almost 100 degrees in the barn and he was sweating profusely.

"Brian and Will brought me here, Cliff and Billy were out front and I heard Dave yelling from inside the house. They have a big truck parked out there that I'm sure they stole from somewhere, and are throwing the contents all over the yard. I didn't see Greg, but you can be sure he's around here somewhere." She seemed to have stopped her slide towards hysteria, as the kids began to get agitated. The act of comforting them tended to settle her down. "I don't know if you realize this, but we are in serious trouble."

"Just keep calm and I'll get us out of here." Barry was loath to show his cards to the woman. It wasn't so much that he didn't trust her. But she had her kids with her, and a mother would do anything to keep her kids safe. And he could see her giving him up if her kids were threatened. "You're not going to see Greg. I killed him when they ambushed us as we were driving that truck down to Wichita."

They sat there as it grew dark, the kids trying to be comfortable. The woman didn't volunteer her name and Barry didn't ask, figuring she would have told him when he volunteered his, if she had wanted too. The little girl whispered in her mother's ear after an hour and she asked Barry to look away while she went to the bathroom. The strong smell of concentrated urine drifted across to Barry's nose, and he knew if he wanted to keep these folks in good enough shape to move, he was going to have to keep them hydrated. He looked over at the cases of booze stacked against the wall, nothing good for them there. He hitched his body around the post he was leaning against and looked around some more. He noticed a coiled garden hose hanging on a hook on the back wall. The end was connected to a spigot.

The three signs were completed to Tricia's approval.

The butcher paper had been stapled to the plywood so the wind would not tear it. The staples had presented an artistic problem until Tricia had each staple adorned with a small flower. She didn't like the fact that the staples looked like ants on her masterpieces. The posters were sure to attract anyone's attention, in fact, Hank was pretty sure they would catch the attention of any Martian who looked up.

The posters had bright yellow backgrounds with multi-colored letters. All of a dark color, because Tricia wanted them to 'Pop'. The letters had flowers that matched the ones used to hide the staples. The message was simple:

Barry-Stop!
Hank and Dad are here at Sheriff Lansdowne's house!
You can get directions at the Medical center
Artwork by: Tricia Lansdowne

They took the posters out to the highway north of town and nailed them across the uprights that held the regular green highway signs. They were able to place all three on the approaches to town, Hank was still pretty sure someone coming from the south would see them. They went by the medical center for a quick check-up for Dale then went to the sheriff's house where they had been invited to stay until Barry showed up.

He never did.

CHAPTER 31

Billy was finally starting to feel better. His leg had been throbbing all afternoon, and the pain had only subsided after he had put down half a bottle of Jack, chased by a six pack of beer. The 5.56 millimeter bullet had punched a hole through the meat of his left leg below his hip. While painful it was not debilitating, and was easily bandaged. He was pretty upset about it however, and after he got his drunk on, went in to torment Barry.

He staggered through the barn door, and stumbled over to Barry. Noticing the slight smell of urine in the air he leered down at his captive. He placed a hand against the short wall and leaned down until his face was inches away from Barry's.

"You are one dead sucker! You know that?" The smell of booze wafted across Barry's face. His expression didn't change and he just returned Billy's stare.

"I'm gonna make you pay for this." He tapped the bandaged leg.

"Here's what you're going to do." Barry spoke in a calm voice and even leaned towards Billy. "You are going to let these folks go."

"And if I don't?" Billy sneered.

"I'll kill you slow instead of fast. Your choice; make it now." The statement was so matter of fact, and Barry's stare so unsettling, that Billy pulled away.

"How are you going to do that when you're tied up in here?" Billy regained some of his bravado once he was out of reach of the somewhat scary kid. "Don't worry though, it ain't your time yet! I got other business to attend to first."

He turned towards the woman and kids and walked somewhat unsteadily towards them.

"You!" He said jabbing a finger at the woman. "Little Miss Suzanne 'I'm too good for everyone one in town' Bonner! You been stuck up since the fifth grade when you started to get them titties! Well your time for being all high and mighty is over…Over Bitch!"

"Billy, I never been nothing but kind to you, and you know it!" Suzanne cringed away from the angry man. "Just don't hurt my kids, they've never done a thing to you!"

"Little stuck up brats is what they are." He said as he unlocked her chain from the post end, leaving the other end attached to her handcuffs. Both of the kids started crying, but quieted down when Billy raised his hand as if to strike them. "You brats shut up and your mom will be back in a bit. We've got some things to discuss over in the house."

"Billy, this is the last chance for you to go easy. Let her go or it will be bad for you."

"Shut up you little shit!" Billy screamed. "Once we're done with her, I'm coming out here and you're next on my list of people who need to be fucked! So I'd cherish these last few minutes of virginity, do you understand me?"

Barry just stared at him and shook his head.

Billy began to pull Suzanne out of the barn by the chain, jerking it to keep her off balance. He kicked the door shut, but they could hear the increase in noise as the men outside cheered. The noise caused the kids to resume crying and Barry had to spend several minutes calming them down. Once they were somewhat settled, he got them to give him their names. The kids were named Carl and Abbi, he was ten and she seven. They told Barry of how one of the men had been able to carjack them and had brought them out here. Their father had been killed a few months ago by a small pack of ferals that had worked its way north from Oklahoma City. Their mom was an accountant for one of the grocery chains in town.

They both complained of being very thirsty, so Barry leaned in close.

"Can you guys keep a secret?" He asked very seriously.

"I can, but she's a blabber mouth." Carl said nudging his sister.

"Am not! You are!" Was the automatic reply from Abbi.

"Hey, hey!" Barry whispered. "If I get you guys some water will you be quiet?"

The two kids began nodding their heads vigorously.

"Okay, wait just a sec, quietly..." Barry used his loid again to slip out of his handcuffs, causing Abbi to cover her mouth with her hands. He went to the back of the barn and turned on the hose. He let the water run for a minute until it was nice and cool and the water didn't stink like hot rubber. He turned the water off and took the end over to the kids. After instructing them on not letting any of it spill because they wanted to keep it a secret from the bad guys, Barry walked back to the spigot and turned a small trickle on. Both kids drank a copious amount of water before Barry turned it off. He retrieved the hose and hung it back up after drinking his fill.

He spent the next ten minutes searching through the barn. The bolt cutters had never been brought back, but he found several other tools that would easily cut the kid's cables. He took a heavy duty pair of cable cutters and buried them under where he sat when shackled. He moved some other things around, stopping occasionally to look out through various apertures at what was going on outside. After making sure that things were arranged to his liking, he sat back down and re-attached the chain and cuffs, albeit loosely this time. He told the kids to settle down and get some rest, they would have to get up early in the morning.

Barry sat in silence waiting.

CHAPTER 32

Hank and Dale helped Jesse with some around the house projects, and helped him expand his 'victory garden'. Since the attacks, the few neighborhoods that survived intact often acted communally to grow vegetables and raise livestock. Interstate commerce was almost non-existent, and food stuffs were the number one target of highway robbers. The only thing that held more value was guns and ammo. A lot of preppers and survivalists came out of the initial crisis in pretty good shape as long as they weren't affected by the toxin. The only upside was that the population had been reduced to the point that there were plenty of manufactured items to go around.

After two days and no Barry, Jesse made a few calls up to Kansas City looking for him. The sheriff up there said he'd look into it and get back to them. They got a phone call the next day asking Jesse what he knew about Barry. Jesse informed him of the Metzler situation and asked why. He was told that they had found out about Barry catching a ride with Oscar heading back down their way, but the truck never showed. The highway had been driven several times since by convoys and no sign of the truck had been found. Jesse said that he would ask over at the airfield if anyone could go look for the truck from the air. After getting a description of the truck, they promised to keep in touch.

At the airfield Jesse was able get one of the volunteer pilots for the Sheriff's office to start searching for the truck. The search was going to be limited because fuel was still a critical issue. The truck wasn't found for three more days and when it was, it was a smoldering wreck parked among some burnt down buildings on a farm twenty miles from the highway. They put a posse together (Which Hank thought was pretty cool and was thoroughly endorsed by Tricia, even though she wasn't allowed to go), and went to the farm. There was no one left alive there but several severely burned bodies were found in the wreckage of the main house.

Two hours after Suzanne was taken from the barn, Barry heard a vehicle start up and drive away. He waited another hour before slipping his restraints again. Moving quietly to the door, he peered around the edge out into the driveway. Not seeing any one, he went back and cut the cables around the kid's necks. He didn't want to do it if they had to run out of there later. The two of them barely stirred, being exhausted from the day they had suffered through. Taking a long flat head screw driver he slipped out the back of the barn and made his way around to the corner where he could observe the house.

The sound of music could be heard quite clearly, even at this distance, so he was pretty sure they weren't going to hear him on his approach. He just needed to do it unseen now.

After waiting for five minutes, looking and listening in every direction, he made his way across to the back of the main house. Pressing himself up against the wall near one of the windows, he again waited to be found out. When no alarm was raised he moved onto the back porch, rolling his feet from heel to ball carefully to avoid making noise. At the back door, he checked the knob finding both the screen door and Dutch door unlocked. He raised his head and peeked through the small window into a mudroom. Seeing it was unoccupied he slipped inside. He made his way through the kitchen to the living room, having to step over trash, bottles, and cans to avoid making noise.

A quick look around the living room revealed a man passed out on the couch and Barry's gear piled over in the corner. Getting through all the litter in what used to be a quaint living room was going to be tough. The trash was literally ankle deep. Barry made it halfway across before he stepped on something that crackled as he put his weight on it. The man on the couch mumbled and rolled away from the noise.

Well if that wasn't a movie moment I don't know what is! Barry thought as he continued to the side of the sleeping man. Using the screw driver, Barry stabbed the man straight through the throat, driving the blade through the esophagus. Ripping forward he pulled it out as the man attempted to sit up and scream. Blood burst from his mouth and the hole in his throat as he choked and gurgled.

Another stab right into the eye socket and the life went out of him like a switch had been thrown. The body collapsed back without further fuss. Blood did however continue to flow into an ever widening pool next to the couch.

Barry immediately began putting on all of his gear, checking his rifle, but finding his pistol holster empty. The magazines and their contents were still there as well as his tac-vest and pack. Once he had his gear on he searched the body on the couch and came up with a Sig 9mm pistol. Not what he usually carried but he put it into the Bianchi holster on his hip anyways. He dropped the only spare magazine he could find in a cargo pocket and called it done. He didn't find anyone else in the house until he was searching the last bedroom.

Billy was passed out naked after having raped Suzanne. His clothes were piled at the foot of the bed, while his revolver was sitting on the nightstand. A shotgun was propped up in the corner on the far side of the room. Barry made his way to the shotgun, making sure to unload it and pocket the shells. He moved back around and did the same to the revolver, checking the drawer for ammo as well before replacing it on the nightstand. Having made sure that the rest of the house was empty, Barry picked up the Remington 870 by the barrel and standing over the still snoring man brought the flat portion of the stock down across Billy's face.

The sound of the man's nose breaking wasn't even as loud as the snoring had been. Billy exploded up into a sitting position putting both hands over his face. He tried to scream through his shattered teeth while blood coursed down the back of his throat. Not waiting for the man to recover, Barry swung for the bleachers, the stock this time slamming into the hands that were pressed to Billy's face. This knocked him flat on his back again and caused him to pass out. Barry rolled him on his side and handcuffed his hands behind his back, then propped him that way with a pillow so he wouldn't choke on his own blood. He was going to gag him but didn't for the same reason. He was going to need Billy alive to find out where Suzanne was.

Barry went outside after turning the music off and began looking around the property for a radio or some other form of communication. He'd found a couple of cell phones in the house, but the batteries were dead and it was apparent they hadn't been used in a while. He went straight to Oscar's truck and was disappointed to find that the CB had been removed already. He checked the pickup and didn't find anything. Hoping for another 'Movie Moment' he flipped down the visor hoping the keys would drop into his hand. No such luck, so he moved his search on to the equipment shed.

It was obvious that this is where the gang had been storing their loot. Boxes of all sorts of random items were stacked haphazardly throughout the open structure. He came across a good supply of rifles and ammo stacked next to the work bench. Barry replenished his one magazine that was only missing four rounds and shook his head. He removed all the bolts from the rifles and put them in a bucket. He then hid the bucket outside in some bushes. He found a set of keys hanging on a peg, but they were for the tractor and didn't fit any of the vehicles out front. Barry didn't know how far away from the highway they were, but it was his intention to get the kids back home after he found their mother. He went in search of keys for any vehicle.

While he was going through the pockets of the dead guy on the couch, he heard moaning from Billy's room. He walked in to the room and looked down at the quivering blob of a man. Double checking the cuffs, he stepped up to the edge of the bed and poked Billy in the hip with the barrel of his rifle. Billy let out a bloody blubber and began trying not to show that his breath was starting to hitch.

"Well Billy, how do you feel about that decision you made earlier? Hmm?" Barry tapped him on the head with the rifle barrel. Billy winced and tried to roll away, but Barry grabbed his arm and rolled him back so he was facing his captor. "I asked you a question Billy. Don't make me ask it again. When I ask you where Suzanne is, I will get an immediate answer."

"I don't know where she is. Cliff and the guys took her." He sobbed.

"I didn't ask you that yet Billy, what I asked you was 'How do you feel about that decision you made earlier?' Answer me." Barry kept eye contact with the man as he began to squirm.

"They would have killed me if I let you guys go, come on man please!" He whined through the bloody bubbles that were still coming out of his mouth and nose.

"Ahh, and I suppose you were kidding about fucking me right?"

Billy looked away to avoid eye contact with the scary young guy who was looking down on him. He finally gave in to his urge to cry. He let his head droop forward and began sobbing. The bloody snot bubbles were too much for Barry and he stepped away from the mess. He picked up Billy's pants and finally hit the jack pot, pulling out a key ring that he recognized from the truck. He pocketed the keys and took the jeans over to Billy and helped put them on. He then walked Billy out to the barn and chained him up in his place, but only after wrapping the chain around Billy's neck and looping it through his cuffs.

Barry got the kids awake and cleaned up. Carl managed to kick Billy in the arm in passing, letting him know there was still a little animosity there. They then began loading some supplies in the truck. Barry was in the barn when Abbi came running in and said that their mom was coming back. Barry stepped outside and could see a blue Honda Odyssey mini-van driving up from a half mile away. Barry hustled the kids around to the back of the barn and gave them instructions to run straight away from the farm if they heard gunshots. He made sure they had a canteen full of water each and some protective clothing.

Barry hustled over to the equipment shed and got set up for his ambush. It had taken too long to get the kids settled and Cliff saw him darting into the shed. He stopped the car sixty yards from the shed and rolled out into the high grass next to the drive. Realizing that he had a fight on his hands, Barry began laying down suppressive fire at where he thought Cliff was. He saw some movement and fired a series of single shots into the area.

Cliff was still a little fuzzy after dropping the guys and the bitch off at their place. It was late and he had tied one on. He just wanted to get into bed and sleep. He almost missed the fleeting shadow that darted into the equipment shed. He could tell right away that it wasn't somebody who was supposed to be there, the shadow moved like his grandpa did, fluid like. None of the guys there knew how to move like that. He stopped the mini-van and rolled out of the door. He had to get to the house and get to a long gun there because the pistol on his hip wasn't going to keep him alive very long. As if in answer to his thoughts, he heard bullets start snapping by his face. He stopped rolling and began slithering, since the rolling was moving too much vegetation, allowing the shooter to zero in on his location. He made it back behind the Odyssey and lifted the rear hatch. It was a mistake since the light went on and immediately drew a small barrage of rifle fire.

Cliff had a fleeting thought that it might be the kid they had caught the day before since he'd had a suppressor on his rifle and this was definitely suppressed fire. He couldn't see the guys being so careless as to let him loose though. After ten or twelve rounds, the fire tapered off and Cliff assumed he was reloading. He was pretty sure there was only one person out there because otherwise they would have flanked him. In a moment of panic he looked around to make sure that it was not in fact what was happening. After taking in his surroundings, Cliff reached into the back of the van and pulled a case of vodka out and down onto the ground with him. The clinking of bottles brought about another round of bullets tearing up the van. He was pretty sure it wasn't going anywhere, since he could smell hot radiator fluid from the front of the van.

Whoever was shooting at him knew what they were doing. The rounds were randomly timed and they impacted under the van and along both sides. The shooter was being very effective at pinning him down. He was relatively safe since the shed was at a slightly higher elevation and with both front tires flat, he couldn't get rounds under the van. The occasional rock kicked up would pepper his face and bring on a bout of cussing but it was essentially a stalemate. The shed held several cans of military ammo, so the shooter wouldn't be running out anytime soon. Cliff didn't think anyone would be coming out this way for some time so he was screwed on any back-up arriving.

Pulling a folding knife from his pocket, he cut the sleeves off of his shirt and sliced them into strips. He then unscrewed the tops from the vodka bottles he had pulled out of the van. After stuffing his sleeves in five of the bottles, he took a long slug out of the sixth and jammed his last strip of cloth into it. Putting the knife away, he pulled out a Bic lighter and lit the wick on the first bottle. Backing a few feet away from the rear of the van, Cliff surged to his feet and threw the bottle for all he was worth. It arced high in the air, but fell short of the shed by a good ten feet. It also landed in the dirt and didn't break. It lay there with the wick on fire until Barry used a shovel to toss some dirt on it.

Swearing profusely at this turn of events, Cliff was surprised to hear the kid's voice calling out to him.

"Why don't you give it up asshole? I can plink at you all morning till the sun comes up, then you're screwed because I'll be able to see you and then it's over." Barry had been moving things around in the shed and had a pretty good firing hide as long as the yahoo by the van didn't have a rifle.

"Help! You guys, I'm in the barn!" drifted faintly out to Cliff. He shook his head and considered giving up to the kid if he'd let him Flay Billy alive first.

"Yeah, why don't you come help Billy in the Barn?" Barry punctuated the question with a few rounds from his M4. "Is that you Cliff? Why don't you come out here with a knife and face me like a man!"

Cliff couldn't believe what he was hearing. The kid had balls that was for sure. Cliff had doubts about the kid actually fighting him. Cliff had some pretty good skill with a blade. His grandfather had taught him when he was young as part of his Apache heritage and Cliff had taken it seriously before he started drinking.

"Come on out then you little shit, and I'll carve you up like a Christmas turkey!"

Barry wasn't about to expose himself for any reason and sent a few rounds into the van.

Billy kept up a constant plea for help until there was the sounds of conflict in the barn. Barry was worried about being surrounded so he pulled back and looked at the barn. The noise stopped and Carl poked his head out and gave Barry a thumbs up. Barry turned back around just as another Molotov cocktail sailed through the air. This one crashing into the roof of the shed and shattering.

Cliff had used the distraction to break cover and rush towards the shed. Throwing with momentum, the bottle of vodka easily covered the distance and shattered on the edge of the roof. Flaming liquid ran down the side of the wall and splashed through the open window. Only a few drops got on Barry, which he calmly patted out.

Cliff had his gun out and fired a few rounds into the shed. Barry snapped a few back towards him and trotted across to the house. He watched as Cliff's head poked around the corner of the shed. Dark smoke was starting to billow out of the doors at both ends. Barry could see Cliff keeping his body behind cover with just an eye and his pistol aimed along the wall. It was obvious he still thought Barry was inside and would have to retreat out this door, since Cliff had seen that Barry had blocked the other door with furniture.

Barry aimed carefully at a point where he estimated Cliffs head to be. Maintaining the sight picture he pressed off a round. If the round would have travelled straight, Cliff would have died. The bullet however impacted the wall a few inches from Cliffs face and was deflected enough that it missed him with less than an inch to spare. It did, however, blow several wood splinters into Cliff's forehead, eye, and cheek. He reeled back swearing as blood began to flow down the right side of his face. Realizing that the shot had come from the house and feeling the heat radiating off the fire from the shed. He picked up the other Molotov that he had brought with him and lit it from the flames licking along the wall in front of him. He switched the gun to his left hand and hurled the flaming bottle at the house.

Barry had been waiting patiently for Cliff to expose himself and got his chance as the man stepped into the open to make his throw. The M4 made two *chutt clack* sounds and Cliff fell to the ground. He wasn't dead though and tried to crawl behind the shed again. Barry was able to hit him in both legs before he was behind cover on the other side of the shed again. Grimacing at all the wasted time, he went behind the house and moved over towards the barn. He noticed several burning embers from the shed had floated over and were starting to smolder on the roof of the barn. Looking inside he could see where the kids had tied a towel around Billy's head. Looking out back he could see the kids half way across the field looking back at him. He waved them over.

"Okay guys, Listen up." Barry said as they crouched next to him. "Cliff is out there hurt, maybe dead, but I doubt it. We need to take Billy with us to find out where your mom is. I have to load Billy into the truck before we leave. I need you guys to watch for Cliff while I'm doing that, okay?"

"Okay, Barry!" Carl said as Abbi nodded along with him.

Barry went into the barn after checking out front. He could see Cliff's legs from this angle and he may well have bled out. Keeping the truck between him and Cliff, Barry went back into the Barn and Hobbled Billy using the same cables from the kid's collars. Once that was done he rolled him on his belly and connected the neck collar through the handcuffs down to the leg restraints. Billy was not going anywhere fast.

Looking at Carl and getting a thumbs up at his *pssst,* Barry leaned in next to Billy's face and removed the towel. The corpulent face squinted at the light and cringed back.

"Okay you piece of filth. You have a choice. I leave you in this building to burn, or you tell me where Suzanne is. This is a yes or no question and you get only one chance to answer it. Are you going to cooperate?"

Barry could see Billy looking at the ceiling behind him as it started to smoke. The equipment shed across the driveway was a boiling mass of flames. "Yes or No?"

"What happened to Cliff?" Billy asked.

Barry slapped him so hard across the face that he slumped over. He immediately started to blubber again.

"I killed him. Last chance. Yes or No?" Barry emphasized this last with a prod from the gun barrel making him sit up again.

"I don't know which house they took her to..." This time the rifle cracked into the side of his face. He saw the blow coming but even flinching away from it didn't save him. He felt his cheek bone crack and let out a wail.

"Okay, okay! I'll tell you where all the houses are! Just stop!"

Barry helped him to his feet and walked him to the door where Carl and Abbi both frowned up at the shirtless man.

"Stay behind me guys, we're going to the truck now alright?"

They formed a line behind Billy and walked to the truck. Barry made Billy climb into the driver's seat from the passenger side then followed him. He made sure the two kids got in behind him and closed the door. He put the keys in the ignition and started the car. Placing the muzzle of his rifle into Billy's crotch, Barry gave it a firm nudge.

"Put the car in gear and turn out towards the field between the house and the barn. Make a wide loop through the field to the left until we meet back up with the driveway."

"That's stupid. Why can't I just drive out on the driveway?" Billy asked as he turned to do just that.

Barry jabbed the rifle painfully into his thigh, causing him to use both his hands to try and push it away. Barry slapped him across the face, rocking his head against the rear window glass.

"Do it, or I'll shoot you in the kneecaps! Got it?"

"Okay, okay!" Billy's face had taken so much abuse lately that the whole thing was on fire.

He angled the truck out towards the field and drove out between the barn and house. Once in the field, they bounced in a wide circle around to the north. They were only a hundred yards from connecting back with the drive when a bullet smacked into the rear quarter panel of the truck. Barry crouched a little lower and told the kids to get down into the foot well. Billy let off the gas to look around, this got him another smack from Barry. He got back on the gas as a few more rounds zipped by the truck. Not all of them missed however and a couple hit the engine compartment.

Once they were back on the driveway, Barry started to interrogate Billy.

"Where are your buddy's houses? I want to know every place where they could have taken her."

"I thought I was going to drive you there?" Billy looked over with a worried look on his face.

"You are. But I want their names in case, we come across Some Law Enforcement and you try to use your right to remain silent. Right now talking to me is the only thing keeping you alive. If you don't tell me right now, I'll leave you in a hole out here." Barry emphasized this with another prod from his M4.

"Well then why would you keep me alive after I told you?" The whiney tone in his voice was starting to grate on Barry's nerves.

"Because it's faster to have you drive us there!"

Billy spilled the name of several probable locations. Carl was familiar with a few of them and pointed them out on Barry's map. They were discussing the locations, and had gone about eight miles back towards town when the truck started to sputter. Barry looked at Billy to make sure he wasn't doing anything to cause it, but the worried look on Billy's face and the fact that his hands were still at 10' and 2' on the wheel got him off the hook.

"Uhm, the temperature is way up."

"Stop the truck and let's see if we can fix it."

They stopped right in the middle of the road, and after giving the surroundings a good once over, they got out. Once the truck was stopped, the leaking steam from the radiator became noticeable without the wind whipping it away. Lifting the hood revealed that a bullet had impacted the radiator overflow hose and torn it off. The bullet had also cracked a weld on the radiator fill spout and they were losing fluid from there as well.

"We still have twelve miles to go to the freeway and another fifteen to town!" Billy whined. "No one is going to find us out here!"

"Shut your mouth and sit down."

Barry used the boxes from the bed of the truck along with the tarp from his pack to make a shelter for the kids behind the tailgate. The sun was well above the horizon and it was already warming up. He pulled out some metal epoxy and got it ready to go. He didn't want to use some of their precious water to cool the radiator prior to repairing it. If the repair didn't hold he would have wasted the water they would need to get out of there on foot. They would have to wait for the engine to cool.

Barry ate breakfast with the kids and made sure they had water. Billy was given water, but when he complained he was hungry, Barry slapped him on the gut and said he could stand to miss a few meals. While they waited under the shade, Barry went through and double checked all his gear. Someone had rifled through it back at the house but left it all in the pack. He used a leftover foil packet from the kid's breakfast to mix some of the epoxy. He repaired the crack as best he could plugging the over flow stem where it was broken. After recovering as much of the radiator fluid as he could from the overflow reservoir and putting it back in the radiator itself he used a little water to top it off. They would have to stop every couple of miles to let it cool, but it sure beat walking.

They repacked the gear and started back down the road. They kept a close eye on the gauge and stopped whenever they came across some shade near the road. It was mid-afternoon by the time they reached the first of the houses where they might find Suzanne. Barry had Billy stop at the edge of the property. The farm house was visible in the distance. The fields on this property were overgrown and untended just like the last one they were at. Barry made Billy turn around and backtrack a mile until they found some trees.

They parked the truck in a small copse of pepper trees. Barry took Billy over to a tree to tie him up. As they were walking to the tree, Billy made a break for it. It was the most ridiculous thing Barry had ever seen, the shirtless fat man hobbling towards the farm house. They all stared for a minute before Barry easily caught up with him and kicked his legs out from under him. Billy immediately attempted to roll into Barry's legs so he could grapple with him. Barry nimbly danced away from the attempt. When Billy rolled to his stomach and tried to gain his feet, Barry slipped in and delivered a butt-stroke to his head that knocked him back down.

Barry prodded him back to a tree, and cable locked him to one of the trunks. Next a sock went in his mouth which Barry then cable locked in place. After making sure that there was no chance what-so-ever that Billy was going anywhere without someone's help, he pulled the kids aside.

"Okay guys I need you to listen up. I have to go and see if your mom is in that house we saw a little while ago." Barry had squatted down so he was looking at Abbi eye to eye. "We're going to eat and then I want you guys to get in the truck and get some sleep. I will be back with your mom if she's here, if she isn't then we'll continue to look for her tomorrow."

After receiving nods, Barry got the kids fed watered and bathroom breaks taken care of. He made them promise not to go anywhere near Billy, and if for some reason Barry didn't return they were to continue walking towards town down the road. He made sure they had some supplies already packed in case such a contingency was required. Barry really hoped it wasn't, they were still ten plus miles from town.

After going over to Billy and whispering in his ear for a minute, Barry set off into the gathering dusk. It was full dark as he crept up to the house. He was moving around to the backside of the house when a dog started barking. He took a knee and reevaluated his situation. It was unlikely the dogs were outside without being in a kennel. Too much chance of them getting bit by an animal affected by the toxin.

The dog stopped after a few seconds and Barry slipped further around the house, He had covered less than a hundred feet when he came within sight of the kennel and the dog started up again. This time it went on for a couple of minutes before one of the guys that Barry had seen at Cliff's farm came out onto the back stoop. He soothed the dog down with some words and looked out at the field for a few minutes. Barry was slowly bringing his rifle up to take a shot at the guy when he abruptly turned and went back inside. Barry saw a pistol on the guy's hip as he went back through the door.

The faint sound of the dog growling drifted across to Barry, and he was just starting to back away so he could approach the house from the front when the guy came back out on the stoop with a pump shotgun in his hands. He was smart to take the dogs warning seriously, it didn't help him though as a 5.56 mm slug entered his right eye and blew out the back of his head. He collapsed to the ground as if his skeleton was turned to water instantly. The shotgun only made a lite thump as it hit the porch. The dog however went nuts. It's barking picking up in intensity.

Barry felt bad about what he did next. He put a round right in the beast's mouth. The bullet tearing through the back of its throat and into its spine. The startled yelp was cut off by the damage done and the dog collapsed. Feeling horrible, Barry rushed the back of the house, pausing only to put another round through both the dog and the guy lying on the porch in a rapidly expanding pool of blood.

He took up position next to the back door and listened. He was rewarded with the sound of someone shuffling through the house. A shadow shifted in the window but no footsteps approached the back door. Barry bent down and took the shotgun and what turned out to be his own pistol from the body. He set the shotgun in the tall grass alongside the house. He then shoved the corpse off the porch.

After listening at the door again, he slipped inside with his rifle leading the way. After checking both directions in a short hallway he began to step across towards the living room when a board creaked.

"What was the damned dog barking at this time? Those coons again?" A voice asked from out of sight.

Barry continued his glide into the room sweeping to his right, catching a man on the couch watching the TV.

"Nope, just me." He said as the man turned towards him with a startled look on his face. He leaned back and then lunged for the end of the couch where an AR-15 was propped up. Barry put two in his upper chest near his shoulder. He flopped back with a cry of pain and Barry butt stroked him into unconsciousness. Turning towards the other doorway and the rest of the house he waited for anyone to respond to the commotion. When nothing happened he finished clearing the house.

He found Suzanne in one of the bedrooms. She was in terrible shape after being raped and abused multiple times. She was naked and handcuffed to the head board, lying on her side facing away from the door. Barry could see her tense up when she became aware of his presence.

"Suzanne?" He whispered. "It's Barry."

He walked around the foot of the bed as she started to lurch up out of the bed. He shushed her into silence as she began to ask about the kids.

"Sshh!" He put a finger to his lips. "They are fine and waiting for you. Let's get you cleaned up and get out of here. Do you know how many there were here?"

"Four...There were four of them." She barely managed to croak out. Her face was bruised and she was missing a tooth. She smelled to high heaven, some of the abuse involved the men degrading her by urinating or defecating on her. Barry gave her a small drink from his hydration pack and took her to the bathroom. It wasn't in much better shape than she was but they managed to get the water on and shower the grime off. Barry was getting twitchy not knowing where the other two men were, and kept a constant vigil out for someone entering the house.

Suzanne came out of the bathroom drying herself off with the cleanest of several dirty towels. She was still naked as they day she was born. A search for her clothes came up empty, so she finally settled for cutting the bottom off the legs of a pair of jeans that were eight inches to long and had a waist four inches too big. Barry pulled a piece of 550 cord out of his pack and fashioned a belt for her.

The next obstacle they had to overcome was footwear. There was no way she could make it the few miles to the truck in bare feet and in her condition. They checked both of the bodies and finally settled on the smaller pair of boots and two pairs of socks. She was lucky and found a clean pair that she wore next to her skin with a pair of somewhat less fresh socks on the outside. While Barry was out back, he recovered the shotgun and pistol. He also took the belt off the guy lying next to the porch since it was the locking slide kind made of canvass. After donning the belt and holster, she picked up the AR-15 and faced Barry.

"Let's go!"

They went out the back door. It was evident right away that it was going to be very slow going as Suzanne limped along at a snail's pace. They were lucky that the moon was up early and made their going easier. Barry took them out through the field, looping back to the road. They stopped off to the side and rested while Suzanne drank some more water. After too short a time Barry had them on their feet and moving again.

An hour later the small copse of trees came into view and they trudged off the road towards it. Barry approached cautiously but the kids were asleep in the cab of the truck and Billy was snoring, still tied up to the tree. Suzanne was looking in the window at the kids when she realized Barry was checking on Billy. He hadn't told her that he was there on the way back.

"You left my kids here with him?" The look of outrage on her face caused Barry to step back. He was about to explain his actions when Billy moaned behind his gag and looked up at them. Suzanne stepped over and reversing her grip on the shotgun so she was holding the barrel, swung it towards Billy's face. He tried to duck away but had limited mobility. The shotgun stock hit him in the neck, bruising his Adams apple and collapsing his carotid artery. The next strike shattered his skull, leaving him lifeless.

Barry had stepped a few paces away and didn't try to interfere with the execution of justice. He waited as she stood over the body breathing heavily. Her labored breathing turned to sobs and she turned into Barry's arms. He held her until she was done and then took her back to the truck.

Suzanne gently woke her kids and held them the rest of the night.

CHAPTER 33

Dale and Hank were at their wits end. The farm where the truck was found had a body burned beyond recognition in the house and was obviously the scene of a gunfight. There was a blood trail in the driveway and shell casings galore. All three structures were smoldering heaps, and the Honda mini-van that was shot to hell in the driveway, belonged to a missing family.

There was very little forensic support, but they were sure it wasn't Barry or Oscar in the house. There was no other sign of Barry or Oscar other than it was their truck that had been looted and was parked in the yard. They drove the roads back to the highway but didn't find anything until Oscar's body was found in the ditch. An expanded search didn't turn up any sign of Barry.

Hank and Dale left for Bemidji two days later.

Barry was woken up by the kids getting out of the car. He had left Suzanne and the kids in the cab of the truck and had strung his hammock in the trees nearby. After a cold breakfast, they got cleaned up and got ready to get on the road. Barry checked the radiator and saw that there was still a small leak. He replaced the lost fluid with some of their water and made a mental note to replenish their water supply at the next creek.

Suzanne drove while Barry took the window seat and the kids rode between them. They were only on the road a few minutes when Suzanne let out a muffled curse. Barry looked at her and she nodded her head towards the rearview mirror. Barry turned around in his seat and saw a second dust cloud half a mile back and closing quickly.

"I'm pretty sure that they came out of the Sutton place." She saw the confused look his face. "Where they were holding me."

"Ahh, well is there any place where we can get something between us for a few seconds."

"Not for a few miles." Suzanne had been unconsciously pressing down on the gas pedal and Barry had to calm her down, they couldn't afford to slide off the road.

The pickup behind them quickly closed the gap. Barry had the kids crawl down into the foot well and plug their ears. He turned on the seat and knelt facing backwards, he opened the small sliding window and got into the best firing position he could.

"Tell me when we are getting close to the turn!" Barry shouted over the noise of the wind rushing through the cab. It wasn't necessary since she was right there, but the adrenaline was flowing in both of them.

"Another mile."

"Okay." Barry counted to twenty slowly, then began pumping rounds into the front of the truck behind them. He walked a string of shots across the grill hoping to disable the vehicle. As soon as the rounds began impacting, the driver began to swerve back and forth, then he backed off, opening the distance between them. Barry then lowered his aim and tried for the tires. It was futile and he wound up wasting half a magazine on the endeavor. He did notice some steam starting to billow out from under the hood before being whipped away in the slipstream. The other truck dropped further back. He used the break to change magazines.

"Here's the turn for the creek!" She slowed the truck enough to keep from sliding off the road. They made the turn as the road dipped to follow the creek bank, Barry could tell it wasn't going to provide the cover they needed to get the kids away from the truck before whoever was chasing them would catch up.

"Won't work! Keep going!" Barry watched as the truck rounded the corner and he could see a man leaning out of the passenger side window holding a long gun. Barry pushed Suzanne's head down as the report from the rifle drifted to their ears. The bullet hit the rear bumper with a twang. Barry put the front sight of his rifle on the windshield and walked a second string of rounds across the windshield this time. The truck swerved violently for a second, but the driver recovered and it straightened out. The passenger popped out again and another shot hit somewhere on the back of the truck.

The road curved onto a small bridge spanning the slow moving creek below. Suzanne turned left onto the bridge and after lining the truck up on the center line punched it. Steam was already starting to curl from under the edge of their own hood and they could smell the metallic scent of the radiator fluid. Their truck wasn't going to make it much further without a chance to cool down. Suzanne brought the temperature gauge to Barry's attention.

"I'm painfully aware of it! Nowhere else we can lose them huh?" Barry asked wistfully.

"We're still more than twelve miles from town! There are nothing but straight country roads out here." She gestured at the arrow straight stretch of road in front of them.

Barry just shrugged and got back on the rifle. A few more rounds into the windshield caused the truck to back off several hundred yards. It became a long range game of potshot. Both trucks had steam billowing out of them and it was anybody's guess as to which one would die first. Barry finally decided that it was better to set the time and place of the ambush. Glancing ahead he saw a slight dip in the road and decided that they would take the high ground. He instructed Suzanne to stop the truck at an angle at the top of the rise on the far side.

The engine was starting to make unfriendly noises as it struggled up the incline. The truck slid to a stop and Barry had Suzanne and the kids hustle off to the side of the road. He told her to hold down their flank as they settled into the tall grass. He would have kept them behind the cover of the truck but it was soon going to be a bullet magnet and he didn't want them near it.

After getting them all settled down he rushed back to the truck and lay down prone behind it. The other truck was just coming to a stop down in the dip. The driver angled it across the road to the right and they both scrambled out the passenger door. *Well not everything can be easy.*

From his slightly elevated position he began to fire on the men below. They weren't going to be able to leave the cover of their truck without him being able to take them under fire. In the meantime steam billowed out from both the trucks. Barry scanned his target area and finally saw some movement by the front of the truck. Placing the red dot of his scope on the piece of fabric that he could see, he pressed the trigger. The round hit a little low but skipped up into the leg of whoever was behind the truck. He was rewarded with a yelp, and a flurry of movement.

Chris Sutton rolled away from the stinging pain in butt. Barry's bullet had ricocheted into the meaty part of his buttock, tearing a gash across it into his thigh. He cursed at whoever it was driving Billy's truck and swore vengeance upon them.

He had come home this morning after passing out at Will's house, hoping to get a little from the bitch they had tied up in his room. Instead he found Joe dead in his back yard, and Mike shot and bleeding on his couch. The girl was gone along with his shotgun and Mike's AR-15. He was driving Mike into town to get his wounds looked at when Billy's truck went past the farm. When they tried to catch up to the truck, someone began shooting at them. This was a pretty good indicator that they might have had something to do with what had happened at Chris' place.

Mike had a bandage around his chest and shoulder, and the side of his face was swollen and a dark shade of purple. He was not looking well after the truck ride and blood was starting to seep through bandage from his newly reopened wounds. He was sitting with his back to the rear tire and snarling at Chris.

"Well now what the fuck do you want to do?" He hitched himself up. He was woozy and almost slumped over. "I told you we should have let whoever that is go once they shot at us! How are we going to get to town now?"

"I don't know asshole. It's not like it was going to be all flowers and sunshine when we got there. The Doctor was going to ask how you got shot!"

"And I would have told him the fucking truth! Some guy I didn't know came in and shot me!"

"And when the cops came out and started poking around my house? What do you think they wouldn't notice that we had a couple of dead chicks buried in the back yard?"

Another round zipped by ending the conversation for the moment. Then the rear tire went flat on the other side of the truck, followed shortly by the front. They weren't going anywhere now. At least the truck settling on the rims on the other side prevented any more rounds from coming under the chassis.

"I say we light these fuckers up!" Mike looked at Chris who was grinning.

"Let's do this!" He shouted. They had pumped each other up, but it didn't change the situation. As soon as they rolled out from behind cover and started shooting, Barry took them both out with well-placed shots to the torso followed by head shots once they were down.

Barry called everyone back to the truck, which had been hit a few times but didn't appear to be much worse for the wear. After getting them in the truck, he went down to the other truck to see if there was anything they needed. His scavenging run only took a few minutes and yielded just a little ammo. He carried their guns back to the truck, since they would make good barter goods once they made it back to town.

It was all for naught though because the truck wouldn't start. Barry checked the fluid in the radiator and saw that it was dry, but he didn't want to risk using their drinking water to fill the radiator. The creek they had crossed was two miles back and Barry was not looking forward to hiking there with an empty igloo cooler, and back with a full one. The cooler being the only container capable of carrying enough water to make a difference.

They discussed their options. Suzanne was in no shape to make the walk to the creek and back, and she really didn't want Barry to leave them alone for the hour+ that it would take for him to go to the creek and bring back the water. Barry had pretty much reconciled himself to doing it because they would need the water if they had to walk into town. Suzanne finally agreed that they would need the water and Barry set off after making sure that they had shade and drank some of his water.

Barry pulled his baseball cap down low over his eyes and set back off towards the rising sun. He had made a sling for the cooler, attaching it to his tac vest. The trip there was an easy stroll, and Barry drank almost his entire water bladder getting there. He was trying to get as hydrated as possible.

He used his water filter to fill first his bladder then the cooler. He soaked a wash cloth that he wrapped around his neck and began the much slower walk back. The cooler held five gallons of water and the extra thirty-five pounds were very uncomfortable. Whereas the trip to the creek took twenty-five minutes, the return trip took twice that with all the rest stops. He collapsed under the tailgate when he finally made it, joining the kids who seemed to be okay with their situation now.

Suzanne had the hood up on the truck, and told Barry that she thought the damage was permanent and they probably shouldn't waste the water on the radiator. She had divided what few supplies they had and made up kits for the kids to carry. Unfortunately the cooler was still the best option for carrying the water, but she offered to help carry it. Barry told her that the Marine Corps had made sure he was fit enough to do it and he would take care of it.

They slept through the hottest part of the day, hoping that someone would come by, but the road remained empty. They did see a plane circling off to the east of them but it never came within two miles of them. They would travel mostly at night with the help of the moon which was just becoming full.

They only covered six miles the first night. Suzanne's injuries were just too severe to allow her to go further. The second night was better and they covered almost eight. They hit pay dirt the third night coming across an occupied home before midnight. The owners let them stay in the guest bedroom and drove them into town the following morning.

The Sheriff took their statements and drove them back out to the various crime scenes. He wasn't too sure what to make of Barry, but after getting a hold of Jesse he made sure that Barry was taken care of and free to go. A quick stop at the pawn shop to barter the guns for some supplies and ammo, then he was off.

The Sheriff had promised to post an update on the website for Hank and Dale.

CHAPTER 34

Hank and Dale had an easy trip north until they started getting closer to home. The terrorists who had initiated the attacks had used Hill River State Park as one of the areas to test their toxin prior to their full attacks. This was done for several reasons. To help eliminate the population around Bemidji so that the airport could be used as a jumping off point for the second attack, and because the environment had a lot of bodies of water, so they could see the results of the chemical on the local ecology.

This resulted in a far greater amount of the chemical being introduced into the area, causing a higher percentage of both the animal and human population being affected. Animal attacks were just as much a threat as human ones. The watershed also drained towards the Mississippi river, resulting in a concentration along the rivers ecosystem. All of these factors combined to make the last leg of their journey the most dangerous.

They made it to Des Moines Iowa without incident, and were told to not travel any further north alone. The packs were just too large and everything was trying to kill you. They stopped in Ames, a smaller city to the north of Des Moines and waited for a large convoy to form up. They were lucky in that it was almost ready to go and they were only delayed twelve hours before it left for Minneapolis. They were thirty miles short of the city when they were attacked by a large pack.

The ferals used rocks thrown from an over pass combined with a wave attack to swamp the convoy's defenses. All of the cars were hit, and the attackers climbed on every vehicle, pulling the broken windshields out of their frames to get at the people inside. Of the 115 people in the convoy they lost nine people killed and three were bitten so badly that they had to be put into restraints for when they succumbed to the toxin. They lost a truck and a mini-van.

The convoy that rolled into Minneapolis was made up of battered vehicles and disheartened people. There wasn't a car or truck that had a windshield left. A slight drizzle and an overcast sky contributed to the overall dampening of spirits. Hank and Dale were especially downcast in their mood, returning without Barry.

Hank pulled into his condo complex and parked in his spot under the carport. The Durango had not been spared in the attack and the windshield was missing and blood stains were slowly being washed away on the hood. A particularly aggressive young man had clung to the wiper while trying to get through the cracked windshield. Even after Hank, who was riding shotgun, had literally shot the man to pieces, the body had stayed on the hood. They dared not stop to remove it, so it sat there with the blood draining into the firewall and dash area of the SUV as they travelled the last thirty miles into Minneapolis.

With the windshield broken, they had run the heater until the smell of the blood being heated up caused them to put up with the slight chill instead of the stench. They were miserable by the time they unloaded the truck and got inside. It wasn't until they had dried off and were sitting next to the fireplace getting warm, that they could finally relax, the stress of their journey falling away. It was bittersweet however, with the whereabouts and health of Barry being unknown.

Barry was in Des Moines, only two days behind them and catching up fast. He finally got a post on the website stating he was on his way home. After a day layover, he wrangled his way onto a small convoy heading north. He had met one of the drivers at a small restaurant/bar at the north edge of town. Barry had wandered in for a meal and wound up sitting at an elevated table next to a tall dark haired guy with a goatee. The man had turned and looked at Barry as he came in with all his equipment and his rifle dangling from his harness.

"You look ready for a war there buddy."

"Yes sir, it pays to be prepared in these times." Barry said in reply.

"Well you sure look like you're a Boy Scout, that's for sure."

"Just trying to make my way back home, sir"

"Oh, where's that?" The man asked with a raised eyebrow.

"Up in Bemidji, sir. That's where I grew up."

The man stared at Barry for a little bit and was about to say something when the waitress showed up. He waited while Barry ordered a rather large amount of food.

"You expecting someone else?"

"No sir." Barry replied with a frown on his face. "Why do you ask?"

"I just noticed you ordered enough for two is all." The man let out a gruff bark of laughter. "Didn't mean to be nosy."

Barry put out his hand and said "Name's Barry."

"I'm Shawn, Barry and I have a small convoy heading to Minneapolis in the morning. Are you any good with that rifle?"

"Yes sir." Barry didn't elaborate and Shawn could see that he didn't have to.

"Well if you're interested, be at the clover leaf where the 235 meets the 6 tomorrow morning by 7:00 AM. I could always use another guy riding security."

"Thank you Shawn, I'll be there."

The waitress brought Barry's food and they chatted as he ate. Barry learned that Shawn had worked his way out from San Diego to help with his family. Barry told him of recently being there and how he came to be so far from home. Barry was impressed to learn that Shawn had ridden his Harley out from San Diego right after the attacks. No small feat with the ferals popping up and the lawlessness overtaking the land.

They agreed to meet the following morning.

The vehicles looked like something straight out of a Mad Max movie, with iron bars welded across empty windshield frames and spikes sprouting in every direction. Barry rode in the open bed of a pickup truck, holding onto the roll bar. The convoy was moving north by 9:00 AM.

The convoy was attacked in the same location and by the same pack that had attacked Hank's convoy two days earlier. They had to slow down at the same overpass because of a mini-van that was on its side lying in the slow lane. The attack was just as vicious as the one on the previous convoy and the fight was furious as they tried to get the cars past the choke point.

The driver of Barry's truck was killed when a feral landed on the hood and drove an angle iron fence post through the grid of mesh bars and into his neck. The piece of green painted metal was not sharp by any means and tore its way into his neck more than cut. The end struck below his Adam's apple and ripped through half of his neck.

The driver slumped down and the truck swerved into the center divider, striking the K-rail and then rolling over. Barry jumped clear and rolled right back to his feet, coming up with his rifle to his shoulder and putting out rounds at the pack members. After eliminating the immediate threats around him, he began looking for the alpha, finally seeing him off to the side gesturing at another pack member.

Barry sent a bullet his way but the man moved as the shot broke, striking him in the side and spinning him around. Barry had to divert his attention back closer as a female charged at him with her hands raised like claws. Barry did a step slide to the side and put two bullets in her as she flew past, noticing the extended belly of obvious pregnancy. Combat was so second nature to him now that he pondered the fact that she was pregnant and its implications while he moved to put his back to the overturned truck, reloading as he went. He did not let the thought distract him though, as he kept up the constant barrage of fire at the numerous pack members.

The convoy was in dire straits. Three vehicles made it through the ambush and fled northward. Five were caught in the main attack and the trailing two had turned and hightailed it back south. The defenders from the middle vehicles were putting up a vicious defense but were horribly outnumbered. Barry once again found himself with a free space around him and knelt down to check on the people in the cab of the truck at his back.

The driver, Ben, was dead and lying on top of the two passengers who were having a tough time getting around the corpse and climbing out the driver's side door which was above them. The woman and teenaged girl had to struggle with their seat belts and maneuver around the body lying on top of them. It was going to be a minute before they could get out and Barry was worried he might get overrun before they could make it out. He put his back to the hood, and yelled encouragement to the two girls.

He fired at another charging feral and stepped aside to let the body slam into the truck when his left leg was yanked out from under him. The feral that had killed the driver was pinned under the front of the truck and Barry had stepped within his reach. It had pulled on his leg, yanking him off balance and into the splits. Barry was limber, but he still felt the strain in his crotch as his legs went in opposite directions.

Twisting his body to alleviate the pull he placed the rifle to the forehead of the feral who was trying to sink its teeth into his leg and fired. The head snapped back and the body went still. Barry turned as he heard screams from the cab of the truck. Several ferals were on top of the driver's door and another was reaching through the wrought iron grid that covered the windshield opening.

Barry shot the two off the top and moved to get an angle on the one reaching into the cab when he had to engage another feral charging at him. After taking care of the immediate threat, he saw that one of the ones he had shot on top of the truck had fallen on top of the door and was preventing the girls from opening it and getting out. Barry screamed for them to break out the rear window and get out that way, but they either didn't hear or didn't understand. Either way it was their undoing. Barry had been keeping the attackers at bay, but had to give ground to make a magazine change.

The cab was swarmed and more spears were jabbed into the cab as the women screamed. A few seconds later they went silent and Barry was the last person standing. A few pops sounded from one of the vehicles but there were thirty-plus ferals between him and the car.

Barry decided that a tactical withdrawal was in order, and he began backing away from the scene. The pack for the most part had had enough as well and he was allowed to trot off into the woods.

CHAPTER 35

The soft thud of running footsteps broke the early morning silence as a figure slipped past trees and over downfall. Even with the variations in the terrain, the steps fell with metronomic regularity. The slumped shoulders on the figure showed the fatigue of running all night. The ache in his muscles didn't stop the young man from continuing on. He was on a mission of survival, and slacking off wasn't going to further that. Coming across a game trail, the figure only slowed slightly before veering onto it. The noise of something behind him drifted through the shrouded trees.

The shadow glanced back but maintained its pace, its footfalls even more subdued on the trail. A second later there was a *ssnaap*, and the head of the shadow jerked back, and the figure crumpled to the ground. Moments later seven other pack members came upon the body lying on the trail. Looking about, three of them began to howl and continued down the path. The other four weren't about to leave a meal behind and immediately fell to eating the free meal in front of them.

A quarter mile ahead, Barry continued his jog. The stop and shoot game had been going on all night. Initially there had been twenty or so ferals running through the woods after him screaming and trying to run him to ground. He had been using every trick they had taught him to keep the crowd off his back. He had reloaded his magazines from the bandolier he had kept across his chest. After a magazine was empty he would wait until he was jogging again and shove rounds into it as he ran. This was somewhat awkward since he dared not lose any rounds, while his rifle banged into him constantly on its sling causing him to do just that.

He thumbed the last of his loose rounds into a magazine and shoved it back into the empty pouch it had come from. He was about ready to turn and start eliminating the last of his followers when he heard the sound of a diesel engine drifting faintly from up ahead. He didn't want to bring a pack of ferals onto a group of unsuspecting survivors, so with his decision made he turned and lowered himself to the ground. Adopting a good prone shooting position, he used five rounds to drop the three pursuers that he could see. He lay there for a moment catching his breath before shoving himself to his feet. With still no sign of pursuit on his back trail, he turned and jogged towards the sound of the motor.

The game trail turned and skirted a meadow. Peering through the trees, Barry could make out several armed guards forming a perimeter around a couple of trucks. One of them had a towable log splitter behind it that was running full tilt. Barry wasn't about to just pop out of the brush and get shot so he tried to whistle and get their attention. The noise from the splitter was too loud and no one noticed it. Next he tied his 'Do' rag to the end of his rifle and waved it from behind cover. It only took a second before one of the men noticed and gestured for the splitter to be shut off.

"Who's out there?" He called out as soon as the noise died down.

"My name is Barry and I have a couple of ferals after me, can I come out?"

"How many people are with you? And how many ferals are chasing you?" The man asked as the two men who had been running the splitter picked up shotguns.

"Just me, and I think less than ten are following me now."

"Well come on out before you get eaten out there!"

Barry rose slowly to his feet and came forward, glancing back over his shoulder once at a noise. He kept the muzzle of his rifle pointed towards the ground but in his hands. With his luck lately he couldn't be sure he hadn't given up one set of predators for another. Once among the men introductions were made and they agreed to give Barry a lift the rest of the way into town.

The rest of the logs were split without interruption, and they piled into the trucks and took off. As soon as they left the clearing a lone feral loped out into the middle and looked around before turning around and heading back into the woods.

CHAPTER 36

The farm was a wreck. Dale shook his head at the overgrown weeds and brush. Hank closed the door on the battered blue Durango and walked around to stand by his father as they took in the result of two years' worth of neglect. Hank frowned at the plywood over the windows and doors. It had not been there the last time he was here. *Must have been a neighbor or a Good Samaritan.*

They walked up onto the front porch and tried the door. It was locked and the deadbolt was newer then the one that had been there when things went crazy. On a hunch Dale walked over to a flower pot which had nothing in it but desiccated soil. Lifting it up he looked at the bottom and saw a key stuck to the bottom with some rubber cement. Pulling it off he went to the door where the lock turned without a problem.

They walked into the entry foyer and set their bags down. Looking into the living room, they saw that the coffee table had been moved over against one wall and a huge section of carpet and padding was missing. There were patches of discoloration on the walls where some stains had been scrubbed off. A quick walkthrough showed that the place had been cleaned sometime after the incident. Dale's emotions got the best of him and he sat on the couch with his head in his hands until Hank got him moving. They spent the rest of the day removing the plywood from the windows and cleaning the house.

They found the small graveyard when they went outside. Set in what used to be Cassy's flower bed, four wooden crosses sat in a row with

Dale's girl's names on them. The fourth cross was smaller and had Bert's name carved into a bone shaped piece of wood. They stopped and stared for a while before going to the barn for some tools.

Barry was having a tough time finding a ride north out of Minneapolis. The ferals, both human and animal were just too dangerous for anything short of a military convoy. Barry who was confident in his ability to survive on his own grew frustrated. He finally found transportation in the form of a boat headed upstream along the western branch of the Mississippi river. That would take him almost all the way home.

The boat left from the dock at the Dunn island spillway and made its way north and west. The trip was easy at first with there being nothing to do while they were still in town and there were relatively few ferals. Once they left the city behind though, it was common to see single ferals or even packs of them trying to keep pace with the boat as it fought the current upstream. They made it to Clearwater without incident. The crew was going to split the watches but Barry insisted he take two shifts so the crew could get their rest, He was perfectly okay with sleeping during the day while the crew drove them up stream. They were leery at first but, after they checked on him a couple times the first few nights, they appreciated the rest. Barry had no trouble sleeping during the day and the arrangement worked out well for everybody.

The only incident came when a feral jumped from a bridge onto the deck of the boat. They had completed their portage at St. Cloud and Sartell, a big industrial crane had lifted the boat above the spillways and they were north of town when they heard a scream and looked up.

A feral leapt off the 125th Street Bridge and almost landed right on Barry who was sleeping in his hammock. The fifty year old woman had been a resident of Rice, the town nearby, and just happened to be near the bridge as they approached.

Barry unassed his hammock and was diving for his rifle when one of the deck hands used a gaff to pull her down. Barry came up with his knife in one hand and his pistol in the other as he looked for his rifle which he had kicked while rolling out of the hammock. The woman screamed and tried to roll towards the man pinning her down with the hook. Barry slipped behind her and grabbing her head pulled it back and slit her throat. He held her still as her struggles became weaker. There was no clothing to speak of, it was all in tatters, and no ID, so they threw her in the river.

They continued upstream and made it to the Mill Island spillway in Little Falls. The cargo was offloaded and Barry was left on his own. He managed to thumb a ride into Brainerd and had to stop for the night. The following morning saw him out looking for a ride again. He was so close to home now he could taste it. Another short ride left him in Walker, just a few miles south of Bemidji. Another few hours and he got a ride to Cass Lake.

Barry was tired of being on the road and tired of being alone. He set out on State Route 2 on foot. He didn't see a single vehicle going his way. He remembered the countless miles spent going up and down the hills at Camp Pendleton, and consoled himself with the fact that at least the road was flat and easy to walk on.

He caught a feral female stalking him, but she ran off when he pointed his rifle at her. The road stretched out before him and he had to play mental games to keep alert. The sun was just above the horizon when he walked into the Hotel command post where he had shared a room with Mag what seemed like a lifetime ago.

He stepped into the court yard where the evening meal was just about to be served and looked around. The conversation stopped as everyone stared at him. Suddenly a voice called out from over at one of the bench tables.

"Well? Are you hungry?" Barry recognized Yavi's voice and broke into a huge smile. The crowd began clapping and Barry was mobbed in short order. Half of the residents had no idea who the skinny stranger was, but as the name Barry floated around, people who didn't know him stared at this kid who somehow had become a legend.

As he was getting pounded on the back for the twelfth time, he looked up and almost drew his pistol.

Standing in the archway next to Captain Crowe was Justine Allensworth. She was staring very hard at Barry and he was starting to get nervous. She finally walked forward and wrapped her arms around him and put her face into his neck. He noticed that he was taller than her now, and it felt funny/weird that she was crying against his shoulder. Her muffled sobs slowed down and she whispered against his neck "Thank you."

Blushing from the attention Barry held her at arm's length and looked at her. Her skin had a few blemishes from acne that she had suffered through, but she was still a beautiful woman. Her eyes were still an intense green and he thought she was still very pretty.

"They told me that I have you to thank for my survival, and I have these flashes of memory with you in them." She said. "I'm sorry if I attacked you or any of your friends or family."

"No ma'am, you never hurt anyone that I saw who didn't deserve it."

"Oh thank God!" She hugged him again as the crowd closed back in on them.

Dan and Scott Preston were there along with Yavi and Roy. Barry was brought over to a table and a plate stuck in front of him. He didn't turn down the food, but he told them he had someplace to be. He ate quickly and then told everyone he would be back soon.

Dan drove him in one of the Park Ranger trucks out to his old house. Barry could see that the plywood he had put up before leaving was down and some of the growth had been trimmed back in the front of the house.

The trucks headlights cut through the darkening twilight as they pulled into the driveway, splashing a brief wave of light across the front of the house. The front door opened as Barry climbed out of the front seat of the car. He stared as first his brother then his father stepped out of the front door. Barry broke into a run and rushed towards them.

Hank and Dale made it down to the bottom of the steps before Barry plowed into them, wrapping them in his arms. The three men stood there holding each other as Barry, who hadn't shed a tear since the day Mag died sobbed in joy.

CHAPTER 37

The front pipper wobbled slightly in the rear sight as the shooter strained to hold the bow perfectly still. Even though the compound bow got easier at full draw, the tension still caused a little shaking. Barry's trigger finger pressed the trigger on the release, and the arrow shot forward with a snap, streaking across the twenty-five yards to sink up to the fletchings in the bull's-eye of the target.

Barry had come home to find that his father had built an archery range out beside the barn. Dale had said that it was the last promise he'd made to Barry, and he intended to follow through. A small strip of ground had been cleared and a stack of hay bales set up for a backstop. Dale had even spent some time in the shop making a bow stand that held the bow and quiver while the shooter was down range.

It had become a weekend past time for an archery contest to happen during the Sunday BBQ that was a regular occurrence at the Metzler farm. This Sunday the party was bigger than usual since Mark had brought Mel and Jake out to visit. He couldn't take the pressure anymore from his youngest child as she threatened to walk to Minnesota if he didn't take her.

A small crowd watched as he knocked another arrow and let fly. This arrow seemed to follow the exact same course and struck the target barely an inch from the previous one. Hank and Dale walked over towards Barry as Mel and Mark clapped. Jake scowled in mock anger at the kid and went to take the bow from him. A slight glint in the woods off to the side of the range caught his eye.

Jake's combat instincts were too well honed not to react.

"Cover! Shooter in the—"

The warning was too late as the .308 slug tore through Barry's upper right chest and exploded out the back. The bullet wasn't done though, it continued on into Hank's chest. It entered his upper left chest and came out his back as well. Both of them collapsed.

Jake ripped his .45 from its holster and began placing rounds into the wood line as he sprinted towards the trees. He knew he only had to distract the shooter for a moment while some of the others got to their rifles and could return fire. He made it to the trees with only one other rifle round going past him. He didn't see any other movement, and the length of time between shots was a pretty good indicator that it was a single shooter, armed with a bolt action rifle.

Mel had immediately tried to rush towards Barry, but her father had snatched her and thrown her to the ground before covering her with his own body. A brief few seconds of pandemonium ensued as People scrambled for cover and went to retrieve weapons. Dan Preston had been closest to the Park Ranger truck and had his M4 in seconds. He saw the area that Jake's rounds were impacting and as soon as he brought his scope up, saw movement. He sent a burst into the figure and moved towards the wood line at a sprint as well.

Lovell was less than five feet behind him as they hit the cover of the trees. Calling out to Jake they were soon on line and advancing in bounding over watch. One man dashing forward while the other two covered him. Less than a minute later they saw a man limping away through the trees. All three men opened fire and the figure went down. Approaching cautiously, they found a dark skinned man lying on the ground with a bolt action gun a few feet away where it had fallen from his hands.

Making sure to stay out of the line of fire, Jake circled around the figure and then rushed in and grabbed him, pulling both of his hands away from his body. The man was quickly stripped of his belongings and hauled to his feet. It immediately became apparent that the reason he had been limping was from old wounds to his legs. The only fresh gunshot wounds he had were on his torso. Jake spun the man around to look at him in the face.

"I got that little fucker!" Cliff Bluefeather spat out. "I only wish he would have taken longer to die!"

Cliff had gone through Barry's belongings when they had first taken him captive. Among his papers was the note requesting that Barry receive assistance returning to his address in Bemidji. After surviving the shootout at the farm, Cliff had made his way north with only one thing on his mind: Vengeance. His friends had told him that the Law was looking for him, and he was too well known near Wichita to stay. Having his life interrupted by the punk kid made him furious. It took him two months to make his way to the farm of the kid who had caused him so much trouble and pain.

Jake didn't even hesitate, he slammed his hand into the man's throat, lifting him off his feet and slamming him back down onto his back. Jake's fingers dug in and closed off Cliff's windpipe. The man only struggled briefly before becoming unconscious. Jake would have kept the pressure up until the man was dead but Dan and Lovell pulled him off. They carried the unconscious body back to the farm.

EPILOGUE

Dale stood and stared at the piles of freshly overturned dirt in the back yard. Tears ran down his face as he wondered what he had done to deserve losing so much. Staring at the new cross that had been placed at the head of the grave he heaved one more sigh and turned to the people next to him. There was not a dry eye in the crowd and they murmured condolences as he headed to his truck.

He had to get back to the hospital, He may have buried one of his sons this day, but the other one still needed him, and he planned to be there for him.

The End

ACKNOWLEDGEMENTS

I could not have completed this book without the help of several people and they need to be mentioned here. My kids TJ, Abbi, Alexis, Tessa, and Maris, who are the inspiration for the kids in my books. If a kid did something weird (or stupid) in my books, you can bet one of my kids or their friends did it in real life.

I want to thank my fellow authors of Braveship Books. It is an honor to write with the best military fiction writers in the world.

Thanks to Chic and Brenda, my first Beta readers.

Please enjoy this preview of

The Other Side of Me
Gone Feral Book III

CHAPTER 1

The change took Pastor Eland Matthews overnight. He had been at a church picnic all day Saturday until the news of the terrorist attacks sent people into a mild panic. The gathering had broken up in an orderly fashion, as people went back home to make sure that their extended families were okay. Eland had stayed with Cory Monroe to help clean up, then load the church's van. Sunday was spent calming the members of his congregation who came to the church for comfort. He had to have Corey and Julia make extra lemonade and sweet tea for all the people stopping by. The attacks seemed to have been relatively ineffective, there had been some casualties at the power plant where one of the planes used in the attacks had crashed, but none were from his congregation. He went to bed Sunday evening feeling a little warm. His ebony skin didn't show the rash that was creeping up his neck.

Eland had served in the United States Navy as a Corpsman or 'doc' attached to a Marine Corps infantry unit. Although he had never declared himself a 'conscientious objector' he felt that he would best serve his country by saving lives instead of taking them. After completing his tour he had served in several roles at his ministry before becoming ordained and taking over. At just over six feet two, with smooth ebony skin, his features were handsome. His smile was a strip of pearlescent white that sent waves of charm out to his congregation. The musculature he had developed while serving with the Marines, and which he maintained with a rigorous workout regimen in the basement gym, filled out his Sunday suit nicely. There were few women who didn't get butterflies when he spoke to them in his rich baritone voice. His grooming was capped off with a faint dash of cologne that tended to make people lean in closer to identify it.

The toxin that had been dumped into the city's water supply was in the sweet tea he had been drinking. He had ingested enough toxin during the day, to overload his neural network five times over. While his body did its best to eject it from his system, the toxin still concentrated itself in his brain. During the night his saliva became a thick serum which held enough toxin to contaminate another person if they were bitten. His body temperature rose to 102 degrees and he began to sweat freely. He was tossing and turning in his bed when a commotion outside caused him to snap upright. He looked around at his small room, recognizing it as his, but somehow feeling that it was also not his. Another noise from outside his window turned his attention away from the room. He stalked over to the window which faced out towards 25th Street in Gulfport Mississippi. He looked down upon a woman who was backing away from a man. The woman had what appeared to be a large doll in her hand and she was swinging it repeatedly at the man. He finally caught her arm and bit into the doll.

Food. The thought flashed across his mind. Other images of vandals on the street flashed in his head as well. He immediately became enraged at the activity and bolted out the door. His small apartment was attached to the side of the church and was above the kitchen. He ran down the stairs leading up to his loft and through the cooking area. He slammed into the door leading outside, and leapt down the short flight of four stairs. He charged towards the gate on the side of the church yard.

The sound of the fight was easily heard as he pulled open the gate and ran towards the sound of the conflict. Rounding the side of the church, he saw both the man and woman crouched in the street tearing strips of flesh off of the young child the woman had been carrying. The man had been able to grab the child's leg and twist the torso away from the woman. She had maintained a grip on the arm however, and the already ravaged skin had torn as the child's arm came off.

Eland saw that the male had the bigger piece, and instinctively knowing he posed more of a threat, Eland attacked him first. The two people were so busy chewing and growling at each other, that they didn't notice that Eland was on them until it was too late. The impact of Eland slamming into the man's back knocked him flat on his face and drove the air from his lungs. Eland easily bent down and bit into his victim's neck, tearing out a huge mouthful of flesh before he could recover.

The woman had scooted away on her butt when Eland first ran into the man, but she darted forward and grabbed what was left of her son's corpse as the one sided struggle played itself out. She threw aside the arm she had been chewing on and ran off down the street dragging the small body by the leg. Eland had growled at her for taking the child but there was nothing he could do while he finished killing the man underneath him. Once the body stopped twitching, he continued to tear at it for several minutes, grunting in pleasure as the hot blood filled his mouth, and the chunks of flesh filled his belly. The toxin which had been flowing in the man's blood now sat in Eland's stomach and was slowly absorbed.

After eating his fill, Eland stood up and looked around. There was a building on fire a few blocks over, and the sound of a siren could be heard in the distance. None of these things affected his immediate needs, so he ignored them. What he wanted was a drink. His metabolism was going overtime, and his body craved water to flush his system. The thick serum in his saliva was mixing with the blood coagulating in his mouth. He worked his mouth a few times and swallowed. He went back inside the church kitchen knowing that he should be able to get something there to satisfy his craving. He walked in and suddenly drew a blank on how to get a drink. He immediately became enraged and began slamming utensils into the shelves and counters. The fit took a better part of ten minutes before he collapsed to the ground breathing like a locomotive.

Once he had calmed down he went exploring, and instinctively found the men's restroom. He immediately began splashing the water from the toilet bowl up into his mouth. After rinsing the slime and blood from his mouth in one stall, he went to the next one and drank his fill. The fluids and meat were sloshing around in his belly as he stood up and wandered back out into the rectory. The early morning physical activity coupled with the lack of sleep and a full stomach were making him drowsy. He finally curled up in a corner of the chapel and fell into a troubled sleep.

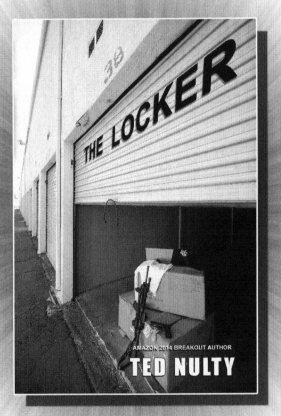

CUTTING-EDGE NAVAL THRILLERS BY

JEFF EDWARDS

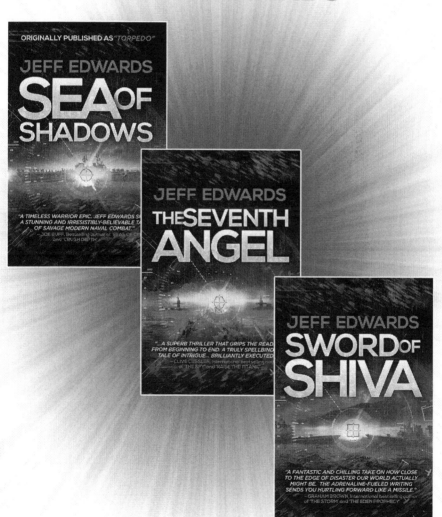

HIGH COMBAT IN HIGH SPACE

THOMAS A. MAYS

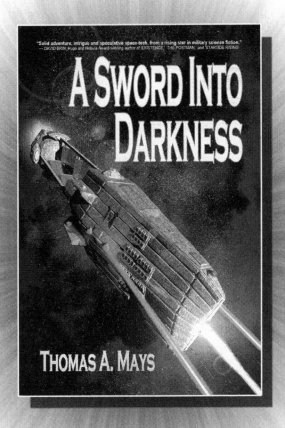

The Human Race is about
to make its stand...

www.BraveshipBooks.Com

WHITE-HOT SUBMARINE WARFARE
BY
JOHN R. MONTEITH

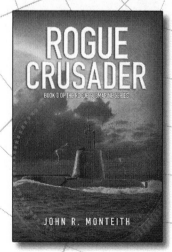

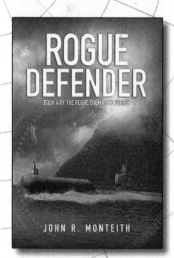

HIGH OCTANE AERIAL COMBAT

KEVIN MILLER

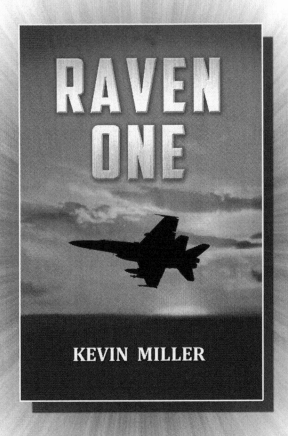

RAVEN ONE

KEVIN MILLER

Unarmed over hostile territory...

www.BraveshipBooks.Com

A THRONE WITHOUT AN HEIR...
A MURDEROUS LIE...

LARRY WEINBERG

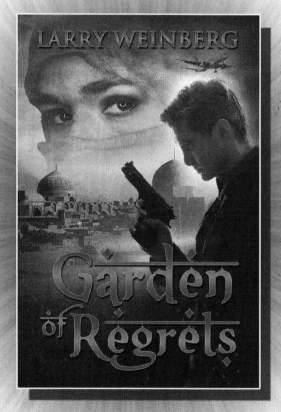

A truth that can only lead to war...

66905841R00130

Made in the USA
Charleston, SC
02 February 2017